THE WATCH

An AJ Garrison Crime Novel

Barb — You are going to love AJ.

Book 1

JERRY PETERSON

This book is a work of fiction. Names, characters, places and incidents are products of the author's imagination or are used fictitiously. All characters in this book have no existence outside the imagination of the author and have no relation whatsoever to anyone, living or dead, bearing the same name or names. All incidents are pure invention from the author's imagination. Any resemblance to actual events or locales or persons, living or dead, is entirely coincidental.

Grand Medallion Books

ISBN-13: 978-1479345243
ISBN-10: 1479345245

Cover Design and Interior Layout Design © Melissa Alvarez at BookCoversGalore.com
Individual Image Copyrights @DepositPhotos.com: ©choreograph, ©kilukilu, ©S_Razvodovskij, ©whitesnakeamirb, and ©alinute.

October 2012

Printed in the U.S.A.

Dedication

To Marge, my wife and chief copy editor.

To the members of my writers group who keep my writing honest.

To a friend and one-time colleague who prefers to remain unnamed.

ACKNOWLEDGMENTS

No longer do those of us who are good storytellers and good writers need a traditional publishing house. We can be independents–indies.

I am now one of them with the publication of *The Watch* as an ebook and a trade paperback, the first book in my new AJ Garrison Crime Novels series.

We indies, if we want to put the very best books in the hands of our readers, do not work alone.

To make sure I had an absolutely clean manuscript–no typos or awkward sentences–I put out an appeal through Facebook for a few good proofreaders willing to help a writer shape up his book.

Four responded saying pick me, pick me.

So I picked them all: Judy Beatty in Madison, Alabama, a retired staff analyst who worked for Boeing; Denise Brooks in Maryborough, Queensland, Australia, a singer/songwriter; Sean Patrick Little in Sun Prairie, Wisconsin, a teacher and writer; and Quackgrass Sally, way out west in Montana, a writer and ranch wife.

To make this book look good, I went to Melissa Alvarez, a cover designer and formatter of manuscripts for the print books, and Sue Trowbridge who does the magic of turning the manuscripts into ebooks.

They are excellent.

Who can write some good words about our book that we can put on the cover? For this book, I went to James Mitchell who writes a detective novel series set on the Arizona border with Mexico. Jim is a lawyer and a pilot, and *The Watch* is a crime novel whose central figure is a young lawyer who's training for her private pilot's license.

In Jim, I have a good match with my sleuth, AJ

Garrison.

Every writer needs a photographer to take his or her picture for the back of the book. For me, this time it was Adam Sorge, a lineman at Wisconsin Aviation in Watertown. Adam, it turns out, is a fellow writer. We had met at an author fair the previous spring. I went out to the Watertown airport because I needed to borrow a Cessna 152, a more recent version of the Cessna 150 in this novel, for a prop for my back-of-the-book picture. There was one there . . . and Adam who manned my camera for me.

I always close with a note of appreciation to the librarians around the country. They, like you and your fellow readers who enjoyed *Early's Fall*, my first James Early book, have been real boosters and most gracious in their comments.

Without them and you, there would be no reason to write.

ALSO BY JERRY PETERSON

Early's Fall
Iced

"Peterson is a first-rate storyteller." – Larry D. Sweazy, Spur-award winning author of *The Badger's Revenge*

Chapter 1

Questions

"News from the battle near Cam Duc in South Vietnam yesterday. American headquarters in Saigon said Marines of the Third Division E Company killed one hundred twenty Viet Cong."

AJ Garrison stared at the transistor radio in her hand.

"Lies," she said to the reporter delivering the latest, as if he could hear her. She snapped the radio off and went on toward her elderly VW parked on the street.

"These hawks. We ought to–" Garrison cut her thought short. Before her, there under the windshield wiper of her car, a white envelope with a question on it in large print: WHO MURDERED DR. TAYLOR?

Doctor Walter Taylor.

The leader of her city's medical community.

She shot her gaze up the street, then to the houses across the way. Who had left this? Could they be watching?

Garrison spotted one person on the sidewalk–a mailman sorting letters as he strolled from one home to another, and he appeared to be unaware of her as he stepped around an abandoned tricycle.

She pulled the envelope out–no one had talked of the doctor in almost three years, at least not to her–and fingered the flap.

Odd.

Not sealed.

Garrison flipped it open. A newspaper clipping laid

inside the envelope. She brought the clipping out, the clipping smelling of must, like an old book shelved in a damp room.

The dateline: Morgantown.

The lead paragraph delivered news as disturbing today as it had been three years ago—

Prominent physician, Dr. Walter Taylor, 56, died last night of a gunshot wound sustained outside the Ballard County Courthouse.

According to Sheriff Clarence Bogle, Deputy Daniel "Bunch" Jeffords found the body minutes after hearing the shot.

"It wasn't suicide. We know that," Bogle said. "We didn't find no gun."

But he refused to call it murder. "We just don't know what happened out there," the sheriff said. "We got no witnesses. We got nothing. Old Doc was about the nicest man around, helped just about everybody in the county. There's no one would want to do him harm."

The story went on to say that robbery had been ruled out because Bogle had found forty thousand dollars in one-thousand-dollar bills in Taylor's trouser pocket.

Forty thousand dollars. That perplexed Garrison. What could he have been doing carrying that kind of money around?

The story went on to say the sheriff had placed himself in charge of the investigation, that he had refused offers of help from the city and state police.

His investigation had gone nowhere. Garrison knew that and wondered whether it would have been different had Bogle accepted assistance.

She skimmed the next two paragraphs, details of the Morgantown resident's life, all familiar—he'd graduated from Memphis Hospital Medical College in 1935, had served in the Army Medical Corps during World War II, had returned to Morgantown after the war to establish a private hospital, that he had sold the hospital to the county in 1959 and stayed on as chief of the medical staff, that he had built Tattersall Park, funded the expansion of the city library, and endowed the Taylor Chair for Humanities at John Morgan College.

The last paragraph puzzled Garrison. It reported that Taylor had recently become interested in tracing his family's lineage. "Dr. Taylor had gotten back as far as A.D. Taylor, one of Ballard County's early doctors," the newspaper quoted Martha Cunningham, chief librarian and genealogist at the Morgantown City Library, as saying. "That Dr. Taylor came here in 1853 from Washington County. Like our Dr. Taylor, he also was an Army surgeon, having served with the First Tennessee Cavalry during The Late Unpleasantness."

Garrison turned the clipping. Someone had scribbled a date along the side–*May 18, 1965*–and the words *Knoxville Sentinel.*

Not even the Morgantown Democrat or The Chief.

Garrison was in first-year law up at the University of Tennessee when the shooting occurred. She had come home for the funeral, had sobbed through it as had so many others.

Taylor had brought this willowy young woman into the world at his hospital. As a kid, she had tagged after him when she wasn't tagging after her father. In high school, she had worked at the hospital as a candy striper. Taylor encouraged her to go into nursing, telling her he would always have a job for her. And she would have gone into nursing had she not injured her back helping an aide lift a woman into bed, a woman who weighed more than Garrison and the aide combined. On bad days now Garrison still had to wear a brace. So she chose the law, where she could help others with her brain.

She examined the envelope–just a cheap number ten, the paper so thin one could read through it.

Hammond MacTeer–Garrison's mentor–shambled up.

"Whatcha got there?" the old lawyer asked.

She held up the clipping. "The newspaper story of Doctor Taylor's murder. It was under my windshield wiper."

"Strange place for it."

Garrison put the clipping, envelope, and her radio in her attache case, empty except for several file folders and a legal pad. "You never talk about it, do you?" she said. "At least you never have to me."

"The killing of old Doc? There's not much to talk about. How about you come with me to a funeral, and I'll tell you what little I know in the car."

"Whose funeral?"

"Teddy Wilson. You know the Wilsons. The First Morgantown Bank? Maybe we can get you some clients."

"You want me to do business at a funeral?" she asked.

"Never know who might need a lawyer, particularly a young pretty one like you." MacTeer's eyes twinkled with a hint of mischief as he took out his cigar cutter. He clipped a lavender rose from a bush by the sidewalk and inhaled the rose's perfume as he tucked the flower's short stem through the button hole in his lapel. "Do love this one," he said. "A hint of spice."

Garrison straightened her charcoal suit jacket.

MacTeer appraised her. "You know, girl, I wish you wouldn't wear those damn suits. Show some leg and maybe a little up here." He waggled his fingers at Garrison's cleavage.

She shook her head. "We've had this discussion before. I'm a woman, and I'm a professional. I dress the part, just as you dress like the old-time Southern lawyer you are, you with your white suits."

"I do, don't I?"

"A little beard and a cane, and people would think you were Colonel Sanders."

MacTeer opened the passenger door of his decade-old Cadillac for Garrison, the car parked next to her Volkswagen.

White Cadillac, white leather seats, white carpeting, MacTeer employed an eight-year-old black boy–Clement Downey–to keep his car clean and polished. He called him Ajax. Clement thought that had something to do with the kitchen cleanser his mother bought at the store until, one day, MacTeer explained that Ajax was a mighty Greek warrior. Ever after, the boy walked tall around MacTeer. When Clement wasn't around, MacTeer called him "my little darkie." He also employed Clement's mother to clean the mansion that served as offices for him and Garrison.

Garrison settled into the passenger seat. "Mister MacTeer–"

"My gawd," he said as he wrenched the key in the ignition, "when you gonna stop callin' me Mister MacTeer and call me Hammond?"

He stepped down on the gas. The engine roared, and he let off and slipped the transmission into drive. Brakes squealed as MacTeer pulled out into the street.

Garrison shot her hand to the dashboard. She twisted around in time to see a mail driver hammering at the steering wheel of his truck. "You cut him off."

"Oh, I did not. Now when are you going to stop with this mister business?"

"Maybe when I'm as old as you. You've always been Mister MacTeer to me. You helped me get into law school. Calling you Mister MacTeer, it's me showing respect."

"Well, gawddammit, missy, if you won't call me Hammond, at least call me Judge."

"All right, Mister Mac–Judge."

MacTeer grinned. "You hear the radio news this morning? Looks like our boys got the Cong on the run again."

"Judge, we have no business over there."

"I know that's what you think, AJ, but the country is committed."

"What country are you living in? Judge, I have friends at the university who can turn out a thousand students in protest."

MacTeer held up his hand. "All right, how 'bout a truce for the moment?"

"Truce," Garrison said.

"Okay, now what do you want to know about the murder of poor old Doc?"

"Anything you can tell me, like who could have put that clipping on my car?"

MacTeer swung wide onto Maple Street and headed toward the Methodist church. Three cars stopped short in rapid succession. "Can't imagine. You remember much about the murder?"

"Very little."

"Oh, that's right, you were up in Knoxville, weren't you?"

"I took off classes to come home for the funeral."

"Real sad affair."

"I remember," Garrison said, "there were some whispered speculations at the church, but, after the funeral, I don't recall that anybody ever talked about it again. Not even my father."

"Well, it kinda hurt too much." MacTeer glanced out the side window. He waved to two women on the sidewalk. "There wasn't anybody wasn't friends with Doc, and you know that included me."

"Yes."

"We were on the fiscal court together some six years. Damn Yankees who move down here, I have to tell 'em they call it a county commission up where they come from. They just can't get their heads around our terminology. Anyway, I talked Doc into running for it when Abner Rumple died. Abner was a good man on the court." MacTeer snatched a look at Garrison. "I'm proud to say Doc was even better."

"But you aren't telling me what happened."

MacTeer stuck his paw out the window. He waved it at the church parking lot, intending to turn.

"Why don't you use the signal?" Garrison asked.

"Don't believe in it. Besides, it didn't work right when I

got the car."

"That was ten years ago. Why didn't you get it fixed?"

"Hand never fails me. Everybody sees me waving where I want to go, they know what it means." MacTeer herded the Whale across a lane of approaching traffic. He cut in front of a milk truck, ignored the driver's horn blast as the great white whale lifted itself across the sidewalk and into the church lot. MacTeer wheeled the car into a spot marked 'Reserved for Rev. Donnelly.'

Garrison fired a look at him that would shrivel apples.

"Hey, Al won't mind. Nice day like this, he probably walked to church anyway."

MacTeer opened the door. He worked at shifting his bulk outside while a man in a black suit trotted up with a small 'Funeral' flag. The man's nose looked like it had been flattened one too many times in a bar fight. "Going with us out to the cemetery, Judge?" he asked.

"Day wouldn't be complete without standing by the grieving family when you lower the dearly departed into the ground, Wilsey."

Wilsey James, a partner in the funeral home of Roberts & James, gave off a crooked grin as he planted the flag's magnetic base on the hood of the Whale. "There isn't a funeral you've ever missed, is there?"

"Well, couple years ago, just about. I was down with the flu."

"I 'member that. Yeah, you had your wife bundle you up–"

"And you picked me up so I wouldn't have to drive."

"Yup, the Harris funeral."

"Haw, me riding in the front of the hearse." MacTeer's jowls jiggled. "I expect there were a lot of people wishing I'd been ridin' in the back."

"Oh, come now, Judge."

"You know AJ? Amanda Jane?"

"Surely do," James said. "Nice to have you back, Miss Amanda. Robby and me handled the funeral for your mom, what was that, ten years back?"

Garrison gave a weak smile.

"You surely growed up to be a handsome young thing."

Her face tinged pink.

James produced two small folders. He gave one to each of the funeral guests. "Teddy's obituary. I expect you'll want to be getting inside. Another five minutes, they start the service."

"I expect you're right," MacTeer said. He extended his arm to Garrison. She took it and they walked on, MacTeer speaking to the other late arrivals hurrying toward the side entrance of the church.

That entrance opened into the chancel.

Everyone else turned left and went to the back of the church, to sign the guest book and go on to their seats, guided by Jefferson Roberts, the senior undertaker.

MacTeer, unlike all others, went straight into the front of the church. He stopped and shook hands and spoke with each member of the Wilson family, all in the front pews.

Garrison trailed behind, introducing herself to those she didn't know. She had known Teddy Wilson in high school, had had a crush on him–those dimples and a smile that could have been in a toothpaste commercial. He was three years older than she, and Garrison knew he had hardly been aware of her.

When MacTeer ran out of family to console, he went over to the side of the church, to the pallbearers. There he spoke with each man, and several muffled their laughter over something MacTeer said. Garrison thought she saw one of the pallbearers slip him an envelope.

"Well, I expect we'd better find us a seat," MacTeer said on returning. He peered up the center aisle to Roberts motioning to him, the undertaker gesturing toward space open at the end of a pew.

The steeple bell started its long toll as Garrison slid onto the pew. MacTeer settled his wide frame in the space remaining.

Reverend Donnelly, in a black robe, came away from his chair on the platform. He stepped up into the pulpit and, on seeing MacTeer, tilted his head in the lawyer's direction, gave a quick nod.

MacTeer waggled his fingers in response.

Donnelly pushed his glasses up on the bridge of his nose. "Dearly beloved," he began.

Garrison heard little. She became absorbed in this great stone church that smelled richly of lilies. Garrison gazed up at the high-pitched ceiling, the polished oak rafters, and the stained glass window in the east wall, brilliant with the mid-morning sun illuminating the picture story of Christ's ascension. This was nothing like the little Baptist church outside of Genesis that she had grown up in. Every Wednesday night, Sunday morning, and Sunday night, her father and mother had driven up into the mountains, Garrison riding in the front seat between them. Often they drove out to the family cemetery in Paradise Cove where four generations of Clicks were buried, her mother now the most recent addition to that gathering of the dead.

Garrison became aware of the comfort of the padded seats. There's money here, she thought. This is indeed the church of the bankers.

She glanced to the side, to MacTeer. He had put on his dark glasses.

His jowls sagged.

And he breathed deeply, asleep.

****

"How could you do that?" she asked when they were back in the Cadillac, rolling in the procession toward the cemetery. "How could you go to sleep at a funeral for heaven's sake?"

MacTeer scrunched a shoulder. "Missy, when you get to be my age, you'll find yourself falling asleep at the damnedest times. One thing's sure."

"What's that?"

"Good old Teddy didn't notice."

"Because he was dead. Judge, I was afraid you were going to snore. And don't call me Missy."

MacTeer patted his breast pocket for a cigar. "AJ, look, if we're going to be partners, you got a job when you're with me. You've got to wake me up before I do snore."

"Where'd this partner thing come from? I've only had my bar license for three months."

"Hon, sometime I'm going to set my valise on Millie's desk, walk out, and never come back. You better be ready to take over the practice."

She twisted in her seat. "Judge, you're never going to quit. Pop says you're going to be pleading cases from your casket."

MacTeer roared. He pounded the steering wheel, swerving the car toward the ditch. "He could be right, you know," MacTeer said between guffaws as he jerked the Whale back into the westbound traffic lane.

"If I may," Garrison went on, "way back before we got to the church, you were telling me about Doctor Taylor."

He pulled a now-found cigar from his breast pocket. MacTeer stuffed the end of the stogie in his mouth and chewed. "It's the damnedest thing. Judgeson Lattimer and I didn't hear the shot. We were back where the court–" he snickered at a memory.

"What are you laughing at?"

"Judge Judgeson, isn't that something?"

Garrison stared at him.

"Well, anyway," MacTeer said, "old Bunch comes gallopin' back, shouting the doc's been shot. I send him to call the sheriff and the ambulance, and we run outside and there in the alley, near where we park our cars, there he was just slumped down on the gravel."

He rolled the cigar in his lips. "I've seen more than a few dead bodies in my time, and, AJ, Doc was dead."

"And that was it?"

"I'm sure that newspaper story told you there was no gun. There were no witnesses either. Poor old Sheriff Bogle, he had nothing to go on, but he shook the bushes for a couple weeks before he hung it up." MacTeer's speed rose as he looked away, the Whale closing the gap on the car ahead.

Garrison blanched. She slapped MacTeer's arm, and he turned toward her. Garrison gestured ahead. "Slow it down. The car!"

MacTeer glanced out the windshield. With the quickness of a toad hopping across hot asphalt, he tromped on the brake. That threw both of them forward.

He let off only when he had slowed the Whale to half its speed. "Hooeee, wouldn't that have been exciting, rooting the mayor in the rear."

Garrison shook her head.

MacTeer rolled his cigar again. "Were you about to ask me something?"

She squared her shoulders. "Couldn't the state police have done anything?"

"About what?"

"About Doctor Taylor's murder."

"Maybe, but it wasn't their jurisdiction. It was either going to be the city police or the sheriff, and gawddammit, it happened on our property. The man didn't have an enemy in the world, you know that."

"Then whoever did it, could they have murdered the wrong man?" Garrison asked.

"It's possible I suppose. Bogle checked that idea out. Judgeson never offended anyone and me, I've had to defend some real mean ones in court. But they did their crimes, and now they're doing their times at Brushyfork." MacTeer stuck his hand out the window. He waved it over the Whale's roof as he turned the steering wheel with his other hand and followed the procession of cars into The Green Chapel Cemetery. "I've always had Bogle warn off any when they come out of prison. They usually find it real agreeable to move to west Tennessee."

The procession wound through the old cemetery filled with garish monuments to Ballard County's fathers and mothers and their children and their children's children. MacTeer pointed to a limestone slab, most of the carving worn away by weather and time. "Old Robert MacTeer is buried right there. That's my grandfather, AJ, six generations removed, the first white man in the county. The way the county's grown up, he probably wishes he'd shut the door behind him."

The procession drifted over a rise and down into a new section dotted with monuments more modest, many flush with the sod. MacTeer nosed the Whale off the gravel drive and in beside a Ford pickup that belonged to Henry Tingle, head of the county road department.

"How you doin', Henry, Alva?" MacTeer called out as he disgorged himself from the Whale.

Tingle, in a black suit worn shiny in the seat, waited beside his wife for MacTeer to catch up with them.

"You know AJ, AJ Garrison? She's got a practice in my office," MacTeer said by way of introduction. "She's Will Click's little girl."

Garrison shook hands with Missus Tingle and gave Tingle the expected greeting.

"Oh, of course, you wouldn't," MacTeer said. "You were farming out there at Rocky Gap, and AJ grew up here in town. We didn't get you that job with the highway department until, what, five years ago?"

"'Bout then," Tingle said.

"That's what I thought. Well, by then AJ was up at the university."

MacTeer put his arm around Tingle's shoulders as they strolled on. Tingle handed something to the judge. MacTeer looked away as he slipped it in his pocket.

"What did he give you?" Garrison asked, hushing her words when MacTeer and she were away from the Tingles and again standing with the Wilson family.

"Hmm?"

"What did he give you? Mister Tingle."

"Campaign contribution. It's a gawddamn election year. You going to contribute?"

"With what? I haven't even billed my first client."

"You've done four cases pro bono, right? It's time you started charging."

"Those people didn't have any money, and you know it."

"That's why I wouldn't take their cases."

"So justice is only for the wealthy?"

"If you want to pay your bills, it is." MacTeer put the back of his hand beside his mouth, so no one would hear. "Let's see if we can snag you a wealthy client out of this funeral."

"Judge, you're hopeless."

"Just bein' practical."

Reverend Donnelly raised a hand. When all eyes had turned to him, he bowed. "Our mighty God, we bring You one of Your children, Theodore McKinley Wilson, taken so tragically from us, to place his body here in this holy ground, to rest here until You call all of us forth–"

Garrison's mind wandered. She knew fewer than half the people gathered around the grave and only a handful well, yet MacTeer seemed to know them all, could even ask after the babies and the relatives who had moved away. This old man was a people's lawyer. Could she ever be half as good as he? She envied him that his ten-minute walk from the office to the courthouse often took an hour because people stopped him to tell him their problems and ask for his help and advice. And he always listened, Garrison knew–never walked away from anyone.

"–we now commit the body of our brother to the soil, in the name of the Father, the Son, and the Holy Ghost. Amen."

Donnelly stepped back. As he did, Teddy Wilson's widow came from the row of chairs at the side of the grave. She held her small daughter in her arms and said something to her somewhat older son beside her, the boy's hair brushed just so, he looking every bit the little man in his new suit, although his tie was askew.

The boy tugged a lily out of a funeral spray. He placed the flower on the casket, going up on his toes to reach the center. His mother grasped the collar of his coat lest he tumble. The boy came back beside her and gazed up, the sorrow in his eyes matching the sorrow in hers.

The parents came next–Teddy's parents, the senior banker holding his wife's arm, she weeping. She waved a damp lace handkerchief at the casket, as if that would make it go away.

MacTeer moved up beside her, the rose from his lapel in his hand. He bent down. "You can do this, Mae," he said. "It's for your boy. I got a boy out here, too. I know how it hurts."

He placed the rose in her hand.

Mae Wilson held back her tears. With an effort, she reached out. She put the rose on the casket, and then, sobbing, asked her husband to take her away to the car–the Roberts & James limousine.

MacTeer touched the shoulder of Averrell Wilson as the banker and his wife passed by. "Sorry, Ave," he said.

"That was awfully good of you to do what you did with Mae Wilson," Garrison said when the two strolled back to the Whale.

"Hmm?"

"With Missus Wilson."

"Yes, well, come a time, you'll do that for others, too. Comes with lawyering."

CHAPTER 2

Boots and the pilot

A man's voice called out to Garrison as she entered the front hall of the house she shared with her father, "Anybody I know?"

"That you, Pop?" she asked, her attention on the envelopes she had taken from the letterbox.

"Last time I looked at the name on my pilot's license. Boots, come back here in the kitchen and give your old man a hug."

Garrison slipped out of her jacket. She dropped it somewhere near the newel post, then kicked off one shoe and the other. She padded away, opening an envelope as she moved along. "Now would you just look at this? I'm hardly out of law school, and the bank's dunning me for my student loan."

"How much they want?"

"Two hundred forty-six dollars and seventy-three pennies," Garrison said when she came into the kitchen, reading from the bottom of a printed statement. "I can pay the seventy-three cents."

Click glanced up from his workstation at the stove. "I've had a good month. Give it to me."

"Huh-uh. You'll pay it out of your retirement check."

He held out his hand, wiggled his fingers. "Really, Todd-a-o and I made some money this month. I know you don't believe it, but we're going to write each other an honest-to-God paycheck."

Garrison sniffed the aroma coming on waves of heat from the oven as she handed the bank bill to her father. "Pizza."

"Poppa Will's best."

"Dad, nobody makes pizza like you."

A grimace twisted its way onto Will Click's face. "When you say 'Dad', that tells me it's been a rough day."

"The judge and I went to Teddy Wilson's funeral." She drifted to the table. There she set about rearranging the plates and glasses.

"I'm sorry for you. Teddy was a good kid."

"Dad, he wasn't a kid. He was twenty-nine." Garrison turned to him, a glass in her hand. "Death doesn't bother you, does it?"

"Oh yeah." Click leaned on the palms of his well-floured hands. "Boots, I've been to three wars in your lifetime. Death bothers me a whole hell of a lot, but Teddy was a fool behind a steering wheel."

Garrison studied the glass, a water stain on the rim. She rubbed at it. "I guess he was, wasn't he? Can I get you a beer?"

"Dew if you don't mind."

She went to the refrigerator of the old-house-plain kitchen, the walls, cabinets, and ceiling painted a high-gloss white, white appliances, white enamel sink, the only color in the Formica counters and the linoleum on the floor–a beige flecked with gold. Garrison opened the refrigerator. She plowed a pathway through a forest of containers of leftovers, to a lone can of Mountain Dew and a can of Budweiser. "We really ought to have a fridge cleaning party."

"Go to it, kid."

"Yes. You're no hand at cleaning, are you?"

Click snorted. "Hogs. That's all we old men are is hogs."

Garrison handed the Mountain Dew to her father. "You know I demonstrated against your last war."

"Uh-huh, and I bailed you out of jail twice before I went over to Nam."

She touched his hand. "Why'd you never get mad about it?"

He pulled the pop top and, with a studied deliberation, dropped it back into the can. "Amanda, your mother and I raised you to be your own person. Knew we might not like what we got, but we determined to love you anyway."

"Thank you." She kissed his cheek, then brushed the tips of her fingers along it. "You know, you ought to shave twice a day."

"Your mother never said that."

"She was nicer than I am."

Click looked away, and Garrison put a hand on his arm. "You miss her, don't you?"

"Every day."

"Maybe we should go up to the cemetery."

"That'd be good."

A timer, shaped like a miniature beer stein, dinged on the counter.

Click wiped a sleeve at his eyes. "It's ready," he said.

"I'll get the plates."

"And I'll get the pizza."

Click, shorter than his daughter and trim for a man of forty-eight years, had the hard muscles that said he could still do calisthenics with the young men he had known in Vietnam. They were jet pilots, he a piston man who had learned the stick-and-rudder art back in the late 'Thirties. The U.S. had been slow to enter World War II, so Click went to England and joined the Royal Flying Corps. He had flown rescue missions in Europe. Later in the war, Click transferred to the American Army Air Corps and flew spotter missions low and slow in Piper Cubs–dangerous work. Any soldier with a pistol or a fool with a pitchfork could put a hole in your wing, he told his friends. Click transferred again to the U.S. Air Force when Congress created that branch of service.

The Air Force called him back for Korea. When he volunteered for Vietnam, the colonels put him in Cessna's hot new twin, the pusher-puller O-Two-A Skymaster.

There his orders were simple–go out and find enemy missile sites, make them light up their radars, then get the hell out so the pilots in the Phantoms could rocket them.

Click cut two slabs of pizza from the pan. He lifted each onto a plate, winking at his daughter as he did. "If I hadn't found this good ol' Bisquick recipe book at the Food Lion, you'd be eating that miserable thin-crust stuff."

"You do like a tall pizza."

"Double the portions for toppings and she stands up there a full two inches thick."

Garrison cut a forkful from her slab. She ate it in silence, sipping from her beer.

Some of the browned hamburger, seasoned with chili powder, rolled off Click's pizza when he cut a bite. He scooped up the meat and squished it back it into the cheese. "Anything else happen today?"

She gazed out the kitchen window. A hummingbird helicoptered there, in front of a plastic flower on the hummingbird feeder. "You remember Doctor Taylor?"

"Boots, he was our family doc forever. Shame how he died."

"Do you think someone intended to kill him?"

Click rubbed the palm of his hand across the top of the soft drink can before he raised it to his lips. "What's brought this on?"

"There was this newspaper clipping in an envelope. I found it under my windshield wiper this morning. Someone put it there. Someone wanted me to read it."

"Wonder why?"

"I don't know." The Ruby Throat zipped away, and Garrison turned to her father. "Do you think it was murder?"

"Boots, I was in Nam. All I know is what you told me in your letters at the time, and a little story and Doc's obituary in the Chief."

"You ever get concerned?"

"A couple minutes, maybe."

"That's pretty cold."

He waved his fork over his plate. "Look, back then my concern was flying fast enough so some black pajamas guy didn't shoot my fanny off."

"What did happen?"

"To Doc?"

"To you."

Click drew a hand down his face, stretching the leathery, sun-crisped skin, then he pushed his plate aside. "Boots, the only hazard for us helicopter and piston pilots was the enemy on the ground. They could put up a lot of bullets, so we went to sitting on our flack jackets when we were out flying. The senior officers didn't like it, but a bullet in the butt was going to go on up and tear hell out of our innards. If we weren't dead in the instant, we were going to be dead in the crash."

Garrison listened, horrified yet fascinated.

"We figured a shot in the arm–" Click slapped his biceps "–or in the leg, we could survive that. For me, I had blundered on a Cong supply depot. I wheeled my O-Two around and put a smoke rocket in there so the Phantoms could see it, then I put my bird in a steep bank to get out of there."

He gave a tug on the front of his tan shirt, a Vol-Air patch over the breast pocket. "Some lucky bastard on the ground got off a one-in-a-million shot–one bullet through the thighs of both my legs–blood spilling out like I was the proverbial stuck pig and no way to stop it."

"You must have been terrified."

"Hell no, I was mad. I was the one who was going to have to scrub the blood out of my airplane. I screamed into the radio, Lordy, I screamed into the radio. Anyway, all I knew was I needed seven hundred feet of airstrip to get down and the closest was twenty minutes away. Echo Two, one of the Phantoms I was working with, called to me, said he'd fly high cover." Click pulled his pizza back. He picked at a black olive. "A Cobra gun ship came out of nowhere. The pilot tells me on the radio if I go down, he's gonna land and pull me out. Talks to me all the way home. Last thing I remember him saying to me was my landing was an embarrassment to all pilots everywhere."

Click twisted his head to the side. He rubbed the back of his neck. "Probably was. I was so low on blood I was barely conscious. A one-in-a-million shot, two million-dollar wounds, the medic said as he worked on me. They sent me home and just as well. War isn't for old men."

"You weren't old."

"That Cobra pilot? Nineteen. I could have been his father. You didn't really want to know about this, did you?"

"You never talk about it."

"I'm like most of the vets, never felt there was much point."

"Your legs, they still hurt?"

"Only in the nightmares."

"You yell a lot at night."

"Yeah, I s'pose I do."

Garrison ran a finger along a crease in the yellow-and-red checked cloth that covered the table. "I wish there was something I could do for you."

"Kid, you do plenty, just being here, sharing this old place with your old man."

"It's home."

"I know."

"This is where I grew up."

"Most parents would say, at your age, you ought to be out on your own."

"You aren't most parents." She finished her pizza and went back to the pan for another slice. "You want more?"

"Sure." He held out his plate.

"Do you think it was murder? Doctor Taylor?" Garrison asked when she returned to the table.

"Unless Doc shot himself, then buried the gun, and that isn't likely." Click tapped on the table. "Murder is the only thing that makes sense, and that doesn't make any sense at all."

"Could he have surprised someone? Could someone maybe have been trying to break into his car?"

"It's possible, although I doubt Doc ever locked his car. Boots, I'm not the person to ask."

"Bunch?"

"Yeah, Bunch."

CHAPTER 3

The widow

"The judge in?" Garrison asked as she walked into the Freyberg Mansion, the house that served as offices for Hammond MacTeer and Garrison.

The old place needed paint, outside, not inside. Inside, the oak floors, the woodwork, and the glass gleamed, and Rachel Downey, Judge MacTeer's cleaning woman, had put new wallpaper in all the downstairs rooms. She didn't select the papers. That job had fallen to Millie Purkiss, MacTeer's secretary for longer than Garrison could remember. Purkiss had hectored the judge for years about the shabby condition of the old paper before she won her argument.

"The courthouse, Miss Garrison," Purkiss called from the file room that in a previous life had been the household pantry, the bell system still in place above the door that summoned the butler or serving woman to whatever room in which their services were needed. Only MacTeer used it now and only when he knew Millie Purkiss was in the file room.

Garrison turned toward her back-parlor office. Before she got to the doorway, Purkiss appeared at the end of the hall. She gestured at Garrison's office, mouthing the words "You have a client."

Garrison picked up her end of the silent conversation, asking "Who?"

"Anne Wilson."

She stared at the secretary.

"Yes," Purkiss mouthed. "Get in there."

Garrison switched her briefcase to her left hand, the briefcase a graduation gift from MacTeer. She carried it, not for need because it usually was empty, but for show. Going in, Garrison dropped the briefcase into a side chair and she went on to the woman waiting for her.

Anne Wilson, in a black suitdress, hat, and veil, rose from the crackled leather couch at the side of the room. Garrison embraced her.

"I'm so sorry for you," Garrison said, her voice husky, as if it were she who had been crying.

"Thank you."

"Is there anything I can do for you?"

"Yes."

Garrison leaned back. "Just name it."

Wilson looked at a spot just to the side of Garrison's shoulder. "Would you handle Teddy's estate?"

"Pardon?"

"Would you handle Teddy's estate? I don't know what to do."

"I don't think I can." She wanted to break off the embrace, but the sorrowing woman held to her arms, her hands sliding down until they grasped Garrison's hands.

For the first time, Anne Wilson looked directly into Garrison's eyes. "Why not?" she asked.

"Judge MacTeer does all the law work for the bank, for the Wilson family—for your family."

"I know, but he wants you to do this."

"Oh."

Purkiss slipped into the room. She carried a silver tray with two cups and a pot of tea. This she placed on Garrison's desk. "Tea," she said. "Earl Grey."

Now Garrison did break away. "Millie?"

"The Wilson file is on your desk."

"Oh."

"If there's anything else, I'll be at my desk." Purkiss left with the silence of a cat, and as quickly.

Garrison poured two cups of tea, then carried the cups

on their saucers to the couch. She handed one to the young woman in black. "How are the children doing?"

"Sue Ellen is too young to understand, you know. She just keeps asking when Daddy will be back." Wilson studied the surface of the tea in her cup, as if there might be some message of consolation there, or perhaps of hope. "James–he doesn't smile anymore."

Garrison sat beside Wilson. "It must be hard for him. I'd see Teddy and James at the park, running together, playing ball."

"Yes."

"They really loved each other, didn't they? You don't see that in many fathers."

"I know. It was special." Wilson sipped at her tea.

"Well, what do I need to know?" Garrison asked, moving the talk to business.

The widow pursed her lips. "There is no will."

"I see."

"We never got around to it. We always figured we had a lot of years before us."

Garrison shook her head. She could hear her law professors clucking. *You young people think you're going to live forever, that you don't need wills right now, and your clients are going to be the same way.* To get a grade in that course, each future lawyer had to draw up his or her own will. Garrison found it a sobering experience, deciding who should get her few possessions and her thin-as-six-o'clock bank account upon her death. "Did Teddy have any life insurance?"

Wilson set her cup aside. She brought an envelope out from her purse.

Garrison took the envelope. She opened it and scanned the documents, turning from page to page as she read. "This is generous, fifty thousand."

"Teddy bought it so I could pay for the house if anything happened to him."

"How much do you owe?"

"I don't know. Teddy never talked money with me.

When I'd ask, he'd laugh and say it was his job to make it and my job to spend it, that I didn't have to worry."

Garrison picked up a pen and a yellow legal pad from the side table. She made a note to check with the county clerk, to see whether a mortgage had been filed on the property. The filing would tell who held the mortgage. That information and a phone call, and she would know how much was owed. Garrison also made a note to get a death certificate from Wilsey James, to file with a claim she would have to send to the life insurance company.

"Any other obligations that you know of?" Garrison asked without glancing up.

"There could be, but I don't know."

"I'll ask Teddy's father, if that's all right with you."

"Would you?"

"If I'm to be your lawyer, that's my job."

Anne Wilson pressed one hand over the back of the other. That motion drew Garrison's gaze to the widow's hands and the ring she wore. The size of the diamond cluster in the setting–impressive. What might its worth be should the estate turn out to have so little in it that she would be forced to sell the ring? A sad affair should it come to that.

Anne Wilson continued pressing one hand over the other. "I feel so much better, having someone to help me. I have absolutely no head for this. It's all I can do to get out of the bed in the morning."

"What about the children?"

"Mae is taking care of them."

"That's good. That's what family's for."

"I'm scared. I'm scared all the time."

Garrison set the pad and pen aside. She took Anne Wilson's hands in hers. "Look at me."

Wilson did, her aura one of fear.

"Anne, you don't have to be frightened. There's going to be a lot of paperwork, filings that have to be made. It's going to look overwhelming to you, I know, but I'll take care of those things for you." Garrison raised a finger, and the woman focused on it. "There is one thing I have to ask."

"Yes?"

"Without a will, it's going to take time to probate Teddy's estate, maybe several months. Do you have money to live on until we get this thing settled?"

Wilson's head bobbed. "The night Teddy died, his father went to the bank. He took everything out of Teddy's accounts and put them into new accounts he opened under my name. He said he didn't want me to be hurting for money."

"That's good." Garrison pushed up from the couch, a cue to the widow that the meeting had reached an end.

Wilson also got up. She pulled her veil down over her face, and, clutching her purse, she hugged Garrison. "Thank you," she whispered.

"You'll take care of yourself?"

"I will," Wilson said, slow to release her embrace. When she did, her hand quaked, so she pressed it to her other hand. "I should be going."

"Yes. I'll come by to see you."

Wilson went to the hall door where Millie Purkiss waited. The two walked on together, to the front door where Purkiss said goodbye.

"You know," Garrison said when the secretary returned, "I wonder if she should be driving?"

"You needn't worry. Hoppy's driving for her today."

Hoppy. Real name Dawson Albanese, Morgantown's one-man, one-car taxi company, the Hop-In.

"I'll get the probate file for you," Purkiss went on. "It has copies of all the forms you'll have to file with the court." She dawdled. "Did you read that newspaper story about Doctor Taylor?"

"You put it on my car? Why?"

Purkiss stood in the doorway, a hand on the frame. "The doctor was a good man. In the months after, I tried to get Judge MacTeer to do something, but he wouldn't."

"Why not?"

She shrugged. "Just said there was nothing there. But I

know there has to be something."

"Why do you say that?"

"It's a feeling. No one should be permitted to take another's life and get away with it."

CHAPTER 4

The deputy

Garrison spotted Judge MacTeer leaning over a bubbler in the hallway of the courthouse, slurping at the stream of water jetting up. She came up beside him.

"Low cal?" she asked.

MacTeer patted his expansive mid-section as he straightened up. "No cal."

"Judge, if you don't mind me saying it, you smell of onions."

"Do like them with my scrambled eggs. Is it too much?"

Garrison brought out a roll of peppermint Lifesavers from her jacket pocket. "Have one?"

"My, aren't you prepared for everything."

"Why don't you take them all," she said as she pressed the roll into his hand. "Oh, and thank you for the client."

MacTeer brightened. "So Anne came by?"

"She did."

"You'll do right by her, and, AJ, if you string the probate out long enough, you'll make a nice pile of money in fees. You know the number one rule of probate."

"There's a rule?"

He winked. "The lawyer gets all of the estate he can."

"Are you serious?"

MacTeer's eyes glistened. "Welcome to the world of lawyering. You here to see old Floyd?"

"I thought the county clerk would be a good place to start."

"You greet him for me," he said and hauled away, toward the fiscal court's meeting room.

Garrison took to the stairs, wondering what he meant about the number one rule of probate. None of her law professors had ever mentioned such a thing. She moved on up to the second floor. *Maybe it's a joke, and I'm too dense to get it.*

Beyond the top of the stairs hung a sign–Office of County Clerk. Garrison stepped out of the way as a short, dumpy man in bib overalls and a seed-corn cap came out of the clerk's suite of rooms. Then she went in, to the counter. Garrison leaned across, craning to see into the records room.

There by her elbow sat a ring-for-service bell and a bowl of M&Ms. Garrison took a candy and touched the button on the top of the bell. That set off a ding, a weak call for help. A buxom woman in a nondescript print dress came out of the records room.

"Is Mister Bitner in?" Garrison asked.

"Floyd?"

"Yes."

"He's in his office." Hazel McIntyre, Bitner's office manager–not overly tall in her low-heeled shoes–crossed through toward a side office. She rapped on the door frame. "Floyd, you have a customer."

"Be right there."

McIntyre, primping her blue hair, turned to Garrison. "Floyd will be with you directly."

"Thank you."

"Not at all," she said and moved toward the neatest of the three desks to answer a telephone.

Bitner, wearing sleeve protectors, emerged from his office. Tall and lean, he moved with deliberation, like a crane stalking a river's edge in search of fish. His thin, beak-like nose added to the effect.

"Amanda," he said, stepping up his pace, his hands and arms rising like wings. When he got to the counter, he settled on them–on his knuckles. "What is it I can do for you?"

"Mister Bitner, I'm helping Anne Wilson with Teddy's estate."

"Ahh, Ham said you'd be up."

Garrison pitched up an eyebrow.

"What can I get for you?" Bitner asked.

"I need to see if there's a mortgage on the house."

"Anne doesn't know?"

"Apparently not. Teddy didn't share the business aspects of marriage with her."

"Huh, old fashioned, just like his daddy. Well, I think I know the answer, but let's go back and look at the property book just to be sure." Bitner opened a gate at the end of the counter for Garrison. She followed his great long strides back to the records room. "Teddy bought that house in 'Sixty-Three, didn't he, Hazel?" he called back to his chief assistant.

"That's right."

"May, wasn't it?"

"Yes."

"I swear," Bitner said to Garrison when the two were in the records room, "I think Hazel's memorized every piece of paper we've got in the place. Don't let this get around, but she's really the clerk. I just put in my time and, every two years, make the rounds of the church suppers, campaigning for re-election."

He edged along shelves of property books. He spied one on the third shelf that had 1963 stamped in gold leaf on the spine. Bitner pulled the book out.

"May, May, May," he mumbled as he paged into the property ledger. "May first, May eighth, May twelfth, here it is."

Bitner laid the ledger open on a table by a side window. Garrison came closer and followed his finger.

"Eight-sixteen Maple, just up from the Methodist church. Really nice house. Bought it for fifty-nine-seven with a forty-two-thousand-dollar loan from the bank. I guess when you work at the bank you can always get a loan."

"Particularly when your father owns it," Garrison said.

Bitner's finger stopped moving along the notations. He tapped the book. "Just what I thought. Teddy paid off the mortgage last year. Here's the note removing the mortgage from the book."

Garrison set her briefcase on the table. She took out a legal pad and a pen. "Do you know how long the mortgage was to run?"

"Standard thirty-year."

"And Teddy paid it off in four?"

"Mm-hmm."

"I wonder how?"

"Maybe his daddy gave him a raise."

"Do you believe that?"

Bitner's shoulders rose and dropped.

"The down payment, do you know where that came from?"

"That I do know," Bitner said. He went back to the shelves and pulled out another property ledger, this one stamped 1961. He returned, paging through it. "Ave and Mae gave Teddy that little house on Fourth Street—a wedding present."

He put the book down, open to that transaction, then paged back in the 1963 book to March 17. "Along comes a baby boy. They need a bigger place. So Teddy sells the little house—see here—for seventeen-thousand-seven, and that becomes the down payment."

"Well, trading up, at least there was no capital gain."

Bitner's hand swept back over his head. His fingers drew several long stands of hair over his bald spot. "There might be now, with Teddy killing himself and you havin' to transfer the deed to the widow. That's a whole new transaction, Amanda. You better check the tax law real close."

"I'll do that."

Bitner looked down from his height. "You want me to draw up a new deed for Anne? I can do that since there's no lien on the property."

"Would you?"

Bitner went for the current year's property ledger. He opened it to the last entry and, with a pen from his shirt pocket, began a new entry. "There's a ten-dollar transfer fee. Cash or check?"

Garrison didn't answer.

Bitner glanced up. "Money tight? Tell you what, why don't I just put it on the tax bill and Anne can pay it when the bills go out in January?"

Garrison finished filling out a request for the transfer of deed. She signed it as Anne Wilson's lawyer and gave the request to McIntyre. "Would you thank Mister Bitner for helping me?" Garrison asked.

McIntyre fanned herself with the request form. "If you really want to thank him, next time you come up, you bring him a cold RC."

"That's his favorite?"

"Never drinks anything but."

Garrison nodded her appreciation. She left. Outside the door she collided with a deputy sheriff, the man a good thirty pounds overweight. A file folder flew from his hand, and the papers showered over the floor and down the top steps of the stairway.

Garrison's face flushed. She grabbed the man's arm. "Uncle Bunch, I'm sorry."

"Amanda, it was my fault," Bunch Jeffords said. He broke away and scrambled after the errant pages. "You know me, I'm always an accident waitin' ta happen."

"Let me help."

"Oh, you don't want to go gettin' the knees of yer pretty pantsuit dirty on our floors. Besides, I got 'em all now." He stuffed the papers, crisscrossed and upside down, back into the folder. Huffing, Jeffords pushed himself up. He swatted at the knees of his khakis, the creases long since gone from them. "What you doin' here, little one? Little one–listen to me, you're all growed up, and a lawyer now. Seems only yesterday yer daddy'd bring you by, just a little tyke. I'd be chasin' after you to get you out of file drawers and such. You was always into somethin'. Oh my, I'm just runnin' on, ain't I?"

"You're just being the dear old Uncle Bunch I know."

"Well, come over here." He pulled Garrison toward an oak bench at the side of the hallway. "Come. Sit. Tell me what yer up to." Jeffords swept imagined dust from the bench with the papers hanging out of the file folder. Then he slapped the bench.

Garrison sat down, and Jeffords sat next to her, his undershirt showing through the open collar of his shirt and his shirttail out over a back pocket. "Well, come on, give," he said.

"Well, I'm working on Teddy Wilson's estate."

"Oh gawd, that was some awful accident that killed Teddy, waddn't it? I was the first one there, ya know. When I saw him layin' there in the ditch, all cut up like he was, I threw up my guts right there. Oh, I shouldn't be tellin' you that."

"Uncle Bunch, it's all right."

Jeffords grinned like a bear with his paw in a honey tree. "So yer officin' with the judge, I hear."

"That's right."

"Oh, that's good. He's a good man, good way for you to start out in the law world."

Garrison leaned forward. She touched Jeffords' knee. "Uncle Bunch–"

"Oh gawd, you still callin' me Uncle Bunch. You know we ain't related."

"Uncle Bunch, what happened to Doctor Taylor?"

Jeffords parked his elbows on his knees. He tucked the file and his hands up under his chin. "You waddn't here, was you?"

"No, I was up in law school."

Jeffords shook his head. "It was an awful thing. I s'pose you know I found him."

"Yes."

"You was real close to him, waddn't you?"

"I always thought so."

"You sure was a favorite of the doc. He'd go on about you at the drop of a hat."

"So what happened?"

"Gawd, hon, I don't know. I was workin' late in the office for some damn reason I can't remember." Jeffords paused. He pulled a bandana from his back pocket and wiped at a watering eye. "I heard this damn shot an' go running out there in the alley, an' there's Doc bleedin', dead right there beside his car. Who'd go and shoot old Doc?"

Jeffords twisted around. "Not a gawddamn soul ta be seen, him all alone there. Well, now, I'm like a crazy man. I run into the courthouse yellin' the doc's been shot, and there's Judge MacTeer and Judge Lattimer, and they tell me to get the sheriff, and I call Clarence at his house. Thank gawd he was home that night."

"Did you find anything?"

Jeffords wiped at his eye again. "Not a gawddamn thing. Oh, I shouldn't be swearin' like this, but I can't help it–"

"That's all right."

"–not a gun, not a shell, which leads me to think it was a revolver. The judge is tryin' to put his jacket over Doc an' I'm yellin', 'Git away! Git away! I gotta go through his pockets!' An' that's when I found the gawd-awful roll of cash, big enough it'd gag a cow."

Jeffords blew his nose into his bandana. He rubbed at the tip as he glanced up the hall one way and down the other. "You know what was gawd-awful amazin'? We didn't give this to the papers." The deputy held up two fingers as a smoker would. "Doc had a lit cigarette. He was smokin' when he died."

"What's unusual about that, Uncle Bunch? Doctor Taylor always smoked."

"Like a chimley, I know, here in the courthouse, in the office. I'm told he even smoked when he was cuttin' on somebody in the operating room. But do you know what that cigarette tells me?"

Garrison shrugged.

"Tells me old Doc knew the bugger who shot him. He

was talkin' to him, comfortable and all, you know, an' that damn fool whips out a gun and shoots Doc before he can even drop his cigarette."

A woman–Mavis Germaine, a secretary in the county treasurer's office–topped the stairs.

Jeffords looked up. "Howdy, Mave."

"Bunch," she said, nodding as she passed, her hips swishing her skirt.

"Handsome woman," Jeffords said.

Garrison jabbed an elbow in his ribs.

"Well, she is," Jeffords said.

"You're married."

"Don't mean I can't look."

After the woman disappeared into the treasurer's office, Garrison asked, "Do you really think Doctor Taylor knew who shot him?"

"Damn right. I'll go to my grave believing that. You know what makes me mad?" Jeffords glanced up and down the hall again, then touched shoulders with Garrison, the musky aroma of his aftershave growing. "After three days, the sheriff told all us deputies to hang it up, that we didn't have anything to go on, an' we didn't."

"But if you didn't have anything–"

"Still an' all," Jeffords said, waving his folder of papers, "we shoulda kept tryin'. Gawd, everybody loved old Doc. He delivered three of my kids, you know."

"Do you know anything about the gun?"

He dropped his volume. "Now don't you go tellin' anybody what I'm about to tell you. It was a Forty-Five."

"How do you know?"

"Hon, a Forty-Five blows a helluva hole in a man at close range, particularly when it comes out the back side. I saw the wounds. I figured, from where old Doc lay, that bullet went on an' either hit the wall of the jail or the telephone pole back there. I searched half the night after ever'body left."

"And?"

"I found it, mm-hmm, buried in the telephone pole,

chest high." Jeffords held up a hand, indicating the height. "I dug it out, an' I still got that bullet to this day."

"Did you show it to Sheriff Bogle?"

"I don't know why, hon, but I didn't. Maybe I figured I could be the Lone Ranger, find the gun an' match the bullet to it." Jeffords tugged at the lobe of his ear. "Someday maybe. I haven't yet, but I check ever' gun we confiscate."

CHAPTER 5

Hiccups and sputters

Sarah–Garrison's elderly Beetle named for a favorite teacher–coughed and hiccupped, snapping Garrison out of the probate maze her mind had been wandering.

The vintage Volkswagen shuddered, sputtered, sneezed, and backfired, slinging Garrison back into the world of the Alcoa Pike, truckers in vehicles the size of houses trundling their cargo to new destinations and commuters racing for home.

Her fingers gripped the wheel, like rubberbands doubled over and doubled over again.

Shudder, shudder-shake, then silence.

Her eye caught the speedometer's needle dropping–fifty-five, fifty.

She tromped down on the clutch pedal, cutting Sarah's wheels free from the dead engine, and the Beetle rolled without restraint. Still, it slowed.

Garrison ground on the starter to no avail. She glanced up at the mirror, her eyes widening at the sight of a GMC diesel's grill blotting out all else behind. She forced herself to search for an out, a break in the string of cars coming her way, a gap she could drift Sarah through to the airport entrance road.

Garrison bit into her lip. She spun the steering wheel and swerved between a Buick stationwagon and a BMW Sportster. Behind, the diesel driver hauled down on his air horn. He blasted by with his trailer load of JFG Coffee, the wind rocking the Beetle.

Tires screeched.

Garrison whipped her head toward the sound, blanching at the sight of the Sportster careening toward her in a sideways skid.

She clung to the steering wheel–thirty-five, thirty–then Sarah cleared the highway.

A woman in an Olds Ninety-Eight hammered her horn, skirting the BMW as it slewed onto the highway's shoulder, its rear end going south.

Garrison pressed her attention ahead, burring through clenched teeth, "Come on, come on. Make the next turn, pleeeease."

Twenty-five, twenty.

She slapped the turn signal down, encouraging, cajoling, willing the Beetle onto an access road that would take her to the trailer that officed her father's flight business.

Fifteen, ten.

Garrison surrendered to the laws of physics. She steered Sarah off the road and onto the shoulder, gravel crunching beneath the car's tires. The Beetle rolled ever more slowly until its forward momentum expired. Garrison took her foot from the clutch pedal, reasoning the dead engine would keep the car where it was, but she also hauled up on the hand brake.

The effort hurt.

It hurt Garrison to sit up, hurt to lean back in the seat. The knotted muscles in her back screamed at her. Why hadn't she worn her brace?

Garrison closed her eyes as a tremor in her hands grew. *Dumb, dumb, dumb. I could've been killed.*

She tried to pound her fists against the steering wheel, but lacked the strength. What would she tell her father, that Sarah had died on the Alcoa, at the height of rush hour, when exiting to the airport was, at best, a gambler's business?

No.

Sarah had died on the access road, where there was no

traffic.

Garrison felt for the door handle. She let herself out of her rusty, dusty, dinged, and dented Beetle. All through law school she had thought of leaving the doors unlocked, of leaving the key in the ignition, of putting a sign on the windshield that said 'Steal me, please.'

Her shoes came down on gravel that had been kicked up onto the pavement. Garrison pushed herself out, the back of her sweat-soaked blouse ripping away from the seat back. With one hand she clung to the door, and with the other, she massaged her twinging muscles. Now she smelled it, the ugly stench of an overheated engine. And her nose wrinkled.

Her father would say it could be worse, but to Garrison nothing was worse than walking when her back ached and sweat dribbled down her temples. A couple hundred yards unless someone came by for a late flight lesson and took pity on her shuffling along beside the road. But no one came, nor did anyone leave from Vol-Air, driving up toward the Alcoa Turnpike.

A Southern Airways twin turned final for Runway Five. Garrison shaded her eyes from the afternoon sun. She watched the high-winged, boxy airliner move with the smoothness of a dancer as its pilot brought the airplane into line with the runway. Her father called the Fairchild-Hiller a bone shaker and maybe it was, but in the air, sliding down the glide path of the approach to landing, the airplane was grace personified.

Garrison limped on. She cut through the ditch and climbed up the far side onto the close-cropped grass that paralleled the taxiway that led to Vol-Air. Two airplanes there, Garrison's father's twin-engined Skymaster and his little One-Fifty, both parked in front of the trailer.

Were the cowling doors off the One-Fifty? Someone appeared to be looking in at the engine. "Dad!" she called out.

A man in tan twills turned. He waved, a wrench in his hand. "Lose your wheels, Boots?"

"Sarah died."

"Again? Where?"

Garrison gestured back in the direction from which she had come.

Will Click gazed at the small car on the horizon. "What happened?"

"I don't know."

"Todd," Click said, turning back to the airplane.

A head came up from the far side of the engine. "I heard," the man said. "You want I should see if I can fix it?"

"Yup."

"Well, we're done here." Todd Arnold Oliver pulled a cleaning rag from his back pocket. He scrubbed dirt and grease from his hands as he strolled around the nose of the One-Fifty.

"Sorry, Todd," Garrison said when she came up.

"You know, if I were Triple-A, I could make a helluva good livin' fixing your car."

Oliver, a large-framed man, hard muscled from years of daily workouts in the Air Force, had been Click's maintenance chief in Vietnam. Now he was a partner in their flight school and charter service.

Oliver moved away to his car, a Ford Fairlane woody–a stationwagon. He closed the toolbox on the tailgate and pushed the box inside. Oliver flipped his cleaning rag into the back seat, climbed in behind the steering wheel, and drove off.

Click gestured at the hinged doors on the tarmac in front of the One-Fifty. "Give me a hand, would ya, Boots?"

She went to the far side. Together, they picked up the door assemblage.

"What happened out there?" he asked.

"I don't know. Sarah just hiccupped and quit."

They lifted the assemblage over the propeller–"You really ought to get a better car, kid."

"I can't afford a better car"–and lowered it into place, closing in the engine.

Click produced a screwdriver. With it, he twisted the

locking screws on his side down flush. "Wanna get those on your side?" he asked as he handed the screwdriver across.

Garrison took it. She twisted the first locking screw down on her side. "What happened with the One-Fifty?"

"Engine got to running rough while I was up on a lesson." Click rubbed his hands on a cleaning rag. He took time to work it around and under each fingernail.

"Yes?" Garrison asked.

"First thought was dirty fuel–crud, maybe water. So I landed and sent the student home, and Todd-a-o and I drained the fuel system." He inspected his nails.

"And?" Garrison asked as she attacked another locking screw.

"We strained the gas. Stuff was clean. Put it back in, then, for the heck of it, we put in new spark plugs. Never know, plugs could have been fouled."

Garrison twisted the last screw down. She handed the screwdriver back to her father.

"Get in, kid," he said. "Let's take her up and see if she runs right." Click wrapped his rag around the screwdriver. He pitched them both in the direction of the trailer's front door, and the screwdriver banged off and fell to the tarmac.

"You want me on the right?" Garrison asked.

"Left seat. You got your sunglasses?"

"Not with me."

"I got extra in the seat pocket."

Garrison had flown with her father for as long as she could remember, but always as a passenger until a month ago. He talked her into the left seat, into taking lessons. She now had six hours of pilot-in-command time. Garrison thought her air work was all right, but landings? She once bounced the One-Fifty half way down the runway before she got it planted on the ground.

Garrison walked around the airplane as her father had taught her to do. She ran a hand along the leading edge of first one wing, then the other, and the tail, checking for dings and dents that would roughen the air flowing over the flying surfaces. She wiggled the ailerons, the elevators, and the rudder–squinted into their openings at the connections to the control cables.

She knelt and peered up under the fuselage. No damage. Garrison checked the brake lines and the tires, the wing struts, and the propeller. She opened the oil access door on the cowling and inspected the engine. She pulled the dipstick out–oil okay. Then Garrison drained a spurt of gas from the sump, where water collects when there's water in the gas.

Done, she dragged a step ladder over. Garrison set it in front of the right wing and climbed up to open the gas cap. Click's rule: Stick your finger in the tank, make sure it's full. Gas gauges, he told all his students, will lie to you.

"Your finger wet?" Click asked after Garrison finished screwing the cap back down on the right wing tank.

She gave him an indulgent smile and toted the ladder to the left wing. Again she climbed up. "You're paranoid about this."

"Darn right. God doesn't build gas stations in the sky."

Garrison stuck her finger in the second tank. "Two fingers wet, one from the other tank."

"Super. Let's go then."

Click laid the ladder aside and horsed himself into the right seat while Garrison worked her way up onto the left. Both buckled their lap belts.

Garrison glanced at her father. "Is that bubble gum I smell?"

"My last student." He motioned to the side pouch, and Garrison pulled out the aircraft's check list. While she ran down it, he rummaged for sunglasses and found two pairs in a seatback pocket. He handed a pair to Garrison.

She put them on, then turned the ignition key. The engine burred to life.

After the pilot and the instructor settled headphones over their ears, Click snapped the radio on. "Ready to go?" he asked.

Garrison gave a thumbs-up.

"Knoxville Ground," Click said into his mic, "Cessna

Six-Seven-Two Charlie Victor at Vol-Air. Ready to taxi."

"Six-Seven-Two Charlie Victor, Knoxville Ground," came back the reedy voice of a controller–a high tenor. "Altimeter setting two-niner-niner-six. Wind north at five. Active Runway Five. Cleared to taxi. You're number two behind the Southern Fairchild."

"Roger that," Click said.

Garrison set the airplane's altimeter. At twenty-nine point nine-six, the altimeter read nine hundred eighty feet above sea level, one foot short of the airport's true altitude. Garrison pushed in on the throttle. That started the airplane rolling as the Fairchild passed by on the taxiway, its turbine engines whistling.

The wash from the airliner's propellers buffeted the little trainer, the air smelling of burned jet fuel.

Garrison touched the brakes. She held the One-Fifty back until its wings stopped rocking, then goosed the throttle and swung in behind the Fairchild.

"Ground, how about an intersection departure?" Click said into his microphone. "We don't need two miles of runway."

"Roger, Two Charlie. You be ready to go before the Fairchild?"

"We'll let you know."

"Hold short of Five for your runup. Contact tower on one-twenty-one-two."

"Roger."

"You hear that, Southern Three Twenty-One?" the ground controlled asked.

"Roger that." The voice of the Southern captain.

"You may have a little bird on the runway ahead of you."

"Okey-dokey."

Garrison pulled back on the throttle, slowing for the turnoff to the intersecting taxiway. After she made the turn, she swung the One-Fifty into the wind and stopped and ran through her checklist, engine run-up, and magneto check. Satisfied all was right, she gave a nod to her father.

He keyed his microphone. "Tower, Six-Seven-Two Charlie Victor, ready for intersection departure."

"Roger, Two Charlie Victor, hurry it along." A new voice, this one a baritone. "Southern Three Twenty-One is taking the active, number two behind you."

Garrison pumped power to the trainer aircraft, and it rolled out onto the runway. She turned the One-Fifty up the centerline and shoved the throttle to the firewall.

"Two Charlie Victor off the ground," Click said into his microphone.

"Roger. Who's at the controls this afternoon?"

"My daughter."

"Nice takeoff, AJ."

"Thanks, Marsh," Garrison said.

"Where you going?"

"Request right departure," Click said, "out to a practice area."

"Roger that. Engine running all right?"

"So far."

"Keep me posted. . . . Southern Three Twenty-One, cleared for takeoff. Cessna ahead is breaking right. You're going left."

"Yup, and thank you. See y'all tomorrow."

Garrison made a guess that, by the Southern captain's accent, he came from Mississippi. She put the One-Fifty into a climbing turn to the right. "What altitude, Pop?"

"Forty-five hundred. Bring her to a heading of one-two-five degrees."

"Any reason we're going that way?"

"Aw, I just like to look at the mountains."

But Garrison saw that her father's gaze was not out the windows, but at the engine gauges to his side, particularly the tachometer. "Everything all right?"

"Engine's purring like a fat old tabby cat."

Garrison rolled the airplane into level flight as the altimeter's needles approached the forty-five-hundred-foot mark. The airspeed crept up to a hundred miles per hour.

She grinned. The One-Fifty was like her Volkswagen,

no speed machine and its interior just as snug.

Click nudged her elbow. "Good day at the courthouse?"

"Are you trying to distract me?"

"A good pilot should be able to fly and talk at the same time."

"I haven't been doing this all that long. There's Clingmans Dome and Mount LeCont over there."

Click scratched at his shoulder. "I'd be disappointed if they weren't. So, you have a good day at the courthouse?"

"Saw Uncle Bunch," she said over the noise of the engine.

"Uh-huh."

"He has the bullet that killed Doctor Taylor. Did you know that?"

"Strange. You'd think something like that would be in an evidence locker."

"Know what's more strange?"

"No."

"Uncle Bunch says Doctor Taylor knew who shot him, that they must have been talking together before the man brought out his gun."

"Know where we are?"

Garrison glanced out her side window. "Genesis under the left wing."

"Where's the airport?"

"Fifteen miles behind us."

"Can you see Knoxville?"

Garrison twisted further to the side. She scanned the horizon, searching for the Tennessee River and the outlines of the city on the horizon to its north.

Click yanked the throttle back, and the nose of the airplane dropped.

Garrison gasped. She hauled back on the control wheel. That brought the nose of the airplane up well above the horizon.

"You'll stall her," Click said. He pushed on his control wheel. That forced the nose back down. "You lost your engine."

"It's still running."

"Not fast enough to keep us up here. And don't touch the throttle."

"Dad!"

"Don't 'Dad' me. Get us out of the sky."

She stared at him, but only for an instant, then spun the trim tab back, slowing the aircraft to a better glide speed. Garrison glanced at the altimeter. Three hundred feet gone. But the rate of descent had slowed.

"Can we get back to the airport?" Click asked.

"I don't think so." Still she laid the One-Fifty into a steep turn, to take it back to McGhee Tyson. "I've lost five hundred feet."

"Then we're not going to get home. Find someplace else."

"We're in the mountains, Dad!"

"Look for some flat land."

Garrison straightened up. She peered over the nose, then out her side window. "Below us, Dry Valley."

"Think you can get us in there?"

"I don't know."

"Look around."

"There's Paradise Cove to the south."

"Bigger, isn't it?"

"Yes."

"Go for it."

Garrison banked the One-Fifty toward the cove, the mountains of the Great Smokies reaching their peaks upward, like so many knobby claws. She winged across Rich Gap, clearing it by a thousand feet with Cerulean Knob off to her left. Garrison skated the One-Fifty between Double Mountain and Paradise Cove Mountain, and slid over Punkin Ridge–all in silence, except for a rush of air beyond her door.

"Where you gonna land?" Click asked.

"The road, straight ahead."

"Good choice, but you're high."

"What do I do?"

"Put your flaps down, all the way."

Garrison jammed a control lever down, and the flaps slid out from beneath the wings. Like brakes, they slashed the forward speed of the aircraft, but they also brought the nose up. Garrison shoved the nose back down, and the aircraft dropped toward the ground like a sick puppy.

"I got it," Click said, not a whisper of concern in his voice. He took the control wheel and leaned the One-Fifty into an 'S' turn, eating up altitude–a double turn that brought the aircraft out over the north-south road that bisected the cove.

Fifty feet.

Twenty-five feet.

The stall-warning horn squalled.

Garrison stared at the airspeed–forty-five, the One-Fifty on the ragged edge of a stall–and the main wheels bumped down.

Click slowed the airplane. He turned it off into a hayfield and stopped. There he cut the ignition. "AJ, you all right?" he asked as he peeled off his headset.

"Can I lie?"

Chapter 6

Mountain home

Garrison sat for a long moment, her hands shaking on the control wheel of the Cessna.

"Could I have done that?" she asked.

Click rubbed at the hair on the back of his neck. "Maybe not the 'S' turn, but you would have got us down, somewhat further down the road." He stepped out of the airplane.

"Would there have been enough road left?"

"Think so."

"You think so. Dad, that's not very comforting."

"Hey, emergencies aren't comforting. If we panic, we're dead. Now hop out and stretch your legs."

Garrison forced herself out, out of the stuffiness of the tight little cabin that smelled of sweat and the dust of the road. She shaded her eyes from the glare of the sun hanging low over Pine Mountain. "You ever lose one? An airplane?"

"I've had a couple shot out from under me. But as a civilian, no, I've never lost one. Well, that's not true," Click said as he went down to the unpaved track. Garrison hurried after him, and they moved away to the south.

"You've lost an airplane?" she asked.

"Ran out of gas on takeoff. Damned embarrassing. Everybody in the tower saw me go down. Gawd, they razzed me."

"That was mean."

"Hey, I deserved it. So yes, I practice this stuff, so if I

really have to make an emergency landing, I won't bend up my bird, or at least not too badly. Boots, your aim as a pilot is always to be able to walk away."

A meadow lark winged up out of the weeds. It circled and landed on a decaying fence post where it puffed out its chest and sang, ignoring the creatures passing by.

"How's the estate going?" Click asked.

"You heard?"

"Stopped at the Sunshine this morning for coffee. The judge was there. He told me."

"Well, I got the house transferred to Anne. Now I've got to work on getting the titles changed on the cars."

"And the airplane."

"What airplane?"

"Teddy was a pilot. He flew an Aero Commander. I s'pose it was his, or the bank's."

"Anne didn't mention it."

"She probably didn't think of it."

"I'll add that to my to-do list."

The road rose near the south end of the cove. Click moved off. He climbed a hillock that had grown wild since the National Park had absorbed the cove. Where the hill flattened out stood a small cluster of gravestones.

Garrison stopped. "You planned this, didn't you?"

"I confess." Click knelt beside one of the gray slabs. He brushed a hand over the lettering. "This is your grandfather's grave."

"I know."

He turned on his haunches, looked up at his daughter. "We haven't been up here for a long time together, have we?"

"Maybe two years."

Click aimed his fingers to the side. "Your grandmother's there. There's my uncle—my dad's brother. Over there, their sister, died in a flood when she was six. Their grandparents over there. And you know that one—my sister, your namesake."

He pushed himself up and stuffed his hands in his back

pockets. "I gotta come up here with a mower, trim all this up, wash the headstones before winter."

Garrison put a hand on her father's shoulder. She leaned against him. "Your dad took care of this place and now you do."

"Yup, and someday, after I'm planted here, I'd appreciate it if you'd do the same."

They strolled together to the newest grave, newest by the dates on the headstone–*Willa Garrison Click, 1920-1958*. Click's gaze came to rest on the name. "Hi-dee, Willa. Meet the lawyer in your family, your daughter."

Garrison slipped her arm through her father's arm. "You still talk to her."

"Oh yeah. I got that from my pa. After my mother died, nights he'd sit out here for hours and talk to her, telling her everything he was doing on the farm, how her apple trees and her flower gardens were getting on. He told me, when I came home from Korea, he'd come out here and read my letters to her, every one I wrote home." Click rubbed Garrison's hand. "If you don't mind, I'm going to sit a spell and catch your mother up on what you've been doing."

She stroked her father's cheek, then ambled away into what had once been a cornfield and a pasture. Beyond had been her grandparents' house and farm buildings. She could still see them in the window of her memory. When Luther Click died, the National Park took possession of the farm. The park people sent in a crew with a bulldozer, to push the buildings over, to burn them, then bury the rubble and ashes. The only thing left–the stonework of the well and the orchard trees, ragged now from age and neglect. The fields went back to native grasses. The cove now looked like it was before the first white man arrived, rangers told park visitors. Maybe it does, Garrison thought, but my family history is gone, except for the cemetery.

A green pickup rolled down the old overmountain road from Punkin Ridge. It turned onto the cove's bisecting road, dust billowing out as the truck picked up speed. It slowed as it passed the airplane, then picked up speed again. Garrison turned back to the cemetery. "Pop, we got company."

Click shaded his eyes. "That'd be Tubby."

"We in trouble?"

"You bet. We're not supposed to land in national parks." He got to his feet and slapped the dust from his trousers. "Let's go face the old dragon."

The truck slurred to the side of the road as Click and Garrison came down the hillock.

"Gawddamn it, Will Click, I shoulda known that was your plane," Frank Tubbs bellowed from his rolled-down window.

Click raised his hands as he and Garrison continued on.

"What the hell's yer excuse this time?"

"Engine trouble."

The park ranger pushed the door of his pickup open, revealing his belly lapped over against the steering wheel. He wedged himself out. Tubbs limped up the rise, his scowl changing to a grin. He and Click fell together in a bear hug, each pounding the other's back.

"How the hell are ya, pard?" Tubbs asked.

"Movin' all right."

"Yer gawddamn lucky not to have my limp. The old war wound still bothers me."

"How's the wife, Tub?"

"Wishin' you'd come by and have supper some night."

"Can I bring my little girl?"

The ranger leaned back. He looked at Garrison. "Gawd, she's a handsome thing, ain't she? Musta got her looks from Willa, sure not from you, old scout." He chucked Click aside and hugged Garrison. "My, you was just a little peanut last time I saw ya. You probably don't 'member me."

Garrison fought for breath. "I do, Mister Tubbs."

"Call me Tubby. Ever'body does. Now what the hell happened?"

"Engine trouble, as Pop says."

"Girl, you lie like yer pa."

Tubbs released Garrison and hauled Click in. "Is that damn thing gonna run so you can get outta here?"

"Now that it's cooled down, I think so."

"Well, climb in my office. I'll give ya a ride."

Tubbs went to the truck. He pushed all the litter on the seat, including his lunch bucket and coffee thermos, onto the floor.

Garrison slid into the center. She tried to find a place for her feet among the junk on the floor as Click took the shotgun seat.

Tubbs pulled the shift lever into 'Drive' and spun the steering wheel, turning the truck back to the road. "Everything all right up at the cemetery?" he asked as he spun the wheel in the other direction, straightening the truck out.

"Yup, but I got to come up and trim the grass. It's gotten shaggy since summer."

"Always does that."

"You know my girl's a lawyer?"

"For real?"

"For real."

A toothy grin came to Tubbs' face. He twisted toward Garrison. "Yer just the person I need to see."

"Why's that?"

"I'm buying a little farm outside Jericho. I need somebody to look over the deed and the contract, to make sure I'm not doin' somethin' stupid."

"She can do that for you," Click said.

Tubbs turned his attention out the windshield. He swerved around a groundhog scurrying across the road. "Where's your office?"

"Do you know where Judge MacTeer has his?" Garrison asked.

"In the old Freiburg Mansion?"

"I'm there, too."

"Well, tomorrow's my day off. Kin I come by, say, around ten?"

Click looked over. "Tubby, AJ will cancel her

appointments to make time for you."

"Excellent."

"Whose farm you buying?"

"The Parsons place." Tubbs wheeled his pickup off the road and into the hayfield. He brought his truck to a stop beside the silent One-Fifty. "I'll wait fer you to get off. Will, it's damn lucky it wasn't my partner found ya. He'd a writ ya a ticket."

Click and Garrison slid out of the seat. She made a quick walk-around of the airplane while he came around to Tubbs' window.

"You come by for supper now," the ranger said.

"When you get moved into your new place, it's a promise."

Tubbs looked beyond Click to Garrison settling into the left seat of One-Fifty. "You got a mighty fine girl there."

"You're good to say that."

"No, I mean it."

Click backed away, waving. "Thanks, Tubby." He turned and opened the airplane's passenger door.

Garrison snapped the master switch on while Click pulled himself into the cabin. The gyroscopes whirred up. In went the mixture control, the throttle cracked, a turn of the ignition switch and the engine sputtered to life. Garrison glanced out through Click's window. Satisfied the plane was clear of the Park Service truck, she waved to Tubbs, then bumped the One-Fifty out of the field and onto the road. Garrison pushed the throttle to the firewall and the plane sped away, lifting into the air well short of the hills that rimmed the near end of the cove.

Click flipped on the radio and the navigation lights as the One-Fifty climbed out of the twilight that had taken up residence in the cove. The land to the west of Paradise and Short Mountains, though, laid in full sun.

Click keyed his microphone. "Knoxville Tower, Six-Seven-Two Charlie Victor coming up over Wind Mountain. What's your traffic?"

"Two Charlie Victor, I have a Convair coming up from

Chattanooga, five minutes out, a Piper Apache inbound from Bristol, ten minutes, and a Cessna One Seventy-Two in the pattern."

"Roger that. We're coming home."

"Gotcha, Two Charlie, you're number two behind the Convair. Tell me when you see him. Wind is calm. Runway Five is the active, and the altimeter here at T-Y-S is two-niner-niner-seven."

Garrison twiddled with the adjustment knob on her altimeter while her father scanned the horizon to the west. He waggled his fingers at a red flash–a rotating beacon on a distant airplane.

"Must be the Convair," Garrison said. She banked the One-Fifty toward it, pushing the nose of her aircraft down.

Click pulled his microphone closer to his lips. "Tower, Two Charlie Victor has the Convair," he said.

"Roger that, Two Charlie."

"Ahh, Convair Three-Three-Six is over the outer marker."

Garrison glanced at her father. A new voice, the captain of the airliner.

"Three-Three-Six, you're cleared to land. There's a Cessna putt-putt off your right wing about six miles. He'll be following you. . . . Cessna Two-Four-Five-Eight Montana, a Cessna One-Fifty will be ahead of you. Extend your downwind."

A woman's voice came through Garrison's and Click's headsets, saying "I have him."

"Who's this pilot?" Garrison asked.

Click shrugged.

She eased the throttle back and leveled the One-Fifty at Knoxville McGhee-Tyson Airport's pattern altitude, then slid down the base leg. Garrison glanced out the windshield at the One Seventy-Two flying the downwind leg, its landing light on, the Cessna above and well clear of her. Below she saw the Convair, rolling off the runway onto a taxiway.

Garrison turned the One-Fifty onto final. She lowered

the flaps ten degrees as she lined up on the runway, as her father had taught her. Garrison stole a glance at him.

"You're doing fine," Click said. "Ride it down. Landing light on."

Garrison pushed a rocker switch up. The airport rose in her windshield, and the One-Fifty came over the runway numbers a hundred feet high. Garrison shot a look of discomfort at Click.

He ignored it. "You got two miles of runway. Let the little bird come down the way she wants."

Garrison forced herself to concentrate, to hold airspeed and the glide. A taxiway, a half-mile beyond the approach end of the runway, flashed by.

Click slipped two fingers under his control wheel. He tugged back, and the nose of the One-Fifty came up into a proper flare for landing with the stall-warning horn squawking. The main wheels kissed the pavement. "Hold it there," he said.

Garrison wanted to slam the nosewheel down, wanted to be done with this landing, but she held the nose wheel off. The aircraft's speed bled away, and the nose wheel touched down on the pavement without the slightest shock, as if the pavement were a pillow.

"Two Charlie Victor, was that AJ's landing?"

"All by herself," Click said into his mic.

"Smooth. AJ, you're going to be as good as your old man."

Garrison said nothing, her mouth dry from fear.

"Two Charlie Victor, pick up your speed to the next taxiway. You have a One Seventy-Two hot on your tail feathers. . . . Five-Eight Montana, cleared to land."

Garrison added throttle. A warm weight settled around her shoulders–her father's arm.

"Marsh is right," Click said. "You're gonna fly circles around your old man."

CHAPTER 7

Money

Garrison yelped.

She scrunched her face and jammed a thumb in her mouth, a hammer in her other hand.

Millie Purkiss ran into the back parlor office and stopped. She stared at Garrison standing on a stool. "What happened?" she asked.

Garrison, the rims of her eyes wet, held her thumb out. "I hit it."

"Why ever for?"

"Millie."

"Are you all right?"

"I smashed my thumb." She climbed off the stool, studying her bruised digit. "Do you have a band-aid?"

"Why?"

Garrison held her thumb out again. "I'm bleeding, Millie."

"Well, so you are. Come on, come with me." Purkiss waved for her to follow.

Garrison laid the hammer on some papers on her desk before she trotted after Judge MacTeer's and now, by default, her secretary, out into the hallway and back to the kitchen.

Purkiss produced a box of Johnson strips from a drawer. "Before we put one of these on, we better wash that thumb of yours. We wouldn't want ourselves getting an infection, would we?" she said, her voice exuding sympathy that to Garrison rang hollow.

The secretary twisted a spigot in the sink. When Garrison hesitated, Purkiss grasped Garrison's hand and plunged it into the stream of cold water. She soaped the wound with a bar of Lifeboy, Garrison wincing from the sting of it.

"This won't kill you," Purkiss said. She let the flood wash the soap away before she toweled the hand and wounded thumb dry. "Whatever were you trying to do?"

"Put a nail in the wall, so I could hang a picture."

"Hold your thumb up."

Garrison did, blood still oozing from a break in the skin.

Purkiss peeled the protective strips from a band-aid, all the time giving Garrison a look one does an idiot child. She placed the pad over the wound and pressed the sticky ends around the thumb. "That's going to throb, you know. You want some ice?"

"No, I'll live."

"Just asking." Purkiss dropped the strips in a wastebasket. She then shook the towel out and hung it on a rod beside the sink. "What picture?"

"My law school graduating class." Garrison breathed on the band-aid, the warmth taking the edge off the pain welling up in her thumb. "Pop framed it."

"You should have had him hang it, and you ought to put up your diploma and your law license."

"People already know I'm a lawyer before they come in."

"Very well. Just trying to be helpful."

The front door opened and banged shut, and the heavy tread of well-shod feet came down the hall. "Anybody here? Millie? AJ?"

Hammond MacTeer.

"In the kitchen, Judge," Purkiss called out.

MacTeer shambled through the doorway, Frank Tubbs behind him. "Coffee klatch going back here?"

Purkiss gestured at Garrison. "Just bandaging the

wounded. Your associate tried her hand at picture hanging. She's not very good at it."

Pink tinged Garrison's cheeks.

"I can do that," MacTeer said.

"Judge, you're no better with a hammer than she is."

"That's likely true, Missus Purkiss, yes, ma'am, well–" MacTeer slapped Tubbs's shoulder. "Frank, here, tells me he's your client, AJ. Is that true?"

"It's good to see you, Mister Tubbs," Garrison said. She held out her hand, but pulled it back when she realized her thumb looked like a small balloon.

"So you're stealin' business behind my back," MacTeer went on. He winked. "Good for you. Frank, I leave you in good hands, except for that." He motioned at Garrison's damaged thumb. He turned away and headed up the hallway, toward his front parlor office, Millie Purkiss following him.

"Coffee, Mister Tubbs? We always have some on the stove," Garrison said.

"Smells good, but I've already had three cups. Don't want to float off."

"Well, uhmm–" She slipped around the off-duty park ranger and into the hall. "Come with me to my office."

He followed, gandering at the pictures on the walls and the massive grandfather clock midway between the two offices, the clock striking the first of ten chimes.

"Quite a place, isn't it?" Tubbs said when he came into Garrison's office, "'cept you don't have much on yer walls, do ya?"

"I was trying to fix that." She picked up the class picture. Garrison held it up where she had intended to hang it.

"How about I take care of that fer ya," Tubbs said. He took the hammer from the desk and, spotting the nail on the floor, squatted down for it. He looked up. "Right about there?"

"Be perfect," she said. She lowered the picture.

Tubbs stood up. He tapped his knuckles along the wall,

humming as he did.

"What are you doing?"

"Didn't yer daddy ever show you how to find a stud? You don't nail into a stud, yer picture's gonna pull its hanger outta the wall. You'll come in some mornin' an' find yer picture on the floor, a big patch of plaster with it."

Tubbs' rapping sounded hollow, then firm, then hollow again. He cocked an ear toward the wall and listened as he rapped back to the firm sound. "Ahh, there the rascal is."

He wet the end of the nail on his tongue, positioned the nail, and tapped it through the heavy, flocked wallpaper into the plaster. He tapped harder until the sound changed as the point sank into the wood. Tubbs drove the nail down until only the head and a quarter inch of the shank remained exposed.

He traded Garrison the hammer for the picture. Tubbs brought it up. He fished around until the wire on the back came down over the nailhead. "Tell me when I got it straight," he said, jigging at a corner.

"Right there. What am I going to owe you?"

Tubbs chuckled. "Say fifty cents. You kin knock it off what you're gonna charge me."

For the first time since whacking her thumb, Garrison laughed. She touched the side chair. "Please, sit down."

She drew her chair up to the desk. As she settled in, she studied the legal pad before her. "I went over to the county clerk's office, this morning," Garrison said, glancing up. "I did a search of the records on the property you're looking at. It's a good deed. There are no liens against it. There were two, for back taxes, back in the Nineteen Thirties, but Ellis Parsons–Ellis would be Walter Parsons' father–paid them both off."

"So I'm not buyin' any trouble."

"Not at all. Do you have a survey of the property?"

Tubbs pulled on the front of his jacket. He smoothed it over his belly. "No. Don't see much point in that. I'm satisfied with the description in the deed."

"You really ought to consider getting a survey."

"Aw, it's an unnecessary expense."

"All right. Is the bank financing the purchase?"

The park ranger took a paper from his back pocket. He slid the paper across Garrison's desk.

She opened the rumpled sheet and scanned down the page, the contents hand-written in ink. "A land contract?"

"Walter didn't want a big wad of cash he'd have to pay taxes on. This way he gets a monthly income for fifteen years, and he gets the interest instead of the bank, for me about half the interest the bank would charge."

"Who drew this up?"

"Walter did."

"Did he do the math on the payments?"

"No. He's got a cousin in the loan department of a Knoxville bank. She knows how to work all that out–amortizing Walter called it–so she did it."

"Do you want me to run the numbers past someone at First Morgantown?"

"You think that's necessary?"

Garrison came forward. "Do you know this cousin?"

Tubbs twisted in his chair, as if a loose spring had poked him in the butt. After he resettled himself, he shook his head.

"It wouldn't hurt to get a second opinion," Garrison said

"I guess not."

She turned the loan paper to Tubbs and touched a particular paragraph. "There's only one thing that bothers me."

"What's that?"

"Right here. If you pay the loan off early, Mister Parsons wants a penalty equal to ten percent of the balance."

"Yeeesss."

"I'd ask Mister Parsons if he'd be willing to take that out of the contract. If you pay off the contract early, he can invest that money and make interest on it. He shouldn't expect you to pay him a premium."

"And if he won't?"

"Then negotiate. Get that percentage reduced. I don't want to see you have to pay out anything more than what's fair."

"Can't argue with that."

"Do you want me to talk to Mister Parsons?"

Tubbs hesitated.

"I can do that for you," Garrison said.

"Amanda, I know you got all these years of law school, and Walter and me, we're just good old boys, but I think the two of us can work this out."

"Well, you let me know."

"I'll do that."

"And about the interest and principal payments, I'm going out to First Morgantown on an estate matter for another client. I'll take this along and have it checked by one of the loan officers. When will you see Mister Parsons?"

"I expect I can run out there now."

Garrison placed the paper on her briefcase. "How would it be for us to, say, meet again here at three o'clock? I'll tell you what I've learned, and you tell me what you've learned."

The day had warmed by the time Garrison came out to her car, a good day to drive with the top down, she decided. She unsnapped the latches that held the top to the top of the windshield. Garrison pushed up on the frame, but the stiff-hinged joints of the convertible top fought against her.

She got out. Garrison pried her fingers between the frame and the top of the windshield, wiggling and pulling and barking her sore thumb in the process. The top gave. The hinges squalled, complaining as Garrison wrestled the top up and forced it over and down into the boot. She mopped her sleeve across her forehead.

"Isn't that girl a strong one?" said a woman to a second walking by.

Garrison flushed. She got in the Beetle and drove away, the breeze toying with her hair.

She stopped at Main and turned northeast to

Washington Street. At Washington, Garrison jogged southeast to the new bank the Wilsons had built next to the Parkway Shopping Center, a project she knew they had financed. She put the clicker on, signaling her turn into the bank's parking lot, but the clicker didn't click. Garrison waited. After the approaching traffic cleared, she did a Hammond MacTeer–waggled her hand in the direction she wanted to go.

A county police car passed, its driver honking. Garrison glanced over in time to see Bunch Jeffords. She waved and drove on into the bank's lot, parked in the slot reserved for Teddy Wilson. Who would get that parking place now that Teddy was dead? Garrison guessed a new vice president should the senior Wilson hire one.

The new First Morgantown was not like the bank where her father did business. First's lobby was open and carpeted, low counters between the tellers and the customers, no bulletproof glass with the speaker holes cut out so you could talk to the tellers but couldn't reach them. Garrison remembered, as a child, going into the old Morgantown State Bank downtown to put some money in her savings account, of reaching up and sliding a bill and a handful of coins through an opening at the bottom of the glass. She remembered the cold marble floor and the barbed wire above the glass of the teller's cages and the old guard who sat by the vault door. Such matters, her father told her, was a response to the bank robberies of the Depression years. At eight years old, she had no idea what the Depression was.

Garrison went up to the desk of Lawrence Frye, a loan officer, Frye talking on the phone.

"That'll work out just fine," he said into the mouthpiece, "you come in at two o'clock tomorrow."

He hung up.

"Amanda," he said, his face wreathed in a smile as he tipped back in his chair, "how long's it been?"

"Six years."

"Well, sit, sit." Frye waved at his side chair. "You're as

beautiful as ever."

"And you're as full of it as ever." Garrison sat down. She held her briefcase in her lap.

Frye, laughing, threw up his hands. "You in need of a loan?"

"No, just help." She brought out the land contract and handed it to Frye. "I have a client who's buying a farm, and the owner is financing it. I just want to know if, based on the interest rate that's offered, the payments have been figured correctly."

He scanned down the paper. "I'd heard you'd become a lawyer."

Garrison saw a picture frame on Frye's desk. She turned the frame to her. "I see you didn't wait for me, Larry."

"Huh?"

She pointed at the photo.

"Yeah, Lydia. Can you imagine back in high school I'd ever marry a Lydia? We got two kids."

Garrison pooched out her lower lip.

"Hey, we weren't that close," Frye said. He tugged at the cuffs of his suit jacket.

"You took me to the junior prom."

"And you threw me in the duck pond when I tried to grope you."

She laughed. "I'd forgotten that."

"I haven't." He drummed his pen on his desk. "Word around the bank is you're handling Teddy's estate. You here to see the boss?"

"Is Mister Wilson in?"

Frye craned around. "I don't see him, but I'll bet he's in the vault. The bank examiner's here today. I'll get him for you."

"No, no, no. I can wait."

"Hey, it's no fun working with an examiner. Averrell will appreciate having a reason to get away from him. Those guys are such sticklers for the nittiest of details. By the end of the day, you want to shoot them."

"Well, then–"

Frye shot away toward the line of tellers and the vault beyond.

Garrison gazed around at the paintings on the walls–mountain scenes and soaring eagles, nothing like the austere, barren marble walls of the old bank downtown. There was warmth here and a cinnamony aroma. The scent of money? Garrison heard a psst and glanced up to see an air freshener above a window jetting a fine mist into the air.

"I got him for you," Frye said, startling her, interrupting her fascinations. She rose, her hand coming out to shake hands with the senior banker.

"Amanda, so good to see you," Wilson said. "It was good of you to come to the funeral."

"Teddy was a friend."

"Yes, well, if I appear to be at loose ends, it's just that Teddy did so much around here, and we're all having to pick up the pieces."

"I understand."

"Larry, here, is doing all the loan work Teddy used to do. Well, Anne's told me you're handling the estate."

"I have some questions."

"Why don't you come with me over to my desk? I've pulled a number of things you're going to need."

"Thank you."

"Don't thank me just yet," Wilson said, turning toward his desk some distance away.

Frye touched Garrison's arm. "I'll check these figures for you. Stop and see me on the way out."

"Thank you," she said and followed after Wilson.

The two stopped at the desk of Wilson's secretary. He bent down to the woman. "Etta, this is AJ Garrison. She's handling Teddy's estate."

"You want me to hold your calls?"

"If you would, please. It may be a while." Wilson went on to the next desk. There he held a leather chair for his guest. "Would you like a coffee, Amanda?"

"No, thank you," she said as she sat.

"Tea? RC?"

"Maybe an RC."

Wilson held up two fingers to his secretary. "Etta, would you get us a couple RC's, please?"

Garrison glanced around. "You surely don't have much privacy here."

"That's what I thought until the architects assured me that, with all the carpeting and the other sound deadening they were planning to put in, the people at one desk wouldn't be able to hear people talking at the next desk, and they're right." He took a stack of folders from the corner of his desk and placed it in the center. "Now where would you like to start?"

"The airplane?"

Wilson brushed his pencil-thin mustache, then sorted down. He pulled out a file and opened it for Garrison. "An Aero Commander. Teddy bought it used. The key is in here. It was in Teddy's flight case. When Teddy started flying for us, he picked up a lot of business up in the coalfields. His commissions on the loans more than paid for the airplane."

Garrison raised an eyebrow.

"Yes, we pay our loan officers commissions. That's why they're so aggressive in getting business for us, why we've grown from a small hometown bank in the past decade to one that can stand shoulder to shoulder with the biggest of the banks in Knoxville."

Garrison twisted the file to her. She lifted a page. "Back to the airplane, if I may. What do you want to do with it?"

"Amanda, that's not up to me. That's Anne's airplane now. If I had another pilot in the bank, I'd offer to buy it, but I don't."

She fingered the file. "May I take this with me?"

"You can take them all. We've made copies."

Garrison opened her briefcase and laid the file in it. "The bank, Mister Wilson, did Teddy own any of it?"

"A third." He opened a file. "This details the ownership agreement. I used to own it all, but when Teddy started with me, I gave him a third. Of course, he didn't get it free-and-clear."

"Meaning what?"

"We set a value on it which may have been half of what it was really worth, and Teddy was paying for it on time, as if we had given him a loan."

"How much does he owe?"

"Nothing. Paid it off, last year."

"Mister Wilson, that's pretty amazing."

He chuckled. "That was my boy. When he wanted something, he went after it and worked hard to get it. Teddy wanted to buy more of the bank, and we were working on that until–"

"I'm sorry."

Wilson pulled out a handkerchief. He wiped at his nose. "That's all right. Things happen."

Wilson's secretary interrupted, carrying a tray on which rode two glasses of RC Cola, ice cubes bobbing in the sodas.

"Etta, thank you, you can put the tray down here," Wilson said.

She set it on Wilson's desk, and the banker helped himself to a glass. He handed it and a napkin to Garrison.

She sipped at the soda. "So Anne now owns a third of the bank?"

"Yes, but the inheritance tax is going to be a killer."

"Why's that?"

"The tax rate, and Uncle Sam wants cash. In most small businesses, when the old man dies, the heirs usually have to sell it to get the cash for the taxes. Now, Amanda, if you're uncomfortable with tax law–and I don't mean to be telling you your business–I'd go get a tax expert and bring him in on this."

"That's probably a good suggestion."

Wilson stirred the ice cubes in his glass. "If it looks like Anne will have to sell, you tell her I'm willing to make an offer. I'll buy her out."

"At the full price or the discounted price?"

"We can talk." He pulled out another file. "Here's our

most recent financial statement and, of course, our books are always open anytime you or Anne need to go over them."

Wilson handed over another file. "This is a list of all Teddy's loan customers, their accounts with us, and a status report on each."

Garrison added the newest files to the collection in her briefcase. "There's certainly a lot here for me to read. Now what accounts did Teddy have with the bank?"

"Checking, a little more than a thousand dollars, and savings, just under ten thousand." Wilson passed along another file folder. "There are copies of all transactions for the last three years there. As Anne may have told you, I closed both accounts and put all the money in a new checking account under her name. Strictly speaking, that wasn't legal, but I did it anyway. I didn't want Anne and my grandchildren to be caught short of money, you know, while the estate is being settled."

"Is there anything else?"

Wilson opened his center desk drawer. He took out two keys and put them on the side of the desk, next to Garrison. "We searched the records, and Teddy's got two lockboxes."

"Two? That's odd, isn't it? Does Anne know about them?"

"I don't know. Both are in Teddy's name. Even if she does know, legally, she can't open them because she's not on the signature cards. That's a banking rule I can't skirt."

She picked up one of the keys. Garrison rolled it over in her palm. "Do you know what's in them?"

"Insurance papers probably."

"Enough to fill two boxes?"

"Obviously more than enough for one."

"Who can open the boxes?"

"You," Wilson said. "You're the executor. I found the keys in Teddy's desk."

She held up the second key. "Shall we take a look?"

Wilson waved at Frye, signaled for him to come over.

"I'll have Larry take you into the vault."

"You're not coming?"

"What's in those boxes is Teddy's business and now your business. I don't need to know."

"Yes, Averrell?" Frye asked when he came up.

"Would you take Amanda to the safety deposit boxes? There are two boxes she needs to get into."

"Right." Frye motioned for Garrison to accompany him to the vault.

She latched her briefcase and went along. At a desk beside the vault door, Frye took the two keys. He looked up the signature cards that belonged to their numbers.

"Oh, they're Teddy's," he said when he saw the name on the cards. "Well, if you'll sign on the next line of each, I'll get you in."

Garrison helped herself to a bank pen. It refused to write, so she drew circles on a deposit slip. Still no ink. "I think we have a problem here."

"Damn cheap pens," Frye said. "I don't know why we buy them. Here, use my Parker."

With that pen, Garrison's signature rolled out on one card, then the next. She gave the pen back to Frye, and he dated the signature lines and scribbled on his initials.

Frye held up the bank's master key. "Shall we?" he said and went on into the vault.

Garrison moved along with him. When they entered the lockbox room, Frye searched for the numbers. He found the first among the small boxes and put the bank's key and Garrison's in the twin locks. He turned them, and the small door swung open revealing a gun-metal gray box. Frye carried it to a table. "Amanda, you can start on this one while I find the other."

She wrote across the top page of a legal pad she had taken from her briefcase 'Inventory for safety deposit box number 216.'

She opened the box. On the top, a life insurance policy in the amount of ten thousand dollars. Next, a Blue Cross-Blue Shield policy and insurance policies on the house, the cars, the airplane, and a property in Ohio. Garrison scratched down the essential details.

"Here's the other box," Frye said. He placed it on the table. "When you're finished, put the boxes back where they belong and come and get me and we'll lock 'em up, all right?"

"Thank you, Larry."

Frye put a hand on the table. He glanced at the mass of papers Garrison had taken from the first box. "If there's anything there you need to copy, we've got a new Xerox just outside the vault. Amanda, that machine is slick, pops out copies like a rabbit does babies."

"That's a cute word picture. I raised rabbits when I was a kid."

"All right then, you're on your own." Frye left, and Garrison went back to her work of inventorying–deeds, titles, tax returns.

She bunched everything together and put them back in the box and returned it to its slot.

Garrison flipped to a new page in her pad. After she wrote 'Inventory for safety deposit box number 408' at the top, she opened the second box and looked in.

The contents made Garrison catch her breath.

CHAPTER 8

Morning tea

Garrison pressed on the doorbell. That set off a cascading of chimes. She waited and pressed the button a second time. Again the sound of celestial bells. This time Anne Wilson opened the door.

"Those chimes, they're wonderful," Garrison said.

Her client wiped her hands on her apron. "They were our one extravagance, well, that and the grandfather clock I made Teddy buy for me. It has a music box in it that plays 'Edelweiss' on the hour. Come in, come in."

Garrison surveyed the entryway and the front room before her as she stepped in. "This is really nice. I envy you having a home of your own."

"It's a bit lonely."

"I'm sorry. I didn't think."

Wilson shook her head. After a moment, she said, "Please come back to the kitchen. I'm on a baking jag–for something to do–and I've just taken out this most beautiful coffee cake. I can't eat it all myself." Wilson led the way down the hall, the walls a gallery of family photos.

Garrison made mental notes of the pictures of the Capitol building in Washington, a sternwheeler riverboat–she guessed that may have been on the Mississippi–and a geyser that was unmistakably Old Faithful in Yellowstone Park, several members of the Wilson family prominent in each photograph. "I see you've traveled some."

"Yes, from the first year we were married, Teddy

always took a summer vacation. We'd go by car or train. I'm afraid to fly."

"But Teddy has–had an airplane."

"I know. It scared me to death, scares me still to think of it."

The hallway opened into a kitchen that struck Garrison as one that could have been a photo spread in Southern Living magazine–a center island, all the appliances in avocado, copper cookware hanging from hooks above the island, and a wealth of flowers everywhere–roses and gladiolas, the air rich with their fragrance.

"There were so many from the funeral," Wilson said when she saw Garrison gazing at the flowers. "I couldn't bring myself to throw them all away, but come, try the coffeecake."

Wilson brought out china plates and lifted a square of fresh-baked pineapple coffeecake from the pan onto each plate, the cake still warm. She carried the plates to the breakfast table in front of a window that looked out on a backyard. A jungle gym and slide stood on one side, a vegetable garden on the other. Wilson gestured at a chair for Garrison as she went back for cups and the tea kettle spouting steam on the stove. "What'll you have, English tea? Camomile? Or I have some of that new Sleepy Bear they make out in Colorado."

"Camomile would be fine."

Wilson came back with the cups and tea bags. She placed a bag in each cup before she poured in the hot water. "I've been drinking a lot of Sleepy Bear, but I'm afraid it doesn't help me sleep. I'm awake most of the night, expecting Teddy to walk in and say, 'I'm back,' but that's not going to happen, is it? Let me get you a napkin."

Garrison reached out to stop her, but Wilson whisked away. She rummaged in a drawer and returned with two cloth napkins the color of apricots. Wilson slipped them into ivory rings.

"Anne, sit down please. You've done enough."

Wilson settled onto a chair. She wiped her hands on

her apron, then poked at her hair although Garrison couldn't see a strand out of place.

"It's terrible," Wilson said. "I just don't know what to do with myself."

"The children?"

"They're still over with Mae."

Garrison lifted the bag from her tea. She squeezed the bag against her spoon, then licked the drops from her fingers. "This is good."

"It is, isn't it?"

"Anne, did you know Teddy had two safety deposit boxes?"

The widow glanced up, puzzled.

"One has insurance policies in it and other legal papers. One policy is life insurance for ten thousand dollars."

"Oh."

"If you like, I'll call the company and get a claim form and get the paperwork started on that."

"I suppose that's good."

"Not only good, Anne, it's necessary, and I'll get the house and car policies changed to your name." Garrison took her legal pad from her briefcase. She jotted reminder notes while she sampled the coffeecake. "Mmm," she said, pointing her fork at the cake, "I think you've got a Betty Crocker winner here."

"You like it?"

"I wish I could do as well." Garrison set her fork aside. "The airplane, I suppose you want to get rid of it."

Wilson stared at her hands, at her fingers twisting her wedding ring. "I don't see any reason to keep it, do you?"

"No, I'll put it on the market. But let me ask, would you be willing to lease it to someone while it waits to sell? It could make you some money."

"What do you think?"

Garrison gazed into her client's eyes. "Anne, you have to look after yourself now and your children. You have to consider everything that will bring in money because your bills will never stop coming."

Wilson looked away. "Who would want to?"

"Who would want to what?"

"Lease the airplane."

"My dad might. He asked me about it. Look, here's what I'll do, I'll make some calls to find out what the going rate is for a Twin Commander. Pop either pays the going rate or he doesn't get the airplane."

Wilson dipped her spoon in her tea. She brought the spoon up and poured the spoonful of hot beverage back into the cup. And she did it again. "Isn't that a bit harsh?"

"Anne, I'm working for you. I'm not working for my father."

"Well, all right then."

A rabbit hopped in from a neighbor's yard. It headed across the lawn for the garden, the movement catching Wilson's attention. She waved her spoon toward the window. "Those rabbits. I'm thinking of getting a dog, to keep them out of the garden, what do you think?"

"Your children would like a dog."

"Yes, they would, wouldn't they?"

Garrison touched Wilson's hand, to draw her attention back to the business she had for her. "Do you know what I found in the second safety deposit box?"

"I have no idea."

"Just shy of one hundred thousand dollars–all cash."

Wilson stared at Garrison, an eyebrow slightly raised, as if she perhaps had not understood what she had heard.

"Anne, do you have any idea where that money could have come from?"

"No," she whispered.

"Assuming that it's legal–and I've always thought of Teddy as an honest person–the money's yours, or it will be after the estate is settled. It could pay the inheritance taxes on the third of the bank you own."

"I own a part of the bank?" Wilson rose from her chair. "Would you like more hot water for your tea?"

"My tea's fine. Sit down, please."

Wilson settled again, her fingers worrying the corner of

her napkin.

"Yes," Garrison said, "you do own a part of the bank."

"Teddy never discussed any of these things with me."

"From what I've seen of the annual statement, the bank could provide you a very good income for as long as you keep it or a very significant amount of cash should you want to sell it."

"There's just too much–"

"I know. Most of these thing don't have to be decided now. Look, first, I'll go after the life insurance for you, then I'll get something going for you with the airplane."

"The money in the safety deposit box, does anyone know?"

"Know what?"

"Know about the money?"

"Only you and me."

CHAPTER 9

Fizz bomb

Garrison watched the water rising in the claw-foot tub while, in the background, a radio played–a newscaster reading from his top-of-the-hour script. "Chicago today, eight hundred protestors injured in confrontations with the Chicago police and the Army National Guard outside the Democratic National Convention. Chicago Mayor Richard Daley, angered by the anti-war rally that triggered it all, said–"

She made a swipe at the radio–to turn it off–but instead knocked it over. Garrison went after the off switch again. "We know what the head of the gestapo is going to say. Why don't they talk to the demonstrators?"

She twisted the faucets closed and threw a bath bomb in the stilled water.

The bomb fizzed.

It bubbled.

It filled the bathroom with the fragrances of violets and lavender.

"Those news reports make me so mad," she said as she tossed her robe aside. Garrison stepped into the tub. She lowered herself into the water and froth, the warmth of the water easing the muscles in her back and shoulders. The bath oils released by the bomb had a luxurious feel to them–soothing–the bomb a gift from a friend who wore her hair long and went about in a granny dress, wire-rimmed glasses, and flip-flops cut from tire treads. The bomb was her newest creation in a line of scented bath soaps she made and sold.

Garrison laid back. Her eyelids became heavy. They closed only to pop open when she heard footsteps clattering up the stairs. The bathroom door banged open.

In strode Will Click in his Vol-Air tans.

"Dad! I'm taking a bath."

"Ooops."

Garrison slid lower under the billow of bubbles, until only her chin and above showed.

"Boots, honest, I didn't know you were home."

"Aren't you going to look away?"

"Hey, I've seen you in the all-together before. In fact, I've bathed you."

"Yeah, when I was a little kid."

"So?"

"Dad!"

Click swivelled away.

"Pop?"

"What?" he asked on his way out the door.

"If you promise not to look at me, put the seat down on the toilet and sit over there. There are things we have to talk about."

"You're not going to rip me on what's going on in Chicago?"

"I could, but no."

"Oooo."

"Don't oooo me."

Click threw up his hands in surrender. He covered his eyes and felt his way over to the toilet with the toe of his shoe.

"Quit being silly, Pop."

"You told me not to look." He kept one hand over his eyes, with his other hand he put the toilet seat lid down and sat.

"Pop, do you want to lease Anne's Twin Commander?"

"Business, huh?"

"Yes."

"I could lease it."

"What's a fair price?"

"Fifty-five dollars an hour dry."

"That means you pay Anne fifty-five dollars for each hour you fly the plane and you buy your own gasoline, do I have that right?"

"Yup. I'll even insure the plane while I'm flying it."

"That's reasonable. The lease price, Pop, is that a fair price or are you trying to get a bargain here?"

"Boots, I'll tell you what. You call Bigger Brothers Aviation over in Memphis. Ask them. If they think I'm too cheap, I'll kick it up to whatever they suggest as long as I figure I can make a couple dollars flying it charter."

"All right."

"Is that all? Can I go now before I embarrass you any further?"

"No."

"Oh." Click tapped the soles of his shoes in a rapid staccato on the bathroom tile. "Well?"

"I went to the bank today."

"And I should be surprised by this?"

"No, but this will surprise you. Teddy's got a hundred thousand dollars squirreled away in a safety deposit box."

Click peeked through his fingers at his daughter.

She mouthed the words 'A hundred grand.'

"Holy–" Click caught himself before he finished the words. "Do you know where it came from? The money?"

"I can't figure it out, and I spent all afternoon reading Teddy's financials."

"I tell ya what I'd do, Boots, I'd get that money into another lockbox. Put it under Anne's name, and I wouldn't tell anybody. Kid, that's tax-free money for her."

"Can't do that." Garrison lathered a sponge. She mopped it over her face. "I'm an officer of the court. I've got to list the money as an asset of the estate."

"Now don't go doing any listing before you talk this over with Ham. He may have some ideas for you." Click squirmed on the toilet seat. "Kid, I gotta pee and real bad.

With you in the tub, I'm gonna race next door and ask to use the Adamskis' toilet."

"I didn't see anybody home."

"I'll whiz in the backyard then."

CHAPTER 10

Ladies' slippers and antique watchcases

Hammond MacTeer sat hunched over his desk when Garrison came through the doorway. "You have a minute?" she asked.

He looked up from something. "AJ, for you, always. Come in. Park yourself in the good chair."

Garrison stared at the bear rug on the floor between her and the good chair—a cushiony leather wingback—the bear rug complete with head, eyes open and fangs glistening. Step on it to get across? That bothered her, so she edged around the rug. Garrison gestured at the flat creature. "Did you shoot him?"

MacTeer peered over his glasses and over the edge of his desk. "Well, I was up in the mountains one time on a huntin' trip, and old Bruno found me. Took a great interest in me, like he was sizing me up for lunch. So, yes, I shot him."

Garrison sat down, unsure whether the story was a MacTeer whopper or the truth. She glanced at a small object in MacTeer's hand. "What's that?"

"A lady's shoe." He held it out.

"Now, Judge, don't tease me."

"I'm not teasing. This was once a lady's shoe."

"Do I hear a story coming on, like that bear story of yours?"

"Well, you asked." MacTeer set the slipper on his desk and came forward onto his elbows. "I saw this ad in the

Knoxville paper for an estate auction. It listed an antique watchcase. So I went up Saturday, and when I saw it, I had to have it."

"Why?"

"Those people didn't know it, but there's only one watchcase like it. I read about it, and this is that case. Now I know you don't care for old stuff, so let me make this quick. You know Mount Vernon, George Washington's home on the Potomac River?"

"I've never been there, but, yes, I know about it."

"Well, after he died–that was in Seventeen Ninety-Nine–the plantation went to rack and ruin and, by the Eighteen Fifties, the house was pretty well falling down. Now here's the interesting part." With his finger, MacTeer turned the watchcase around and around a second time. "A woman by the name of Ann Pamela Cunningham–no relation to our city librarian–saw the President's old home, and she organized the Mount Vernon Ladies Association to buy it and restore it to its original glory."

He gave a knowing smile to Garrison. "Miss Ann Pamela raised a lot of money and one way she did it was with an auction of members' things. One woman, who had very tiny feet, gave one of her pearled slippers that she had made into a watchcase–this very watchcase." He paused. "I can see you're not impressed."

"Judge, it's an old slipper."

"Still I had to have it, and here's why." MacTeer opened the case exposing a pocket watch.

"May I?" Garrison asked.

MacTeer placed the watch in her hand.

She studied the scroll work in the gold case. "Pop has a couple railroad watches, but nothing as intricate as this."

MacTeer smiled like Alice's Cheshire cat. "Open the cover."

Garrison found the latch. She lifted it, and the cover came up, revealing a watch face with two Roman numerals, XII at the top and VI at the bottom. However, it was the inscription inside the cover that captured her attention:

Presented to Robert MacTeer for exceptional service, General George Washington, Seventeen Seventy-Eight.

"The watch is a fake," McTeer said.

"I don't understand."

"There really was a watch like this in my family. Everyone called it the General's Watch. Old Robert, inscribed there, he was my grandfather six generations back, but you know that. Came here in Seventeen Eighty-Five. Built a little fort north of here about six miles."

Garrison closed the cover over the watch face. She handed the timepiece back.

MacTeer caressed it. "Somehow the original got out of the family. When I came across the description in the records, I had this one made up as a duplicate–just to have."

He swivelled his chair around to a bookcase behind his desk. MacTeer gestured up three shelves to a bell jar. "Someday, when I find the real watch, I'm going to display it right there in that bell jar. I got lights rigged up to show it off and everything. That watch, it's the MacTeer family's pride."

"Do you have any idea where the watch is?"

"Not the damnedest." MacTeer swivelled back. He slipped the watch back into its case and the case into his vest pocket. "Well, you didn't come in here to listen to an old man ramble. How can I help you?"

"Judge, I think I need some advice."

MacTeer shifted his bulk back in his chair. He massaged the side of his face.

"You know I'm working on Teddy Wilson's estate."

"Big thing, huh?"

"I had no idea."

"Well, I knew he was into a number of things–a real promoter. Teddy could sell ice cubes to Eskimos."

Garrison pointed a thumb over her shoulder. "May I close the door?"

"Is there something you don't want Millie to hear?"

"I'm not sure."

"Go ahead."

She went to the door to the hallway and closed the door so quietly that the latch did not click. When Garrison came back, she put her hands on the back of the good chair. "Did you know Teddy has almost one hundred thousand dollars in a safety deposit box at the bank?"

MacTeer's eyebrows swept up.

"Judge, I've gone through all of Teddy's financial records for the past three years, and I can't account for the money."

"You think he may have embezzled it?"

"I don't know."

MacTeer swivelled toward the window. He stroked his chin. After a long silence, he said, "AJ, if I were you, I'd call the state bank examiner."

"Why?"

"Tell him you're working on the estate and you want to know, since Anne and the children are going to inherit Teddy's share of the bank, you just want to know if everything is all right, that there are no blemishes on the bank's books that could bite someone. You want to know, have the examiners given the bank their Good Housekeeping seal of approval?"

"Shouldn't I tell them about the money?"

MacTeer turned back. He fixed Garrison with his gaze. "Not a word. If the examiners say the bank is clean, just drop the subject. Cash can't be traced. Just declare it on the estate's inventory of assets and be done with it. You want as much of it to go to Anne as possible and, of course, with that money there, you know you're going to get paid handsomely for every hour you put in on this case."

"You don't want to know where the money came from?"

"Absolutely not. As long as it isn't the bank's money, I don't care and you don't either. Teddy's dead and any secrets he may have had are now in the grave with him. Leave them there."

Chapter 11

The Twin Commander

Garrison approached a reporter beating on the keys of a typewriter, a telephone receiver clamped between his shoulder and ear.

"Is Mister Peamantle in?" she asked.

He gave a head jerk toward a door behind him without either looking up or breaking his typing speed.

Garrison wandered away, back through the junked up office of The Morgantown Chief and into a back room where a man sat at a slanted table, X-ing in columns on a dummy sheet the size of a newspaper page. "Mister Peamantle?"

The man, chewing a cud at a furious speed, continued his X-ing. "That be me," he said.

"I need to place a death ad."

"Ah, that'd be for Teddy Wilson." Peamantle checked his notes and scrawled a headline above two columns.

"How'd you know?" Garrison asked.

"He's the only one who's kicked off in the past couple days." The newspaperman looked up. He tucked his pencil behind his ear. "If this is for Teddy, that makes you AJ Garrison."

She took a half-step back. "And you know that how?"

"Missy, it's my job to know everything that's going on in this town, hell, in the county. I'm the editor."

"Well, then, I guess I'm glad to meet you."

"Damn right."

"And it's AJ, not Missy," she said, recovering that half-step. She leaned forward.

Peamantle leaned forward as well. "And I'm O.C., not Mister Peamantle. Mister Peamantle was my father."

The two, nose to nose, stared into one another's eyes. "You're a rough soul, aren't you?" Garrison said.

He cackled. Peamantle rocked back on his stool. "I think I'm going to like you. AJ, you an honest lawyer?"

"That I am."

"Well, that's a scarce commodity in this wicked world. Let me tell you something, young lady. You're going to need me."

"Why's that?"

"'Cause I'm the only one who'll tell you the truth in this damn town." The editor ripped off with another laugh. "Hope my bein' blunt don't scare you none."

Garrison half smiled. "I guess I can get used to it." She opened her briefcase and brought out a short piece of paper, typed. She handed it to Peamantle.

He scanned down the page, counting the words. "Pretty standard stuff. You can run it as a classified, but I'd spend a couple bucks more and make it a display ad–box it."

"Why?"

"You don't want some dumb yahoo who Teddy owed money to coming back on Anne and saying he didn't see the notice. Make it big, people will see it."

"How much?"

"Twenty dollars. The law says you have to run it once, but I'd run it twice."

"Forty dollars then?"

"Thirty. I got all my work paid for with the first ad. The second run is pure profit. I'm not going to jack you up like my competitor down the street."

Garrison closed her briefcase. "You are blunt."

"Saves time at the big dance. I tell you what, I'll bill Anne because I know you got so little money you can hardly keep gas in that bug of yours." Peamantle took a pack of gum from the side pocket of his suit coat. He shook a stick out to Garrison. "Blackjack. It's good for ya."

She took the stick and put it in her pocket. He spat his wad into a trash can halfway across the room, then stuffed a fresh stick in his cheek.

Garrison had seen Peamantle walking along the sidewalks of town, his suit coat open, a newspaper stuffed in one side pocket and a roll of tan galley paper in the other. Pencils and a pica stick always protruded from his breast pocket, and he kept his thumbs hooked in his belt as he moved along. Her father joked that Peamantle's suit had never seen the inside of a dry cleaner's store. Now that she saw him close up, she confirmed it was likely true.

The man had a recessed chin, an Adam's apple the size of a small child's fist, and a hawk nose that looked like God had carved it with an axe. Garrison gazed at him, and she saw Ichabod Crane.

"You stand to make pretty good money probating Teddy's estate, don'tcha?" Peamantle said.

"How do you know there's not a will and this will be all over when I file it with the court?"

He laughed. "What young dandy's ever written a will? Wills are old men's things."

"You're right. There isn't a will, but why do you think the estate might be anything more than a house, two cars, and a bank account?"

A bulky man in an ink-stained apron pushed in next to Peamantle, a fistful of galley sheets in his hand. "Here's your stuff for the editorial page, O.C."

"Thank you, George," Peamantle said. He gestured toward the spike at the top of his table, and the typesetter jammed the galleys onto the nail. "George, do you know this young lady?"

The typesetter grubbed his spectacles from his shirt pocket and hooked the bows over his ears. "Well, my stars, Amanda Click."

"Mister Boyd?"

"It is. Come here, let me hug ya. I'll try not to get too much ink on yer fine suit." Boyd held his arms out and the two embraced. "O.C., this little girl was in my Sunday School class that I taught up in the mountains when we still had that little paper at Genesis."

"Well, what happened to you?" Garrison asked.

"When the newspaper closed out up there, I hired on at Knoxville. Then a couple years ago, O.C. talked me into coming to work for him."

Peamantle interrupted. "George, the young lady goes by AJ Garrison."

"Really?" Boyd said, looking wide-eyed at Garrison.

"I'm a lawyer now. It just sounds more professional."

"Well, ya took yer momma's family name. What's your daddy say to that?"

"He said it's a proud name and I'll do right by it."

"I hate to interrupt this happy reunion," Peamantle said. He handed Boyd a sheet of paper. "Here's the ad schedule for next week's edition. Would you check to see that they're all made up?"

"Sure thing." Boyd stepped back from Garrison. "Amanda, it's sure good seein' ya. You come by and visit when we're not so busy and this mean old buzzard isn't beatin' on me with a licorice stick."

"I'll do that."

The printer bobbed his head and disappeared around the corner into the type room.

Peamantle folded his arms across his chest. He gazed at Garrison. "Where were we?"

"I was asking you why you think there might be more to Teddy's estate than a house, two cars, and a bank account."

"Because he's got money and property ratted away you don't know about."

"Mister Peamantle, why do you say that?"

"It's O.C."

"All right, O.C."

"I always thought Teddy was a little too slick a fella, so I've watched him ever since he come back to his daddy's bank. I can't prove it, but I've long suspected young Teddy was as crooked as a snake's back."

"And you think that why?"

"Because he's spent a hell of a lot more money than he ever made peddling loans. I'll bet when you went through his papers you didn't find one debt or IOU. Am I right?"

Garrison clamped her lips tight.

"I take that as a yes," Peamantle said. He pulled a piece of blank galley paper from a drawer. He scribbled on the paper and spiked the note with the other galleys. "A story idea comes to me, if I don't write it down, I forget it. Now, AJ, Teddy had his hand in something that was illegal, maybe several somethings. When I find out, it's going to be a helluva story, and it's going to be on the front page of my paper."

"Aren't you afraid of the Wilsons' bank?"

"Hell no." Peamantle took the paper off the spike and dashed a few more words on it. "I do my business with a bank in Georgia, so neither First Morgantown nor Morgantown State's got a hold on me."

"I think my dad would say you're an independent cuss."

"And he'd be right."

Garrison motioned at the dummy sheet. "What's this?"

"Next week's paper." Peamantle spiked his note sheet again, then wiggled his fingers at the lawyer. "Come around here. See, this is going to be the front page. Here–" he pointed to the right side of the page above the fold "–here will be a photo and story about that accident south of town. Down here on the right, the Lions are giving out some kinda Mickey Mouse award and I always like to play those things up big, and over here on the left, the county's letting bids on a couple trucks. You know what bothers me about that story?"

"I haven't the faintest idea."

"Why the county even bothers to take bids. Same outfit gets the contract every time, some rinky-dink dealer up in Ohio. We got two perfectly good dealers right up the road in Knoxville who would give their champion coon dogs for those sales, but–"

Garrison moved her hand over an area of the page that had not been X-ed in, nor had a headline been written there. "How about this open space at the top?"

"Ahh, that's the big one," Peamantle said. He rubbed his hands in apparent anticipation. "Someone's been bleedin' the county's school budget. The S.O.B.'s down at the central office have been trying to hide it, but I got the story. Cage, my ace reporter out front, he's gettin' the last details now."

Garrison studied the editor. "You don't have a bit of fear, do you?"

Peamantle took a pica stick from his pocket and scratched the back of his neck with it. "Not a whit. Like your daddy, I been shot at by the best, only they missed me. Yes, I know what happened to your daddy in Nam. Now on this Teddy thing, are we going to work together?"

"O.C., I don't think I like you that much."

"Now, hon, why would you say that? Hey, my wife would confirm it for you, I'm a gentleman and a charmer."

"And I'm Richard Nixon."

****

Garrison saw something not quite right when she drove down the airport's access road toward Vol-Air, her father's flying business. There, in front of the office trailer, sat a stunning low-slung blue and white aircraft–high wings, two engines, and a tail that reached into the sky–and beside it her father on a stepladder with a bucket and a washrag, scrubbing the leading edge of one of the wings.

"A little presumptuous, wouldn't you say?" she asked after she parked her Beetle.

"What, cleaning Teddy's plane? Last time he flew it, he must have busted a cloud of horse flies. Bug guts everywhere."

Garrison leaned a hand on her hip as she looked over her father's work. "So you're going to get it all cleaned up and Anne's not going to lease it to you."

Click whipped around. His rag dropped from his hand.

"Just teasing, Pop. You've got it at your price, but still,

bringing it down from the hangar without permission–"

"I just had a good feeling," he said. Click came off the ladder and recovered his cleaning cloth. He gave it a sharp snap, flicking away the grit the cloth had picked up from the tarmac.

Garrison aimed her pointer finger toward the end of the wing. "You missed some out here."

"I haven't got there yet."

"Well, before you do, I have the lease. You need to sign it." She opened her briefcase and, from it, brought out a document. Garrison gave it and a pen to her father.

"I trust there's nothing in here that's going to bite me in the butt," he said.

She made a fist.

"Oh yeah, tough now that you're a lawyer." Click signed the paper and handed it and the pen back.

Garrison held out the aircraft's combination ignition and door key. "Would you like this?"

"Can't fly without it." Click let out an ear-piercing whistle, and a moment later Todd Oliver opened the office door. He stood there with a manual in his hand.

"The key, Todd-a-o. Let's take her up." Click underhanded the airplane's key to his partner. He then gathered up his ladder and cleaning supplies and toted them to a storage building that looked like a miniature barn. "Boots, you'd be amazed how much ragging I get about keeping a herd of tiny cows in there," he said after he rolled the door closed.

Oliver ducked back into the trailer. When he returned, he wore his Vol-Air cap and sunglasses. "Going with us?" he asked Garrison. He strode toward the aircraft. When she didn't fall into line, Oliver turned back. "You too good for us?"

"It's not that, but, ahhh, have you ever flown a plane like this?"

He held up the Aero Commander manual. "I've read the book."

"Somehow that doesn't inspire confidence."

"Sweets, I've flown DC-Threes and DC-Sixes. This one's simple in comparison." Oliver unlocked the aircraft's door. He opened it and disappeared into the cabin. As he did, a State Police cruiser rolled up to the Vol-Air trailer. Out stepped a man in civilian clothes–dungarees, T-shirt, and a ball cap, the bow of his sunglasses hooked over the neck of his T-shirt.

"Hey, Super Trooper," Click called out, "how about going for a ride with us?"

"If I'm not in the way."

"Not at all." He ushered the officer along. "Have you met my daughter?"

"Not had the occasion."

"AJ's a lawyer. Got a little practice in Morgantown. AJ, this is Scotty Moore. He's the trooper assigned to our area."

"Three years ago, too?" she asked.

"That's him," Click said. "Figured you two might like to talk. Let's get in before Todd-a-o leaves without us." He pushed his daughter and Moore ahead of him.

Garrison stepped up and into the cabin and settled in the seat behind the pilot. Moore banged his head on the door frame as he came in. He rubbed his scalp while he looked around. He went to a couch against the far wall. Click followed, sniffing the air. "Does it smell like stale booze in here?"

"Does a little," Garrison said.

"I'll bet Teddy spilled some on his last flight. Well, we'll get the air going." Click pulled the door closed. He snapped the safety latch and went forward to the co-pilot's seat. After he settled in, he handed a pair of sunglasses back to Garrison. "Got it figured out?" he asked his partner.

Oliver gave Click the open aircraft manual. "Checklist is on this page." He reached overhead to a panel of switches and snapped several on. "You see the starter buttons?"

"How about those down by your knee?"

"Ah, of course." Oliver cracked the throttles and pushed the mixture controls to full rich.

Click turned on the radio. "Think we need ear muffs?"

"Wouldn't hurt."

Click and Oliver took the headsets that hung on the yokes in front of them and fitted the headsets over their ears. While Oliver fiddled with his boom microphone, Click turned back to Garrison and Moore. "You should find headsets by your seats. Hon, there also should be a toggle switch to your left. Should you only want to talk to the super trooper and not to me and Todd-a-o, flip that switch and cut us out, okay?"

She scanned around for her headset and found it at the same moment Moore found his.

"All right, this is an inside radio check," Click said into his microphone. Oliver started the right engine. "Is everyone with us?"

"Roger," Oliver said. He started the left engine. It stuttered, shaking the cabin until the engine settled down to a steady idle.

Garrison tapped her microphone. "I'm here."

"Me, too," Moore said.

"Good." Click pressed the transmitter button on his yoke–the control wheel for the co-pilot. "Knoxville Ground, this is Aero Commander November Four-Four-Two-One Echo at Vol-Air. We'd like to taxi to the active."

"Roger, Two-One Echo," the ground controller came back. "You're cleared to taxi to Runway Two-Three. No wind at the moment. Altimeter three-zero-zero-one. A DC-Three will be taxiing out behind you. There's a Cessna in the pattern and a twin Beech inbound from Chattanooga."

"Got the numbers, Two-One Echo." Click dialed in the setting on the altimeter in front of him and the one in front of Oliver. Oliver goosed the engines and swung the Twin Commander around and out onto the northeast-bound taxiway.

Without touching the transmitter button–so only those onboard would hear him–Click sang out, "All right, boys and girls, standby for Terry and the Pirates. In today's exciting episode, Terry and his sidekick, Hotshot, find themselves at the controls of an unfamiliar airplane. They must fly it to Saigon in exotic Indochina where they must rescue the beautiful Princess Won-Lee from the clutches of the evil Doctor Chang. Terry, are you ready for takeoff?"

"Not yet, Hotshot," Oliver came back, his voice like that of a ham actor. "First I must have my Ovaltine, Ovaltine, that nutritious hot-chocolate drink made with milk."

Moore motioned at the switch by Garrison's side. She turned it, cutting out the pilot and copilot.

"What's this Terry and the Pirates stuff?" he asked.

"Pop and Todd have had been doing that shtick for years. Whoever's in the pilot's seat is Terry Lee. The other is Hotshot Charlie."

"Oh, the comic strip."

Oliver wheeled the Commander into the runup area. He ran through the gauges and controls as Click called out each item on the checklist. When done, Oliver pointed at Click's radio. "Hotshot, switch us to the tower frequency."

"Roger, Terry," Click said.

A voice crackled through the headsets. "Cessna Seven-Seven Golf turning final."

"Roger, Seventy-Seven Golf. You're cleared to land, or is this another touch-and-go?"

"Touch-and-go."

"Roger that. Keep up your speed, Seventy-Seven Golf. There's an Aero Commander holding short, about ready to depart. And Beech Zero-Eight-Three Oscar, where are you?"

"Oscar's over Maryville."

"I gotcha. Keep on coming. There's an Aero Commander departing ahead of you and maybe a DC-Three, and there's a Cessna putt-putt in the pattern. All right, Aero Commander Four-Four-Two-One Echo, are you with me?"

Click pressed his transmitter button. "Knoxville Tower, Two-One Echo, ready to roll."

"Take the active, Two-One Echo. Cessna ahead just lifted off. When he turns crosswind, you're cleared to go."

"Roger, tower, cleared after the Cessna turns crosswind. We want straight out, then northeast. Going over the mountains for a little practice."

"Copy that."

Click bumped Oliver's arm. He cocked his head toward the Cessna One-Fifty climbing out.

Oliver pushed the throttles up to the top of the control quadrant. The engines came up in a thundering bellow, and the Commander raced down the center of the runway. Click glanced at the manual. "Rotate at seventy-five," he said.

Oliver watched the needle on the airspeed indicator rise. At seventy-five miles an hour, he pulled back on the yoke, and the nose of the Commander came up into an easy climb. "Wheels up," Oliver called to his copilot.

Click scanned for the landing gear handle. He found it on his side of the control quadrant and pulled the handle up. Hydraulic pumps came on. Click peered out his window as the right main gear folded into the well beneath the engine and clamshell doors closed over the well.

Oliver held the Commander in a fast climb. At two thousand feet, he banked left and headed the aircraft for the Smoky Mountains. Oliver leveled the Commander at fifty-five hundred feet and throttled back, the airspeed rising to two hundred miles an hour. "Hotshot, this bird's one speed freak."

"Compared to what we've been flying, she sure is. Comfortable back there, AJ? Scotty?"

"Rides like an airliner, Pop."

"Well, you chil'en relax. Cap'n Terry and I are going to do some slow flight, stalls, and engine-outs to get acquainted with Two-One Echo. The no-smoking light's off." Click nudged Oliver, thumbed for him to make a right turn.

Garrison moved the toggle switch, cutting out the pilot and copilot. She turned to her fellow passenger. "Trooper Moore," she said.

"Scotty. Call me Scotty."

"All right. Scotty, did Pop tell you what I'm working on?"

"He said he thought I might be able to help you."

"I'm in over my head. I need an investigator."

"Well, the Patrol owes me a couple days."

A warning horn squawked. Garrison sensed the aircraft was nose-high, that the engines were working too hard. And she felt the nose fall away.

The Commander plummeted toward the earth. As it did, Moore grabbed at his seatbelt.

"It's a stall," Garrison shouted over the roar of the engines while the pilot wrestled the aircraft back into a climb, hydraulic pumps and electric motors whining.

She heard the right engine fail.

The Commander yawed in that direction, and the wing dropped.

"Engine out," Garrison shouted. "It's just practice."

Moore clung tight to his seatbelt, his jaw muscles rigid. Acid rose in his throat. "When they gonna stop this?"

"Soon," Garrison said. She handed him a sick sack. "You get queasy, put it in here."

Moore mopped the sweat beading out on his forehead. He forced a swallow. "Gawd, I'm dying."

The aircraft rolled back up into level flight, both engines running.

"So, ahh–so, ahh, what's your problem?" Moore asked.

"I found almost one hundred thousand dollars in one of Teddy's safety deposit boxes," Garrison said as casual as if she were at an afternoon tea. "I don't know where it came from. Some people I've talked to think it might be bad money."

"This got something to do with Doc Taylor's murder?"

"I can't think what. But I've got to clear it up so I can settle Teddy's estate. When we get that done, then maybe you can ask some questions for me on the murder."

"I've been wanting to do that for three years."

"You have to know I can't pay you."

Moore choked back another burst of acid. "I've got a

state paycheck."

"What about the alimony?" Garrison asked.

"You know about that?"

"I'm sorry. Divorce shouldn't happen to anyone."

The left engine went silent. Moore blanched. He gestured at the dead engine as the left wing dipped. Moore moaned, his fingers white as they gripped the burp bag.

Garrison toggled the communications switch. "Pop?"

"Yeah, Boots?"

"We've got one here who's about to lose it."

"Scotty?"

"Is there anybody else back here with me?"

"Okay. Todd, get us home."

"Roger that."

Click cranked up the tower's volume on the radio.

"Southern Fairchild, you're cleared for takeoff." A tower controller.

"Ahh, rojjah that. Victor Sixteen fo' Bristol." The drawl, Mississippian.

"Shouldn't be a problem," the tower controller said. "I've got an Aero Commander over the mountains. Let me see if I can find him. Two-One Echo, you got your ears on?"

Click pressed his transmitter button. "Two-One Echo, we're at four thousand feet over Bryson City, coming home."

"Get that, Southern Fairchild?"

"Ahh, rojjah. See y'all tomorrow."

"Two-One Echo, nothing's changed here since you departed. The Cessna putt-putt's still flying the pattern, and we've got a twin Beech inbound from Nashville. Should be coming up on Rockwood. You two might be in a race."

"We'll throttle back."

"Copy that. Call me over the VOR. Twin Beech Six-Eight Whiskey, you hear the traffic?"

"Six-Eight Whiskey, got 'em."

Oliver pulled the power controls back until the Commander slowed to a hundred fifty miles an hour, allowing the plane to slide down toward the Tennessee

River to the northwest.

"This is one smooth aircraft, isn't it, Pop?" Garrison said.

Click looked at his check list. "Real sweet. We'll get some high-class charter business with this one. Put some drinks on ice back where you are for the customers–" He moved his hand in a smooth-as-glass motion, then, for Oliver, pointed through the windshield.

Oliver tilted his head in that direction, toward a red light flashing on the tail of an aircraft low and far ahead.

"Beech Six-Eight Whiskey coming up on West Knoxville at two thousand feet." The eastbound pilot calling the tower controller.

"Gotcha in the glasses, Six-Eight Whiskey. You're number two for Runway Two-Three behind a Cessna One-Fifty on downwind."

"Ah, roger, have him in sight."

"Cessna Seventy-Seven Golf, Tower, what's your intention?"

"Seven-Seven Golf, full stop landing."

"Keep up your speed, Seventy-Seven Golf, until you clear the runway. There's a twin Beech coming out of the sky behind you."

"We can do that."

"Two-One Echo, where are you now?"

Click touched his transmit button. "Fifteen miles east of the airport, out of three thousand."

"Got the traffic?"

"That we do."

"You're now number three for landing behind the twin Beech. Report over the VOR."

"Copy that."

Oliver let the Commander continue sliding out of the sky. He crossed the VOR radio navigation station and banked hard for a straight-in to the airport. "Suppose I give those guys in the tower a thrill, do a Bob Hoover," he said to Click. "I got five hundred ninety horses pulling us through the air."

Click gave him a look that said 'I can't believe you said that.'

Oliver pressed his transmitter button. "Tower, Two-One Echo. Request high-speed pass over the runway at two hundred feet."

"Tower, what ya doing, Todd?"

"I want to ring this bird out. See what it'll do."

"No air or ground traffic. Okay by me."

Oliver slammed the throttles to the top of the power quadrant. He dove the Commander for the airport, the airspeed indicator winding up to the red line–to two hundred sixty miles an hour.

Oliver pulled the Commander out of the dive low over the terrain. As the aircraft screamed across the approach end of the runway, he tipped the right wing up sixty degrees, held it a moment, then tipped it up another sixty degrees, then another, and three more–doing a six-point barrel roll as the Commander streaked past the control tower.

Two words came through the headsets from the tower, "Holy hell!"

Oliver hauled the aircraft up into a steep climb at the far end of the runway.

Behind him, Moore retched.

CHAPTER 12

The hundred grand

Scotty Moore, in the gray business suit his father had bought him when Moore graduated from college, presented himself at the First Morgantown Bank.

"Is Mister Wilson in?" he asked the woman at the first desk.

She glanced back toward the bank president's desk where Averrell Wilson sat reading the Wall Street Journal.

"Just a minute," she said. She picked up her telephone and pressed three numbers. "Mister Wilson? . . . A Mister–"

"Moore."

"–a Mister Moore to see you. . . . Yessir." She hung up and pointed toward Wilson now standing. "Mister Wilson will see you."

"Thank you." Moore smiled when he saw the bank president waving for him to come over. He made the long walk across the deep carpet, springing on the balls of his feet, wondering how much change people dropped and lost in the shag each day.

Wilson extended his hand, a welcome-new-customer grin on his face. "Mister Moore, how do you do?"

"I'm doing fine," Moore said as he pumped the banker's hand.

"Sit, sit. What can I do for you? Are you new in town?"

"New? Not exactly." Moore handed his business card on as he settled into the leather armchair next to Wilson's desk.

"Ahh, a state policeman, but you're not in uniform."

"I'm not on duty. This is my day off."

"Can I get you something to drink? A coffee? Soft drink? Iced tea?"

"Iced tea'd be fine."

Wilson turned to his secretary across the way. "Etta? Would you get us two iced teas, please?" He waved his appreciation as his secretary left her desk for the employees' break room.

"Now what is it I can do for you?"

Moore smoothed the front of his suit coat. "I'm doing some off-duty investigation for AJ Garrison. She's handling your son's estate."

"Yes, I know." Wilson's hand came up to his chin.

"Did she tell you she found close to one hundred thousand dollars in one of your son's safety deposit boxes?"

Wilson whistled.

"I take that as a no, Mister Wilson."

"That's for sure."

"Well, AJ feels that, as an officer of the court, she has to be able to explain that money. She's gone over all of your son's financial records you supplied her, and she can't account for it. Do you have any idea where the money might have come from?"

Before Wilson answered, the secretary bustled up with a tray and two glasses filled to near the rim, ice cubes clicking in them. "Iced tea," she said, holding the tray out to Moore. "Would you care for sugar?"

"Thank you, no." He helped himself to the closer glass, and Wilson took the other.

"Etta," the banker said, "would you hold my calls for the time being?"

"Surely."

Wilson sipped at his tea. "Hmm, a hundred thousand dollars. Teddy brought us a lot of new business from a four-state area, and I paid him well for it. He must have saved it."

Moore touched an ice cube and watched it bob. "No,

your son's wife has all the pay stubs and all the canceled checks, so we've accounted for the money the bank paid him and how he used it. The hundred thousand is still unexplained."

"You're not implying–"

"That your son embezzled from the bank? No. AJ's checked with the examiners, and there are no discrepancies that would explain that kind of money."

"It's a mystery, isn't it?"

"Indeed."

"He didn't play cards or gamble that I know of, and I'm sure he didn't print the stuff."

Moore took a pad from his pocket. He scratched down a note. "Maybe AJ should check to see if it's counterfeit."

"Oh, I can't believe that it would be."

"Even if it were, what would he be doing with it?"

"Come on, I can't believe this–"

"But you can see why AJ has to be able to explain it. Once the money is listed among the estate's assets, the probate judge is going to ask questions."

"This could hurt Anne," Wilson said. "This could hurt the bank."

"Not likely." Moore slipped his notepad back into his inside jacket pocket. "By the time we figure it out, it will probably turn out to be perfectly innocent."

"Well, I certainly hope so."

Moore stood to leave. He extended his hand to Wilson. "I want to thank you for your help."

"It certainly hasn't been much."

"Perhaps it would be best not to talk about this for the moment."

****

A woman, tall, thin, and panicky in a peach suitdress, paced in Garrison's office. "I did not intend to kill my husband," she said.

"But, Irene, you ran over him three times." Garrison paced with Irene McCoskey, nudging her toward a tattered side chair.

McCoskey gave up and flopped in it. She picked at a tear in the leather of the arm. "You need new furniture."

"Yes, but right now you have to tell my why you did this if I'm to defend you in court." Garrison rapped a pencil on her legal pad. "You're up on a murder charge. First, how long were you two married?"

McCoskey still picked at the tear. "Eighteen years."

"Children?"

"I couldn't have children."

"Did you and your husband fight any?"

"Only in the last year."

"What about?"

"That woman."

"What woman?"

"Andrew's secretary. I found out he was over at her house, doing her on her husband's bowling nights and my bridge nights. How am I going to explain this to my bridge ladies?"

Garrison punched the eraser of her pencil at her legal pad. "Your husband's not the first to cheat on his wife. They'll read about it in the Chief and the Democrat."

"You're not going to tell them?"

"Irene, it's all going to come out at the trial. They'll get it there, how miserable a man he was."

"Well, he wasn't that miserable."

"Did he ever hit you?"

McCoskey pursed her lips, so Garrison asked a second time, "Did he ever hit you?"

"Once."

"Where?"

McCoskey patted the side of her face.

"And?"

"He broke my jaw."

"Now we're getting somewhere." Garrison jotted a reminder note to get the hospital report.

"I had to have my jaw wired shut for three months. Andrew was so good about it. He took care of me."

McCoskey choked back a tear.

Garrison threw up a hand. She heard the front door open and close and footsteps come down the hall. Moore leaned in the doorway. Garrison waved him away, toward the file room/pantry.

"Sorry," he mouthed and ducked out.

Garrison glanced at McCoskey who was now smiling. "Where were we?"

"My broken jaw."

"When did that happen?"

"Nine months ago."

"Did you fight any after you healed?"

"Almost every day."

"Did he hit you?"

McCoskey opened her purse. She took out a knitting needle. "I got this. When he threatened me, I told him I would stick this in his liver."

"What triggered the final eruption?"

"Andrew moved out."

Garrison looked up from her notetaking. "That's it? Irene, husbands move out all the time. That's no reason to kill them."

"But he took Buffy."

"Buffy?"

"Our spaniel."

"Buffy's a dog?"

"I don't think of her that way. She's the child I never had, and Andrew took her. So I got in the car and went after them. When I saw Andrew trotting down the sidewalk in front of the Congregational church, his suitcase in one hand and Buffy's leash in the other, well, I couldn't help myself. I bounced the Buick over the curb and ran him down."

Garrison dropped her pencil."Just like that?"

"That's it."

"Weren't you at least afraid you'd hurt Buffy?"

"She was off to the side." Irene picked at the tear again. "I knew I had hurt Andrew. I didn't want him to suffer, so I backed over him, and after I rescued Buffy–she was so happy to see me, her little tail just wagging all over–I drove over him again."

Garrison covered her eyes. "Irene, I think you should make a deal."

The woman sat up as fast as if an electric charge had shot through her. "I will not. Andrew was cruel to me. It's your job to defend me."

Garrison sighed. She pushed herself out of her chair and went to the office door, to wait for McCoskey. When the woman caught up, Garrison said, "I'll see what I can do."

McCoskey stiffened. "You'll see what you can do? For what I'm paying you, I expect results, not 'I'll see what I can do.'"

She huffed away, Garrison calling after her, "How's Buffy doing?"

"Fine. Doesn't miss Andrew at all."

Garrison rolled her eyes as she went in the other direction, toward the file room/pantry. "Mister Moore?"

Moore appeared in the doorway, holding a bottle of RC. "That the woman who ran over her husband?"

Garrison held up three fingers, then waggled them for Moore to follow her back to her office. "What did you find out?"

"Not much," he said as he settled into the side chair still warm from Irene McCoskey. "Miss Garrison, you've got to get yourself some decent furniture."

"You're not the first to tell me."

"She going to pay?"

Garrison held up a check. "A thousand-dollar retainer."

"Good. Go out and buy a new chair."

She raised a warning finger.

"So what's your defense for the old gal?" Moore asked. "She really flattened her husband. The coroner and the undertaker had to scrape him off the sidewalk with a shovel."

"I don't know. He was a wife beater?"

"That's the way, counselor. If you can't defend your

client, blame the victim."

"It's a strategy they teach us in law school."

"The hell of it is, sometimes it works."

"And we lawyers silently thank the jury every time it does. Did you learn anything from Mister Wilson?"

Moore took out his notepad. He flipped it open. "He seemed to be as puzzled as you. When I suggested the money might be counterfeit, he dismissed it, but it does raise a point."

"What's that?"

Moore checked off a note. "You really ought to have some of the bills checked to rule that out."

"You think it could be counterfeit?"

"You haven't shown me the money. Anyway, I haven't got an eye for that stuff, unless it's a really bad job–like the bills were made with Crayons. But I have another idea."

"And what would that be?"

He put his notepad away. "Is your father at the airport?"

"I don't know. Call him." Garrison pushed her telephone toward the trooper.

Moore picked up the receiver. "The number?"

"Nine-seven-oh-three-three-three-one."

He punched it in and waited for someone to pick up.

"Vol-Air."

"Will?"

"Yeah."

"Scotty. What're you doing today?"

"Flight lessons. I got a student up on solo now, so I have an hour free."

"Do you pilots keep logbooks like long-haul truckers do?"

"Yeah."

"Do you know where Teddy's might be?"

"I do. I've got it. It was in his map case in the back of the Twin Commander, why?"

"I need to take a look at it."

"Come on out. How's my little girl doin'?"

"She got a paying customer, the crazy lady who ran over her husband."

Garrison swatted Moore, and he recoiled. "Gotta go. Your daughter's beating on me."

"I am not beating on you," Garrison said as Moore dropped the receiver back on the cradle. "What are you up to that you need to see Teddy's logbook?"

"Ask me later. Do you have the file with the loans Teddy sold?"

Garrison opened a file drawer and worked her way back through the tabs. She pulled out a folder. "Why do you need this?"

"Just a hunch. If I'm wrong in what I'm thinking, you don't need to know. Now can I have the folder?"

Garrison passed it across her desk. He took the folder and left.

She followed Moore into the hallway, but went in the direction of Millie Purkiss' desk. "Who's next?" she asked.

Purkiss motioned to a scruffy man seated by the window, his face clouded, his elbows on his knees. He twirled his cap.

"Okay, Mister Knott, come with me," Garrison said, her voice flat.

The man rose, still twirling his cap. He strode after Garrison into her office and took the hard chair to which she pointed.

Garrison, at her desk, folded her hands. "So what's this about a barking dog that got you arrested?"

"It wasn't my dog. It was my brother's damn dog."

She pulled her legal pad over, turned to a new page. "And your brother is?" she asked, her pencil at the ready.

"Alvin."

"Lives where?"

"Next door."

"And the dog?"

"A gawddamn coon hound. Answers to the name of Old Ned, if he answers at all. Dog howls an' barks, barks an' howls."

"So it bothers you and not your brother?"

"He's deaf."

"Oh. So how did you get arrested?"

"The other night I'd had enough," Knott said. He balled his fists. "After six hours of that howling an' barking, I went out an' made me a bunch of mud with dirt an' rocks an' pitched it by the handfuls at Alvin's house, you know, up there at his second-floor bedroom, the outside wall there to wake him up."

"Threw mud at brother's house," Garrison murmured as she wrote.

"A fistful went through the glass. I guess it did. Anyway, Alvin sicced the cops on me an' I spent the night in jail."

Garrison kept writing–fast. "So?"

"Now the judge wants to fine me, an' Alvin wants me to pay for fixin' his gawddamn window. I want to sue the bastard."

Garrison threw her pencil over her shoulder.

CHAPTER 13

Gambier

Click handed Teddy Wilson's flight log to Moore.

"Can I use your table over there?" the trooper asked. He waved the logbook at an abused table in the corner, a table that slouched at an odd angle, a catalog under one leg in someone's attempt to level the top.

"Help yourself."

Moore opened the loan files folder. He spread the papers it contained, then sat down to peruse the flight log, turning from page to page, reading, stopping to study dates and destinations and comparing them with entries on the loan logs.

Click hunkered over the trooper's shoulder. "Whatcha looking for?"

Moore leaned back. He braced a knee against the edge of the table top, and the table slid away. He and Click scrambled after it, grabbing it before it could crash.

"You know that money AJ's asked me to trace?" Moore said as he stuck the catalog under the leg again. "It didn't come from the bank, and it didn't come from Teddy's paychecks that he managed to save. Maybe it came from some dealings out in one of these towns he flew to."

"So what are you looking for?"

"Patterns, maybe."

Click went over to the aviation map of the United States that covered most of the south wall of his office trailer. "You can use this to orient yourself. Every airport's here that Teddy could have flown into except for the cow pastures he might have landed on."

"Can I mark your map?"

"Only if you buy me a new one."

"AJ's got money for that."

"So you told me. Well, knock yourself out. I'm going out and wash my Skymaster before my next student gets here."

Moore touched a finger to his forehead in a salute as Click left the trailer. He listened for a few moments before he heard the sounds of a hose being dragged away from the trailer.

Moore turned back to the loan log. "Okay, the first loan he made out of town was to–ahh, Handley Distributors, Bristol, Virginia, uhmm March Thirteen, Nineteen Sixty-Two."

He picked up Wilson's flight log and paged back to that year, then that month. "There it is. Old Teddy flew into Bristol on March Tenth."

Moore gazed at the aviation map, puzzling to himself. When he spotted Bristol, he went to the map and wrote in felt-tip pen next to the city 'Handley D., March, 'Sixty-Two.'

The next out-of-town loan, Highland Press, Abingdon, Virginia, March Twenty-Sixth, same year. Moore found a flight to the town in Wilson's log a week before, on the Sixteenth. He put that on the aviation map.

****

Garrison parked her bug next to a rusting Ford pickup at the side of her father's office trailer. When she got out, a Cessna One-Fifty taxied up from Runway Two-Three. The airplane swung around in front of the trailer and stopped, the engine clanking as the pilot starved it of fuel.

Garrison recognized the passenger. She hurried over to open the door for her father. "Teaching today, Pop?"

"Hey, Boots, say howdy to Johnny Cashdollar," Click said, grinning. He waved across to the pilot. "Young John here is about to make his first solo cross-country. Johnny, tell this sweet young thing where we been?"

The youth–Garrison guessed him to be about sixteen–twisted in his seat. "Athens and Rockwood, ma'am."

"Did you get lost?" Click asked.

"Not once. The power lines, railroad tracks, and the river were right where they were supposed to be, and the twin stacks at the Kingston power plant, ma'am, they're amazing to see from the air."

"Johnny, this is my daughter, Amanda."

"You fly, too?" Cashdollar asked.

"A little," Garrison said.

Click slapped Cashdollar's knee. "You fill out your logbook, and I'll go in and write you up a bill. What time do you want to fly tomorrow?"

"Ten o'clock?"

"Ten o'clock it is. Plan Sevierville, Morristown, and back. You're on your own this time, and remember, you gotta get somebody to sign your logbook at each airport."

"All right, Mister Click." The boy dug his logbook out of his soft flight case while Click pushed himself out of the passenger door.

"What's Scotty doing, Pop?" Garrison asked.

Click took off his sunglasses. He rubbed the bridge of his nose. "Damned if I know. Johnny and I have been out for the past hour and a half. Let's go on in."

She closed the airplane's door for her father and slipped her arm through his as they strolled along. "Is he good?"

"Johnny?"

"Yes."

"Boots, he's smooth. He's sharp. Yeah, he's very good."

"But he's so young."

"Weren't we all at one time?"

Garrison punched Click.

"Hey, now!"

"I'm still young," she said.

"And pretty, too."

"Now that makes me feel better."

He opened the office door and held it for his daughter. She went in, to Moore at the map, writing.

"What's this?" she asked.

"Every town Teddy flew to where he sold one or more loans. You see the size of some of those loans?" Moore whistled. "No wonder his father paid him so well."

"He was on commission."

The door opened and Johnny Cashdollar came in. He slipped into a chair next to Click's desk. Click handed him the day's bill, and Cashdollar wrote his check.

"I thank you for your business, young man," Click said after he put the check in his cigar-box cash register. He walked Cashdollar toward the door. "Tomorrow, I want you out here at nine-thirty, to go over all your flight planning, and in the air by ten. I'll block the airplane for you until noon."

With that, Cashdollar was gone, so Click came over to Moore and Garrison. "Whatcha got?"

Moore gazed over the map. "Near as I can figure, Teddy's flying was almost exclusively for the bank. He didn't fly to a resort or Nashville for a show or anything like that that I can see."

"AJ tells me Teddy's wife's afraid of flying, so that wipes out family travel."

Moore swept his hand over the perimeter of the cities and towns he'd marked on the map. "All these, they're within three hundred miles of the airport here."

"Makes sense," Click said. He scratched at his chin. "Three hundred miles, that's an hour and a half flight time in the Commander. Anything further out, his commission on a loan might not cover his expenses."

"Here's the mystery." With his felt-tip, Moore circled Paris, Kentucky, and Gambier, Ohio. "He doesn't have a loan at either place."

"Maybe he tried and failed," Click said.

"Maybe, yet Teddy flew to Paris seven times in the past two years and Gambier once a year for the past six years, always around May Sixteenth, Seventeenth or Eighteenth. If he's not flying for pleasure and he doesn't have a loan customer in either place, why's he flying to those towns?"

Click took his air aid–a small ruler for measuring distances on aviation maps–from his pocket. He placed it on an imaginary line connecting Paris to Lexington. "Lexington is fifteen miles to the southwest. If he had business there, Teddy would go into Bluegrass Field. At Paris, it's Bourbon County Airport."

"Isn't that horse country?"

"Lots of horse farms around there, tobacco and a whiskey distillery, too, as I recall." Click moved to the northeast on the map. He placed his air aid on Gambier. "The airport here is five miles from Mount Vernon. That's a bigger town. Any loans there?"

"I checked. None."

Click went to a shelf. He pulled down an airport directory and paged in to Kentucky. "Bourbon County Airport, Bourbon County, Bourbon County–ahh, here it is. Public airport, twenty-four hundred feet–that's generous. Grass, east-west runway, standard left-hand pattern."

Then he paged on into Ohio. "Gambier, uh-huh, not much bigger than DeLight in our good county, just a crossroads. Airport's a private field, grass, two thousand feet, north-south, a right-hand pattern when landing to the north. That's odd."

Garrison looked at her father. The expression on her face suggested a question.

"It means," he said, "there's something immediately to the west of the airport they don't want you flying near, like a radio tower or a smokestack, some kind of hazard–" Click snapped the book shut "–or a turkey farm."

Moore chuckled.

"Laugh, but the guy who owns the turkey farm doesn't. Low-flying airplanes scare hell out of his birds, and they all pile up in the corner of the pen and smother one another. If he's got a thousand birds, he can lose more than half of them that way. I've seen that restriction for that very reason at another airport–Lone Rock, Wisconsin."

"Turkey farms, radio towers, smokestacks, none of this tells us why Teddy would be going to Gambier." Moore went back to the table. He poked at the loan file pages.

A knock came to the door. Before Click could get to it, the door swung open and in stepped O.C. Peamantle. "Secret orgies going on in here?"

Garrison frowned.

Peamantle plunged his hands into his pants pockets. "Relax, AJ. I stopped by your office, and Missus Purkiss told me you were out here. You quit early and you don't let her have the rest of the day off? Shame on you." He looked at the wall map and the doodlings on it. "Planning a trip?"

"No."

"This got something to do with Teddy?"

Garrison motioned to Moore still at the table. "Mister Peamantle, this is Scotty Moore, and you probably know my father."

Peamantle stuck his paw out to Moore. "Call me O.C. I'm the editor of the Morgantown Chief, and I recognize you, even in civvies. You're our Smoky Bear."

"'Fraid so," Moore said.

"And, AJ," Peamantle went on, "I met your pap two wars back in Korea, when I was a young pup working for the Chattanooga Times, climbing into foxholes and stopping by pilots' shacks to get news of our boys for the folks back home."

Click saluted. "Good to see you, Othello."

"Oh gawddammit, Will, I've tried my best to keep people in town from knowin' my first name, and you go and spill it."

Click laughed, and then Peamantle.

The editor held his pack of Blackjack gum out first to Click, then to Moore. Both waved him off. He shrugged and stuffed a fresh stick in his mouth. "So whatcha got there?" he asked, nodding at the map.

"Scotty's plotted out all the towns Teddy Wilson flew to where he had loan customers," Garrison said.

"Anything interesting?"

"We're not sure."

"Tell old uncle O.C."

"Scotty?"

Moore went to the map.

"We've got two towns of interest." He tapped his pen on Paris. "He's flown here seven times in the past two years, yet he doesn't have a loan customer in the area. Then up here in Ohio, we got this little backwater town of Gambier. Every year for six years, Teddy flew in, and he didn't have any loan customers there or up the road in Mount Vernon."

"Paris, I can't help you there," Peamantle said. "But Gambier, you don't know?"

"Know what?" Garrison asked.

"That's where the county buys its trucks."

Chapter 14

Probing for a connection

Moore glanced at Garrison, then Peamantle. "Wait a minute, what's the county buying trucks got to do with Teddy?"

"Nothing that I can see, but then I'm just a dumb newspaper editor. You're the detective."

Click clamped a hand on Peamantle's shoulder. "There's nothing dumb about you."

"Don't let 'em find out down at the school board, at least not 'til tomorrow when I run my crime-and-corruption story." He cracked his gum as he grinned.

Garrison picked up the loan log. "O.C., why'd you come by?"

"You know, I think I plum forgot, so I guess I'll be goin' on home."

"O.C."

"No, no, my memory's a blank." Peamantle backed toward the door, cracking his gum as he went. When he felt his hand on the handle, he let himself out.

Moore scratched a sideburn with the point of a pencil. "Strange duck."

"Don't fool yourself, Dick Tracy," Click said. "That old boy knows something."

"Then I'd better get him back here."

"Don't bother. He won't tell us until he's ready."

****

Garrison rapped on the door of the county fiscal court's meeting room.

From the other side, a voice roared "Yeah"–the voice of Hammond MacTeer.

"You're alone, Judge?"

"Surely am. Come on in."

Garrison did as invited and found MacTeer seated at a conference table, a stack of printouts and file folders in front of him.

He pushed out a chair for her.

"What are you working on?" Garrison asked as she put her briefcase on the table.

"Oh, just reading through this pile of stuff our county's governors are going to have to take up this afternoon."

"Any of this have to do with the truck bids?"

"No, we don't open those until Thursday next week. They're all in. We could open them today, but the published deadline for bids is next Thursday noon, and we got to abide by that. Why do you ask?"

"I'm not sure." Garrison took her file on Teddy Wilson's estate from her briefcase. "You know I'm trying to figure out where Teddy got that money that's sitting in his safety deposit box."

"You just can't let it go, can you?"

"No, I can't."

"All right, what did the state banking office have to say?"

"That they've never seen better books, that everything balances to the penny, that everything is explained."

MacTeer leaned far back in his swivel chair and planted one of his well-polished number thirteens on top of the table. "I can tell you that's one big relief. The thought that Teddy could have been stealing from his daddy's bank, I couldn't abide that. So what's next?"

Garrison turned to a page in her file. "I've been studying Teddy's flight log. Did you know he flew to Gambier, Ohio, six times?"

"Why would I know that? And you can say 'we've'

been studying because I know you've got Trooper Moore in on this."

"Judge, it's a private matter. He's doing it on his own time."

A smile tugged at the corners of MacTeer's mouth. "You're smart to get help. Good lawyers do that."

"Gambier, isn't that where the county buys its trucks?"

"And endloaders and road graders. I think we even bought a Cat tractor and a blade there."

"Isn't that kind of far away?"

MacTeer brought his foot back down to the floor. "It is that, but as long as Big Gene can underbid everybody else, we're getting a good deal for the taxpayer's dollar, and it's the job of the fiscal court to do just that. If we spent that dollar recklessly, the voters would hang us by our thumbs and we'd deserve it. But what you're wanting to ask is, has Teddy got anything to do with this?"

Garrison fingered the edge of the page.

"No," MacTeer said. "We don't use intermediaries in the bid-and-buy process. We always work directly with the suppliers, in this case, in Gambier, that's Big Gene Prohaska. Calls himself the king of truck sales. With the deals we get, I believe it. Any other ideas?"

She closed the file, slipped it back in her briefcase. "Not at the moment."

A boy of about eight burst through the door, a barefoot black child in jeans rolled up to his knees, his shirt sleeves bunched above his elbows, and a grin as wide as the door wreathing his face. "Gotcher car all shined, Judge."

MacTeer winked at the boy. "Ajax, my good man, did you bring it around front?"

"No, you know I'm too little to drive. Can't reach the pedals, yet."

"Won't be long, though, will it?"

"I surely hope not."

MacTeer excavated his back pocket for his wallet. "S'pose you want to be paid," he said, eyeing the boy, his voice all seriousness.

"Yessir, an' I'm gonna put it away so I can buy Mamma a present for her birfday."

MacTeer, wallet in hand, dug in its innards. "Birthday present, huh? Whatcha gonna get your momma?"

"I can't tell you. You can't keep a secret."

MacTeer rolled his eyes, then thumped a five-dollar bill on the table. "Think that's enough?"

"Yessir, I do." Clement Downey picked up the bill and shoved it deep in his pants pocket.

"Ajax, you on your way home?"

"Yessir."

"Would you do me one more thing before you go?"

"Name it."

He beckoned Downey to come close. MacTeer put an arm around the boy's shoulders and pointed to a weigh scale in the far corner of the room. "Would you turn that wonderful machine there down about three pounds?"

Downey beamed. He dashed for the scale, going down, sliding on his knees up to it. He hunkered around the scales's backside and fiddled with a turn knob.

"What are you doing?" Garrison asked MacTeer.

He came forward in his chair and parked his elbows on his knees. "We got us a group of fat ladies meets up here this evening, one of those diet club things–the TOPS Club. They always start with a weigh-in, see how much each has lost in the past week–"

"Judge, you don't."

A pixie smile came on MacTeer's face. "Oh, but Ajax and I do. We change that thing a little each week. Just drives those women nuts."

"All done," Downey announced. He came up from the scale and marched to the door, head high, shoulders back, a wide grin.

MacTeer slapped his wallet closed. "Ajax, you're a good man. You tell your momma hi-dee for me."

"I surely will, Judge." The boy waved as he went out, pulling the door closed.

"Judge, if those women ever catch on, they're going to

roast you for this."

"You're not going to tell, are you?"

"Noooo, never."

MacTeer tucked his wallet away. He leaned on the table, his arms crossed. "You ready for your first big trial, your murrrrder trial?"

"Did you know Judge Rayfield wants to start Wednesday?"

MacTeer nodded.

"Judge, is there anything you don't know?"

"When it comes to the county's business, not much. Select the jury Tuesday afternoon?"

"That's what he wants to do."

"I feel sorry for you, AJ. You're client's guilty as sin."

"I know, but it's her right to have a trial."

"Ahh, the American way."

"Any advice on selecting jurors?"

MacTeer took a fistful of files from the pile. He opened the top one. "If they're reasonably solid citizens and they aren't senile or mental defects, take 'em. Trust 'em. You'll find most of our Ballard County people, when they sit up there in those twelve chairs, they take that job very serious. They'll be fair."

****

Garrison stalked out the kitchen door in her cutoffs and UT sweatshirt, a scrub brush in one hand and squirt bottle of Joy in the other, snarling, "Where are you, you stinky dog?"

Bart, her father's retriever, poked his head around the corner of the garage. He saw his master's daughter armed and dangerous, and shrank back.

She took a wash tub down from its nail on the back wall. Garrison tossed the tub under the spigot and turned the water on. She squirted in a shot of dish-and-dog soap. Garrison glanced over her shoulder. She caught sight of a black snout and took off at a gallop.

The dog ran toward the far side of the garage, slid, and

swung around the trunk of a Kentucky coffee tree.

Garrison cut sharp. She dove for him, tackled him. They rolled across the grass and into the rhubarb patch, Garrison with her arms around Bart, the dog kicking and flailing. "Gotcha, Stinky, so quit fighting."

She rolled up on her knees, her right hand clutching Bart's collar and a fistful of fur. She dragged him across the lawn to the wash tub. With one hand, Garrison turned the spigot off, with the other, she kept the reluctant bather from escaping.

A truck door slammed.

The dog spun around, twisted free. His rump rammed into Garrison's chest, and she fell backwards into the tub.

He bounded off.

Will Click came around the corner of the house and saw the dog racing toward him.

"Hey, old pooch, miss me?"

"Dad!"

Click, slap-patting his hound, looked up. "AJ, whatcha doin' sittin' in the tub?"

"I was going to wash your smelly dog. He's stinks."

Click strolled over, clacking his tongue. He gave Garrison his hand and pulled her up and out of the water, wet and well lathered from the middle of her back down. "AJ, you just got to know how to do it."

He whistled.

The dog responded, bounding across the lawn. At the last moment, Bart went airborne. He splashed down in the tub and up came a tidal wave, drenching Garrison.

She raked the water from her face and hair.

Click ignored her. He picked up the scrub brush and worked his dog over from nose to fanny–back, sides, and belly. "Get the garden hose and hook it up, wouldja, daughter? We'll rinse him off."

She squished away toward the garage, muttering about damn stupid dogs and men who deserved them because they weren't any smarter. She returned, dragging the hose behind her, to find her father finished and Bart sitting in the tub, his tongue lolling from the side of his mouth.

Click stared at Garrison's sour expression as she twisted the coupling onto the spigot. "Something tells me you haven't had a good day."

"Get the damn dog out of the tub."

He tugged at Bart's collar. The retriever hopped out onto the grass where he stood as firmly as if his feet were rooted in the sod while Garrison, her thumb pressed into the jet of water to make a spray, blasted off the suds. She moved around to soak his face, and Bart bit at the spray, taking in great gulps of water.

Rinse cycle finished, Click let the dog go. Bart danced and shook himself, rolling his hide and hair from side to side, the excess water showering Garrison. She leaped back, turning the hose on her father.

He leaped back, too.

"Sorry," she said, cringing.

"Yeah, I bet."

"Really." Garrison threw the hose down. She twisted the spigot, shutting off the water.

Click came over, his arms out. "Come on now, what is it?"

She fell into his arms, buried her face in his shoulder. "All I wanted to do was wash that damn dog, and I couldn't even do that right."

He stroked her wet hair. "Yeah, but that's not it. Something happen at the office?"

"No."

"The courthouse?"

Garrison's shoulders shook as she sobbed.

"Come on."

Garrison snuffled in an attempt to quell her tears. "I had to argue why Henry Knott shouldn't be fined when it was his brother's barking dog that provoked him. Judge Rayfield fined him anyway. Then he yelled at me for filing Henry's suit against Alvin, a dumb waste-of-time suit he called it, a dumb waste-of-time suit that was going to waste his time having to hear the dumb thing."

Click rocked her as he had when she had twisted her knee running hurdles, losing a high school district championship.

"He yelled at me in front of my client, in front of the county attorney, in front of everybody, and I've got another case before him on Wednesday."

He guided her over to two lawn chairs in the shade of a silver maple turned a toasted yellow beside the remnants of last summer's vegetable garden. After he got her seated, Bart shagged over. He sat beside Garrison and put his head on her lap.

"Smelly dog," she said, but massaged behind one of his ears.

"The Wednesday case is a dumb waste-of-time case, too, isn't it," Click said as he sat back in his chair, "Irene McCoskey running over her husband?"

"Yes."

"She won't plead guilty and let you get out of arguing it, will she?"

"No."

"So what's your plan?"

"I don't have any."

The three sat in silence, the dog content as Garrison rubbed his ears.

Click pulled up a blade of grass. He chewed on it. "Well, when it comes time for you to present your defense, you could tell the jury up front Irene did it."

"I can't do that."

"Why not?"

"The county attorney would move for a bench-ordered decision of guilty, and Judge Rayfield would send Irene to prison."

"Ohh, and you don't want prison for Irene."

"No, she's not a bad person."

"Then, Boots, you're going to have to make one powerful argument for justifiable homicide."

"I can't do that." Garrison peered down at her hand stroking Bart's head. "Murder is never justified."

"Then face up to it. Irene's going to prison."

CHAPTER 15

Flights and trials

Wednesday arrived with the first frost of fall preceding dawn, a killing frost for the tomato plants still heavy with fruit in Morgantown's gardens. Garrison did not consider it a good sign when she had to dig out the scraper from where she had tossed it in her father's box of miscellany in the garage to scratch the white stuff from her bug's windshield. Her father had gotten home first the evening before, so he pulled his truck inside, leaving Garrison to park in the weather. That was their unspoken rule–first home gets the garage.

Will Click had cooked breakfast for her while she soaked in the tub. When she came down, all was on the table, but he was gone. Under the sugar bowl, a scrap of paper with a four-word message, "Gambier. Knock 'em dead."

Garrison bypassed the office. Instead, she drove directly to the courthouse and there idled through the parking lot, muttering words she could not use at church when she couldn't find a place to leave her car. She rounded the corner and found the sheriff's lot equally full. Muttering still, she herded the Beetle back out onto the street. There she found one slot open across from the courthouse. Garrison backed her Volkswagen in and bought an hour on the parking meter for a nickel.

For this she came prepared. Garrison took a roll of Scotch tape from her briefcase and taped six nickels to the face of the meter. She had an agreement with the city police's meter maid to slug her meter each time the time-expired flag went up.

Garrison hurried across the street–jaywalking–and dashed up the front steps. Inside, she went on up to the second floor. There she stopped at the bubbler for a splash of water. As she wiped her lips with the back of her hand, Judge Hezekiah Rayfield came out of the bathroom–tall, distinguished, in his black hangman's suit as the county's lawyers called his attire.

"Good morning, Judge," Garrison said.

"Is it?" he asked from on high. Before Garrison could answer, Rayfield plowed on, "I don't think so because you've stuck me with this good-for-nothing case."

"Judge–"

"Don't give me your 'my client deserves a trial' speech. I just want you to know my hemorrhoids hurt this morning, so you better make this a damn-fast trial. Understood?"

"Yes, Judge."

Rayfield swept away into the courtroom, Garrison trailing in his wake.

The district attorney, Adam Cusick, sat at the prosecutor's table, a series of file folders open before him. He drummed with two pencils on the edge of the table but stopped when he sensed Rayfield. "Morning, Judge," he said, "how's your health?"

Rayfield withered him with a look that would crumble rocks and moved on to his bench.

"Hemorrhoids?" Cusick mouthed to Garrison after she opened her briefcase on the defense table. She responded with a tilt of her head and set out her legal pad, a pencil, and one folder. Garrison settled in a chair to wait for a deputy to bring her client in.

Irene McCoskey appeared in the doorway to the side of the judge's bench accompanied by the ever rumpled Deputy Bunch Jeffords. She came from jail dressed for a country-club tea–pale lavender dress suit, matching lavender heels, a cameo broach at the throat of her ruffled blouse, white gloves, and a hat that might have been designed for Jackie Kennedy. She gave a look of disdain to the judge as she strode with elegance past his bench to the defense table, Jeffords keeping his hand on her elbow.

"Thank you, Uncle Bunch," Garrison said after he seated his charge.

"You all right, Amanda?" he asked.

"Yes."

"Damn shame you got stuck with this one."

"Uncle Bunch–"

Jeffords raised a hand as he backed away. "Sorry, maybe I kin buy ya lunch at the Sunshine if this trial goes to noon."

Garrison gave him an evil look as she brought up a clenched fist. Jeffords only laughed.

Rayfield slammed his gavel down. "Time's come for some testifying and convicting. Let's get the jury in here."

Jeffords opened the door at the back of the jury box. Garrison studied the faces of the twelve people who shuffled past him to their chairs, faces that revealed a range of emotions from utter boredom to high anticipation.

She needed one vote when the jurors retired, but knew she wasn't going to get it.

****

"Columbus Center, Two-One Echo," Oliver said into his microphone.

"Two-One Echo, go ahead."

"We're fifteen out from Gambier. We'd like to leave you now."

"Roger, Two-One Echo. Area weather is scattered clouds at five thousand, overcast at ten, visibility ten miles, winds at the surface generally out of the southeast at five knots, and the altimeter at Columbus is two-niner-niner-seven and falling."

"Two-One Echo." Oliver took his thumb off the transmitter button. He watched as Click dialed in the local settings on the Aero Commander's twin altimeters. "Weather's kind of stinky."

"Could be worse."

"If the forecast is right, we got three hours. Then the front moves in and it's zero-zero. We won't get out until tomorrow."

Click waved at the windshield. "There's Gambier."

Oliver craned around, peering down over the Commander's nose. "What's that I see, a grass strip this side of town?" He throttled back on the engines' power and put in ten-degrees of flaps to slow the Commander.

Click dialed in one-twenty-two-point-nine on one of the radios and pressed the transmitter button. "Gambier traffic, this is Aero Commander November Four-Four-Two-One Echo five south of your airport. We're going to swing around to the north and land to the south."

There was no answer.

"Nobody home," Oliver said.

"Or in the air."

"I got an idea. Pop the gear."

Click yanked the landing gear handle down. He listened to the hydraulics open the gear doors and pump the wheels out into the slipstream. "Green lights on the mains and the nose. Gear down and locked."

Oliver motored the Commander across Gambier at two thousand feet. He laid the airplane over into a steep bank to the left to bring the big twin around to the west of the town, then aimed it east. He dropped down another five hundred feet and dragged over Gambier's main street, landing gear down, flaps extended, engines blatting. At the east end of the town, Oliver pulled back up to two thousand feet. He banked around a second time, cutting back on his power for a landing on the grass field.

"The low pass?" Moore asked from his seat behind the pilot.

"At some of these places," Click said, "that's a signal you need gas and someone comes out from town."

The wheels touched down so gently on the grass runway that Click looked out his window to assure himself the Commander was down. Oliver pulled all the power off.

He pumped the toe brakes, slowing the airplane for a turnaround at the far end of the runway. Oliver taxied the Commander back to midfield, then off to the side and parked in front of a humpback trailer he assumed was the airport's office. Four T-hangars laid to the south of the trailer, each with its doors closed.

Oliver shut the engines down. He snapped off a series of switches as the propellers spun ever more slowly until they spun no more. When all was quiet, Oliver unbuckled his seat belt and went back into the cabin, to the door already open, and outside. There he joined Click and Moore both gandering around.

A Buick Estate wagon rumbled down a graveled road toward the new arrivals.

****

Rayfield tapped his gavel. "So much for the opening statements. Mister Cusick, any witnesses?"

"Just two, Judge," Cusick said, rising. He straightened his necktie that had managed to work itself askew during his speech to the jury. He turned to the back of the courtroom. "Sim Kroizer?"

A city patrolman stood up, the officer in full regalia–gun belt, holster, handcuffs hanging from the side, a traffic whistle on a cord around his neck, the cord draped over his badge to keep the whistle out of the way. Kroizer, creases in his tans sharp enough to slice one's fingers, came forward to the witness chair.

Rayfield leveled his gavel at the patrolman. "Gawddammit, Sim, you know I don't allow guns in my courtroom. Give it to Bunch. Who you intending to shoot, anyway?"

Kroizer's face flushed, but he snapped open the flap on his holster and surrendered his weapon to the deputy. Jeffords tucked the gun in the drawer of his desk at the other side of Rayfield's bench.

"Now Sim," Rayfield went on, "you going to tell the truth?"

"Yessir."

"Sit down."

Kroizer did. He brushed his hand down his necktie, smoothing it.

Cusick stepped up to the lectern that faced the judge. "Kindly state your name and your office for the record, Patrolman," he said.

Kroizer cleared his throat. "Sim Kroizer, senior patrolman for the Morgantown city police department. I've been employed by the department for three years."

"Patrolman, you were the first on the scene?"

"Yessir."

"Tell us what you saw."

"I was coming up Church Street and I saw Missus McCoskey's car coming toward me with a broken headlight, and that's when I saw her husband laying on the sidewalk up a ways from us."

"Broken headlight, you say?"

"Yessir."

Cusick went to the bailiff's desk where he picked up a baggy. He carried it to the officer. "What do I have here?"

Kroizer read the notes written on the plastic with an indelible marker. "This is glass broken from a headlight. And those are my initials."

"Prosecution One, Judge," Cusick said. After he took the baggy back to Jeffords' desk, Cusick returned to the lectern. "Where did you find these pieces?"

"On the sidewalk by Mister McCoskey's body."

"Was he alive?"

"No sir, I checked his pulse. I really didn't have to. I could see he had been run over, busted up pretty bad. Lotta blood."

"And the glass is from the headlight of Missus McCoskey's car?"

"Had to be."

"Objection!" Garrison came to her feet.

Rayfield arched an eyebrow. "What is it, Miss Garrison?"

"The officer testified he stopped Missus McCoskey some distance from the accident. He didn't see the accident happen, so he can't know whether the glass came from the headlight of the defendant's car or the headlight of some other car."

Rayfield turned to Cusick. "She's got you there, Adam. The jury will ignore the officer's assertion that the glass in question came from the defendant's headlight."

Cusick looked again at his witness. "But Missus McCoskey's car did have a broken headlight."

"Yessir."

"Very well. Did you find any skid marks on the street or the sidewalk that would suggest whoever ran down Mister McCoskey," he turned to the defendant, fixing her with a glare, "attempted to stop before hitting the victim?"

"No sir. There were marks of tires going over the curb some thirty feet beyond Mister McCoskey, but that was all."

"That's all, Judge," Cusick said, going to his table.

Rayfield squirmed to get more comfortable on his chair. "Miss Garrison, any questions for the witness?"

"Just one." Garrison stepped to the lectern. "Officer, you didn't see the accident, is that correct?"

"That's correct."

"So you don't know who hit Mister McCoskey, is that correct?"

Kroizer squirmed some himself. "That's correct, but I've got suspicions."

"But suspicions aren't any good in court, are they?"

"No, ma'am."

Garrison sat down.

The judge held his hands out, looking at Cusick. When Cusick didn't respond, he turned to Kroizer. "That's all for you, Sim. Go by Bunch's desk and get your gun and get out of here."

CHAPTER 16

Big Gene

The stationwagon swayed to a stop in front of the humpback trailer, the man inside rolling down his window. "Howdy, strangers. Can I help ya?"

"Can I get some gas for the bird?" Oliver asked, gesturing toward the Commander as he pulled on his leather flight jacket.

The big man began to open the wagon's door but caught his reflection in the rearview mirror. He leaned up and, with his fingers, twisted his right eye. "Damn glass eye's always wantin' to look where I don't want it."

Satisfied, he pushed himself out. "I'm sorry about that, and I'm sorry about the gas thing."

"How's that?" Oliver asked.

"Those of us who fly out of mighty Gambier International, we have to hop over to little Knox County for fuel. I take it you didn't know that."

"No sir, we're on our way to Cleveland and our charter here," Oliver thumbed at Moore, "got complaining he was hungry, so we put down."

"Well, now, there we can help. Got a mighty fine café in town. Y'all want a ride in?"

"No, my copilot and I will stay with the plane."

"Tell you what, I'll keep you company. Name's Gene Prohaska." The man put out his hand, the size of a ham. He shook hands all around, then moved toward the first T-hangar, motioning for all to follow him. Prohaska shoved open the nearest of two sliding doors.

"I got an old beater I keep out here for people to use," he said to Moore. "Why don't you just take it on into town, and I'll keep your buddies entertained?"

Before them stood a Nineteen Forty-Six Ford coupe, the right fender and door dented and scrapes in the paint. Prohaska opened the driver's door. "Go ahead. Key's in the switch."

Moore, in a new suit borrowed for the day, swatted at the dusty seat before he slid his bottom onto it. The old car came to life on the first step on the starter button. "Motor sounds good."

"Oh yeah," Prohaska said. "Looks like hell, but runs like an angel."

Moore pulled the door closed. He stared at the floor shifter and fished around with it until he found reverse. Moore backed out of the hangar and, with a wave to his colleagues, drove off through the ditch and up onto the road toward town.

"Who is he?" Prohaska asked as he watched the beater disappear over a rise.

"Young banker from Knoxville," Click said. "Got business up in Cleveland."

"Well, I s'pose he knows Teddy Wilson, and you do, too, since that's Teddy's airplane."

"You know Teddy?"

Prohaska crossed his arms over his massive belly his suit coat tried to hide. "Sure."

"You know he died last month?"

"Hell no. How'd it happen?"

"Car accident."

"Damn shame. So you bought the plane then?"

"No, we're leasing it from the estate until Teddy's wife decides what she wants to do with it. It's a sweet flyer. How do you come to know Teddy?"

Prohaska kicked the toe of his shoe at the graveled floor of the hangar. "We got a little lake up here Teddy liked to fish. He bought some property on it, and I handled the sale."

Click shoved his hands in the pockets of his jacket. "I thought you dabbled in trucks."

"I do, I do. How'd you know that? I'm not wearin' a sign on my back, am I?"

"I know some of the boys in the county road department down where I live–Ballard County. They told me."

Prohaska dug a massive wallet from his inside coat pocket. He thumbed through the receipts and notes it contained until he came on two business cards. He handed one to Click and the other to Oliver.

Click read the card. "King of truck sales, huh?"

"If it's got wheels on it, I can get it for you cheaper than anybody else. Volume, that's what I deal in. Two, three hundred trucks a month, all sizes, all colors, all kinds."

Beside where the car had been parked stood an airplane covered by canvas. Click, curious, sidled over. He lifted a corner. "Whatcha got under here?"

"Well, I'm not too proud of that," Prohaska said. He shoved the second door open and pulled off one of the canvases.

Click whistled.

"Then you know what it is," Prohaska said.

"Do I ever. I flew one of those back in World War Two–a Beech Staggerwing."

Prohaska pulled off the other canvas, revealing a biplane with an enclosed cabin and a great round engine on the front. "It was the Cadillac of her day."

"And fast," Click said. "The one I flew could keep up with Teddy's Commander without straining. I flew rescue from England into Occupied Europe for the RAF's Moonbeam Squadron."

Prohaska took off his hat. He raked his fingers back through his tangle of hair. "Don't think I ever heard of them."

"Few did, and that's the way we wanted it." Click ran his hand along the edges of the biplane's propeller. "Yours?"

"Yup."

"You fly it?"

"Never have. It's a basket case."

Click went around to the side, to the door. He opened it and looked in.

"You can get in if you want," Prohaska said.

Click took him up on that. He stepped up on the wing, then inside. Click went forward to the copilot's seat, Prohaska leaning in. "Brings back memories, huh?"

"Oh yeah. Most of 'em pretty good. How'd you come to get the bird?"

"History has it the Staggerwing once belonged to Humbolt Petroleum out in Oil City, Kansas. It changed hands a couple times, and I got it a year ago from a fella in Mount Vernon where the old bird was just rotting away. Figured I might like to restore it and had it trucked over."

While the two nattered on, Oliver squeezed around the airplane, a tight fit in so small a hangar. He noted the holes in the fabric of the fuselage and wings, the right aileron hanging loose, one tire flat and the other looking like it suffered from dry rot. He peered inside the engine cowling at the grimy oil that lined it, oil that had stained the belly of the aircraft where it had washed back during flight.

Oliver shook his head. Then he heard the question he knew was coming from his partner, "Want to sell it?"

****

"Mister Cusick, call your other witness," Rayfield said.

The county attorney turned to the back of the courtroom. "Emma Clark."

A silver-haired woman with thick glasses and a cane rose. She wore a gray house dress, black lace-up shoes, gray socks that came above her ankles, and an Aunt Bea-style hat. Missus Clark held tight to her purse, as if she feared someone in the courtroom might try to wrestle it away from her. She came to the witness chair.

Rayfield motioned for her to sit. "Now, Em, you going to tell the truth?"

Missus Clark harrumphed. "You have to ask?"

"I have to ask."

"I will and you know it." She placed her purse in her lap and, with deliberation, folded her hands over it.

"Go ahead, Adam," Rayfield said.

Cusick stepped up to the lectern. "How are you doing today, Missus Clark?"

"Fine. Let's move it along, sonny. My quilting club's waiting on me."

"Well, all right. You live across the street from the Congregational church, have I got that right?"

"Mister Cusick, you know I don't live across from the church. Missus Archer does. I'm the next house to the east."

"But you can see the church."

"Very well from my front window."

"And what did you see on the day that Mister McCoskey was run down?"

"I object," Garrison said, rising to her feet.

Rayfield put a hand to his face. He drew his hand down until it cupped his chin. "What is it, Miss Garrison?"

"I object to the characterization in Mister Cusick's question. 'Run down' suggests it was deliberate."

"Would it be all right it he said 'hit,' like in it was an accident?"

"Yes, Judge."

"So noted. Continue, Mister Cusick."

The county attorney looked at his notes before he resumed. "Just tell us what you saw."

"I saw Irene McCoskey's car hit her husband."

"Did you see Missus McCoskey?"

"Not until she backed over her husband." A juror, her hand shaking, turned away. "That's when she got out of her car, when she went to catch her dog."

"Did you see anything else?"

"I saw her run over Mister McCoskey again as she drove away." A second juror covered his eyes.

"No more questions," Cusick said, retiring to his table.

"Miss Garrison?" Rayfield asked.

She came to the lectern. Garrison stood there, rubbing her lower lip with her index finger. "Missus Clark, you wear rather thick glasses, don't you?"

"Amanda, you know I do."

"How well do you see?"

"Well enough to see that you forgot to button one of the buttons on your blouse."

Garrison's hand went to her blouse front. Her fingers felt for and found the errant button, and slipped it through the button hole. "But can you be sure the person you saw was Irene McCoskey, sure that it was even her car?"

Missus Clark opened her purse. She took out a slip of paper and held it up. "I could see well enough to read her license plate. I wrote the number down."

****

Moore skipped the Gambier Café when he saw the town's bank. He swung the beater Ford around in the center of the street and parked in front of the narrow two-story limestone building. He walked inside, to a woman at the teller window. "Your head teller here today?" he asked.

She pointed to a young man hunched over a calculator at the back of the room.

Moore went on back. The young man, slightly balding, looked up and Moore asked, "You in charge today?"

"I guess you could say that. Mister Winslow is over at our sister bank in Mount Vernon. I'm Neale Harder. Can I help you?" Harder motioned for Moore to take a side chair.

He did and slipped his state police badge onto the desk. "I'm Corporal R.S. Moore. I'm doing some investigative work for the Tennessee bank commissioner."

Harder picked up the badge. He let his fingers play over the surface. "Kind of far from home, aren't you, sir?"

"Guess you could say that."

"How can I help you?"

Moore glanced around the bank. Other than himself and the teller, there was no one in the bank. He noticed the teller studying him. "Any government checks from Ballard

County, Tennessee, ever come through here?"

Harder scratched at his thinning forelock. "Ballard County . . . Ballard County . . ."

He pushed back from his desk and went to a filing cabinet. There he pulled out a ledger. "We're a small bank. We don't get a lot of big checks, so I tend to remember them."

Harder paged into the book. He turned it to Moore and touched a line two-thirds of the way down the page.

Moore took out his notepad. "Interesting. Two hundred ten thousand dollars and, what's this?"

Harder leaned down to look. "Twenty-eight cents."

"A federal check made out to Ballard County, Tennessee, by your notes. You got it on Five-Seventeen of this year. Do you know who endorsed it?"

Harder squinted up at the light fixture, as if the answer might be there. "No, I don't, but I do remember it was signed over to Gene Prohaska. He was the one who cashed it."

"Who's he?"

"Local businessman. I remember we had to call over to our sister bank for more currency because we didn't have enough money in the vault. If Mister Prohaska brings us a check, we know it's good as gold."

Moore continued writing. "And what would this Mister Prohaska be doing with a Tennessee check?"

"He sells a lot of trucks around the country. That was probably it, probably sold some trucks down there."

"Yet he wanted cash."

"He does that often. I think it's mostly for show. I've seen him peel off a thousand-dollar bill to pay for supper at the café, just to see how frustrated he can make Helene Thomas. Then he'll laugh, give her a hundred, and tell her to keep the change."

"Big spender."

"Guess you could say that."

"Any other Ballard County checks?"

Harder tapped the side of his nose as his brain tapped

his memory. Then he went back to the filing cabinet.

****

"Your turn, Miss Garrison," Rayfield said. "Any witnesses?"

"Two, your honor." She went to the bailiff's desk for a file folder and carried it to the lectern. "I call Doctor Amos Detwiler."

A man, one of the collar points of his white shirt lapped over his suit coat lapel and his suit coat stained by driblets of coffee, rose at the side of the courtroom. In an uncertain fashion, he worked his way forward.

Rayfield waved the medic to the witness chair. "You know the rules, Amos. No lying."

"Yes, Judge," Detwiler said after he made a business of settling himself.

Garrison came to the witness chair. She handed the doctor the open folder. "Doctor Detwiler, what is this?"

He held the folder up to his face.

"You can put on your glasses if you like."

"Don't need glasses. This is my report on some surgery I performed on Missus McCoskey."

Garrison went back to the lectern. "And what surgery is that?" she asked.

"Missus McCoskey broke her mandible–her jaw–on the left side." He patted his face, demonstrating the area. "Pretty bad. I had to wire the jaw together so it would heal."

"How did she break her jaw?"

"She didn't. Her husband did. He hit her."

"How do you know that?"

"She told me, in a note."

Garrison came forward and retrieved the hospital report. She placed it on Jeffords' desk. "Defense One, your honor."

"Noted," Rayfield said.

Garrison turned back to Detwiler. "Did her husband beat Missus McCoskey often?"

"Not that I know of."

"Objection."

"What is it, Mister Prosecutor?" Rayfield asked.

Cusick shook a 'shame-on-you' finger at Garrison. "She's implying Mister McCoskey was a wife beater. There is no evidence of that."

"Mister Cusick, he broke her jaw," Garrison said, her face expressing amazement.

Rayfield adjusted his bottom on his chair. "Score two for the defense, Adam. Your objection is overruled. Go ahead, Miss Garrison."

She again turned to Detwiler. "Would you say having one's jaw mashed hurt a lot?"

"Yes."

"Really painful?"

"Yes, the bruising, the multiple breaks in the bone. I believe Missus McCoskey had two teeth she had to have replaced."

"Did you do that?"

"No, that's dental surgery."

"So she had to undergo another operation?"

"That's right."

"A lot of pain?"

"When the anesthesia wore off, yes."

"A long time to recover?"

"Three months."

"Thank you, Doctor Detwiler," Garrison said.

Rayfield turned to Cusick. "Questions?"

The county attorney shook his head.

Detwiler looked from Cusick up to the judge, perplexed.

"You're done, Amos," Rayfield said. "You can go."

"That's it?"

"Yes."

"I canceled all my morning appointments for five minutes of testimony?"

"Afraid so, but we all appreciate it. Now leave." Rayfield waved his hand in dismissal. "Miss Garrison, any more witnesses?"

"Evelyn Carter."

When the woman did not rise, Rayfield motioned for Jeffords to bring her out of the audience.

"Come on, Evie, you gotta do this," Jeffords said in little more than a whisper as he lifted the Carter woman by the elbow. He guided her forward to the witness chair.

"Please note for the record that this is a reluctant witness," Garrison said.

"So noted," Rayfield said.

Missus Carter, chunky and with a generous bosom, brushed at the front of her black dress. Then she patted at her hair near her temple and at the back of her head.

"A little nervous, Missus Carter?" Garrison asked.

"I am," she said.

"Perhaps you have reason. You were having an affair with Missus McCoskey's husband, were you not?"

The woman looked down, then away. "Yes," she whispered.

"How's that?"

"Yes," she said, her voice louder.

"A lot of sex?"

"Two nights a week, yes."

"Did your husband know?"

"Not until now."

A male juror laughed and chucked another in the ribs.

"Did Missus McCoskey know?"

"Not at first. Andrew told me she found out. That's why he was leaving her."

"Do you think she's right to be upset?"

Missus Carter again looked away.

"Your honor, would you direct Missus Carter to answer the question?" Garrison said.

Rayfield leaned forward. He held his gavel between his hands. "Evie, it's all spoiled now, so you have to answer anything either lawyer asks you."

Missus Carter twisted the strap on her purse. She gazed up at the ceiling fan lazily stirring at the room's stuffy air. Finally, she stared at Garrison. "Yes–yes, I'd be upset if my husband was doing another woman."

****

Moore wheeled the beater into the hangar as Click and Oliver threw the canvases back over the wings of the Beechcraft. They draped the inside edges across the windshield and over the engine cowling, leaving only the propeller exposed.

"Food pretty good at the café?" Prohaska asked after Moore got out of the car.

"Excellent." He held up a paper bag. "Got some sandwiches to go for my pilot and copilot–baloney sandwiches."

Click gagged.

"All right, steak sandwiches."

Prohaska asked, salivating, "You get the barbecue sauce, the big Kosher dills, and the string taters?"

"Of course."

He clapped his arms around the shoulders of Click and Oliver. "You boys are in for some good eatin'. Nobody makes a better steak sandwich than our Helene." He escorted them to the Commander where all climbed aboard except Prohaska. He leaned in through the doorway. "So you're gonna buy my Staggerwing?"

Click settled his headset over his ears. "If I can finance it," he said. "Call you tomorrow."

"Roger dodger." Prohaska slapped the inside wall, then closed the door. Moore reached over and twisted the door's security latch into place.

"Ready to start engines?" Oliver asked.

Click waved at Prohaska strolling away. "Big Gene's clear. Go."

Oliver cracked the throttles and pushed the mixture controls to full rich. Only then did he touch the starter button for the right engine. It barked to life as did the left a moment later.

Click dialed one-sixteen-point-seven on one radio and left the second set to the local frequency.

Oliver jockeyed the engines as he rolled the Commander out onto the grass strip and north to the end. Click spun the knobs on the two gyro compasses to settings of three hundred sixty degrees. At the end of the runway, the pilots ran through the checklist, checking controls, flight instruments, and gauges–assuring themselves everything was ready for takeoff.

"Let's do it," Oliver said after he idled the engines back.

Click pressed his transmitter button. "Gambier traffic, this is Aero Commander November Forty-Four-Two-One Echo on the active at Gambier, departing south then turning north for Cleveland." He glanced at Oliver when he said 'Cleveland,' and Oliver snickered.

Silence met Click's transmission, so Oliver pushed the throttles up to the top of the power quadrant. That sent the Commander off down the runway. The twin sprang into the air well before the fence at the end. Oliver swept up the gear and flaps, and Click flipped the transmitter switch to the second radio. "Columbus Flight Service Station," he said into his microphone, "Aero Commander November Four-Four-Two-One Echo listening Appleton VOR. We're off Gambier for Knoxville, Tennessee. Want to file an IFR flight plan and get the latest weather."

Static crackled over everyone's headsets, then came "Roger, Two-One Echo. This is Columbus Flight Service. Ceiling five thousand feet, so stay below the clouds until you get clearance from Columbus Center." The voice droned on through a lengthy weather report that including a mention of icing at ten thousand feet.

Oliver banked the Commander around to a north heading and sped over the Gambier airport and the town. He held that heading until the fog behind him swallowed Gambier, then he leaned the Commander into a long arc to the left and rolled out on a southbound heading for the nearby Appleton VOR.

Click, finished transmitting his flight plan, twisted the radio frequency to one-twenty-point-five. "Columbus Center, this is Aero Commander November Four-Four-

Two-One Echo standing by for an IFR clearance."

"Roger, Two-One Echo. . . . United Three-Thirty-Six, you're cleared to descend to six thousand feet on course for a straight-in to Columbus Regional, Runway Two-Seven. An Aero Commander will be passing below you on Victor Four-Ninety-Three."

"Roger. United Three-Thirty-Six out of ten for six."

"United, what's the icing like where you are?"

"Heavy."

"Commander Two-One Echo, you copy United Three-Thirty-Six?"

Click pressed his transmitter button. "Two-One Echo, copy."

"You still want twelve thousand feet?"

"Roger, best winds there. If the forecast is right, we should break out of the clouds and ice over the Ohio River."

"Likely. A Piedmont captain agrees with you. Called ten minutes ago over Portsmouth. Two-One Echo, stay beneath the clouds until ten DME south of Appleton, then climb to twelve thousand and proceed as filed."

"Over Appleton VOR now."

"All right, Two-One Echo. Copy the traffic, United Three-Three-Six?"

"Copy that, and United is at six thousand."

Radio transmissions went silent for three minutes, until Click pressed his transmit button. "Columbus Center, Two-One Echo is ten south of Appleton. We're going up."

Oliver pressed the throttles to the firewall. He pulled the Commander's nose up into an easy climb and retrimmed the aircraft. Click helped with cockpit business by turning on the wing deicing boots and the windshield heater.

The voice of the center controller came back, "Roger Two-One Echo. . . . United Three-Three-Six, you're cleared to descend to three thousand feet. Contact Columbus tower when you have the airport in sight. You're the only traffic."

The clouds enveloped the Commander at five thousand feet. Rime ice plastered the deicing boots at ten thousand, the boots pulsing, cracking the building ice, letting it slide away over the wings into the slipstream.

Moore gazed out his window. All he saw in the gloom was the propeller chewing through cloud. "You boys know what you're doing?" he asked.

"Heck no," Click said, "we're just making it up as we go along."

****

"Any more witnesses?" Rayfield asked Garrison.

"No, your honor. The defense rests."

He grubbed his father's railroad watch from his pocket. Rayfield pressed a button on the side of the watch case, and the cover flipped open. "It's eleven thirty," he announced, turning to the jury. "What's your pleasure? We can break for lunch or the lawyers can give their closing statements and you can start to deliberate."

A man in the back row, in newly washed Oshkosh-By-Gosh bib overalls and a white shirt, raised his hand.

"Oscar," Rayfield said, recognizing the man.

"Hell, Judge, why don't we get on with it? I got to get home an' pick corn this afternoon."

"Anyone else?" Rayfield asked. When he saw several heads nod in agreement, he pointed his gavel at Garrison. "All right, Miss Garrison, your closing statement. Keep it to two minutes."

She carried her legal pad to the lectern. There she looked at her notes, then the jury. "Let me make this both easy and difficult for you, easy in that Irene McCoskey did it. She ran over her husband, but remember, he had beat her. He had left her. For all we know he was hoping to convince Evelyn Carter to run off with him, so Irene was hurt and she was angry as would you have been if you had been in her place. So when she saw Mister McCoskey on the sidewalk, she hit him with her car."

Garrison put a small check beside something on her pad. "She intended to scare her husband and get her dog back. She wanted to hurt him perhaps, not kill him, but she did. Just about every one of you knows Irene. You know she's not a bad person. She's not an evil person, so here's the easy part, find her guilty. But here's the difficult part, recommend to the judge that he not send her to prison."

Garrison circled an item on her pad for no other reason than to gain time for her statement to sink in with the jurors. She focused on the first juror and each in turn as she continued. "Irene is a registered nurse, 'tho not a practicing nurse. She hasn't worked since she married. Recommend that she work three years as a nurse at the Northside Free Clinic for no pay. Let her help people in our community who need help. Let that be her payment to Morgantown and Ballard County for what she did to her husband."

****

Click saw Garrison standing beside her Beetle as Oliver taxied Teddy Wilson's Aero Commander up to the ramp in front of the Vol-Air office trailer. He waved to her.

Oliver goosed the right engine. He swung the Commander around until it was butt end to the office before he shut down the engines. He and Click then went through the business of snapping off switches. "How do you think she did today?" Oliver asked as he turned to packing his lap full of aviation maps into his flight case.

Click got out of his seat. He reached back down to hook his lap belt together, cinching it tight. "She don't look too tore up, so I guess they didn't throw her to the lions. Shall we find out?"

Moore had the door unlatched and open by the time Click got into the passenger cabin. "Age first," the trooper said and waved Click on.

Click stepped out, then Moore and, last, Oliver with his flight case. The pilots looked like pilots in their leather jackets, their Vol-Air caps pushed back, dark glasses shading their eyes from the late October sun, and Moore looked the part of a banker in a conservative business suit, white shirt, and tie.

Garrison called to them, "Aren't you the handsome

threesome."

Click, smiling, threw out his arms. Garrison came to him, and they hugged.

"I'm buying supper," she said. "Irene's not going to prison."

CHAPTER 17

Comparing notes

They all piled into Oliver's Ford Fairlane woody, gabbling about nothing in particular while Oliver drove to his house on the edge of Morgantown. There his two kids–boys of four and six–clambered into the third seat, and his wife, Hannah, squeezed in front, between her man and Click.

"Hannah," Oliver said in introducing her, "the fella behind us with AJ is Scotty Moore."

She waved over her shoulder. "Good to meet you, Mister Moore."

"Call me Scotty."

"I'll do that."

To his boys in the back, Oliver called out, "Joseph? Samuel? Mister Moore is a po-liceman. So you behave yourselves back there, you hear?"

"Yes, Pa," the older said.

"Samuel?"

The younger stared at the toes of his shoes before he mumbled, "Yes, Pa."

"Where to?" Oliver asked as he backed the woody out of his driveway.

"How about the Cavu," Click said, "at the new Holiday Inn? That all right with you, AJ? I think you can afford it."

"Fine, Pop."

Cavu–'clear above, visibility unlimited', meaning perfect flying weather in aviation talk. The Holiday Inn investors decorated the dining room with propellers and murals of piston passenger planes and jet airliners, and dressed their waitresses as stewardesses for the fictional Holiday Air airline.

Two welcomed the Click and Oliver crowd. They gave out boarding passes and ushered the guests to First Class table seating, the air rich with the aroma of mesquit-grilled steaks.

"How about junior pilot's wings for these two guys?" Stewardess Annie asked. She took a set from her pocket and pinned it on Samuel's shirt, then gave Joseph a set. Both looked at their wings, grinning, Samuel stroking his.

They dealt out menus, then left to greet others at the restaurant's arrival gate.

Oliver opened his menu. "Hannah, you want to order for the boys?"

She inclined her head toward them. "What do you say to spaghetti?"

Samuel, on a booster seat, clapped his hands. "Paghetti!"

"Joseph?"

"Spaghetti."

To Stewardess Annie who had returned with water glasses for all, Hannah said, "Two small plates."

"With meat sauce?"

"Meat sauce and some bread, and milk to drink."

"And for the rest of you?" she asked, looking around the table.

Click leaned on his elbows. He rubbed his hands. "A steak is tempting, but what do you have that's really expensive? My daughter's buying."

"Lobster."

"Oooo, yes. And shrimp cocktails for everyone."

"Whoa, now. Let's not get carried away," Oliver said.

Garrison brought out a one-hundred dollar bill–crisp, not a wrinkle or a crease in it. She laid the bill in the middle of the table.

"Print that yourself?" Click asked.

"Pop, really."

"So Irene did pay you."

"Three thousand dollars, and that's above the retainer."

"Nothing like a happy client. So what's her sentence?"

"Three years community service at the Northside Free Clinic. The first six months, Irene's on work-release which means she has to sleep in the jail every night. The rest of her sentence, she'll be on probation."

Click raised his glass. "To my daughter, the defender of the downtrodden and the guilty."

"Here, here," Moore said, touching his glass to Garrison's and the others around the table.

"Here, here," Samuel said, giggling.

After all tipped a little water, Garrison looked from one man to the next, her eyes glistening in the reflected lights of the restaurant. "So what did my gentlemen do today?"

Click caught Moore's attention. "You first."

"No, you."

"Well," Click said, "we met Big Gene Prohaska. Owns just about everything in Gambier. 'Course, that's not saying a lot. The town's only three blocks long."

Stewardess Annie and Stewardess Lynn came to the table with a tray of shrimp cocktails on ice. They put a bowl of shrimp and a small cup of red sauce in front of each guest. Click took a peeled shrimp by its tail. He dipped it in the sauce and pointed the shrimp at Moore.

"Ah, yes, I went to the bank."

Garrison raised an eyebrow. "Why?"

Moore munched on a chilled shrimp. "A hunch."

"And?"

"It appears that Teddy, on his annual flight to Gambier, carried a sizable check that belonged to Ballard County. At the least, the check showed up on the same day Teddy did, a check endorsed to Mister Prohaska that Mister Prohaska then cashed."

"Sizable? How sizable?"

He took out his pad. "I've got the numbers, but it's sufficient to say the checks ranged from one hundred sixty to two hundred ten thousand dollars."

Garrison stopped eating.

"The head teller guessed the checks were for trucks the county was buying," Moore said, "but if they were, why would they be federal checks? And why would Prohaska be cashing them and not depositing them?"

Garrison glanced at her father.

He gave a one-shoulder shrug.

"Anything else?" she asked.

When neither Moore nor Click replied, Oliver put an arm around his partner's shoulders. "Your dad's going to buy an airplane."

"Another?" Garrison asked.

"If I can come up with the money," Click said. "Big Ed's got a Beech Staggerwing, like one I flew in Europe."

"Except this one's in pretty sad shape." Oliver shuffled his silverware.

"We could rebuild it."

"Who's this 'we,' Kimosabe?"

"All right, you," Click said, gesturing to Oliver, "but I'll help."

****

Keeping Irene McCoskey out of prison brought a windfall of legal business Garrison's way—hoochmakers busted by the sheriff, impatient hunters caught by the game warden shining deer, people with speeding tickets. Her title search for Frank Tubbs and her work on his land-purchase contract brought people buying houses, farms, small businesses, and lots for vacation homes in the foothills because Tubbs talked to everybody. That work paid the bills, but most of Garrison's new clients, in trouble with the law, had no money.

The Wednesday morning she had three cases going before Judge Rayfield, Hammond MacTeer came into her office with a cup of coffee. He set it on her desk and slapped the back of Garrison's weary side chair. "You wouldn't mind if I got you some decent furniture, would you? What you got looks like something stole off the receiving dock at the Salvation Army."

She set the files she'd been reviewing into her briefcase. "I wouldn't mind, Judge, but I've got some money now."

He settled his bulk in the chair. "Yes, and you've been paying your rent for your office. Since I own the place, I ought to furnish it better than I have. You'll let me do it?"

Garrison put her hand on MacTeer's arm. "I've learned not to argue with you, you sweet old soul."

"How you coming with Teddy's estate?"

She rubbed at an itch in her eyebrow. "I've turned up property Teddy owns in Ohio and Kentucky. Would you believe he's part-owner in a thoroughbred horse farm? I have to get those properties appraised."

"Seems to be getting bigger and bigger the more you dig, isn't it?"

"Seems to be."

"The upside," MacTeer said, "is your fee's gonna get bigger. And Doc Taylor?"

Garrison reached for the coffee cup. "Thank you for this. I need the caffeine for court."

"Ahh, Judge Rayfield."

"Three cases today."

MacTeer smiled. "That's the price of success. But Doc Taylor?"

"Judge, I'm sorry. I haven't had time to think about it."

"Just as well. Sometimes it's best to leave the dead undisturbed."

CHAPTER 18

Of fishes and gold pieces

Haggling long distance, Click knocked Gene Prohaska down from five thousand dollars to two thousand five hundred for the old airplane. Oliver estimated renovating the fuselage and overhauling the engine would cost forty thousand dollars, half of that labor that he and Click would supply. If Click were to put in new radios and navigation equipment, bump the price up another ten to fifteen thousand, he said.

"You still screwball enough to want to do this?" Oliver asked as Click banked Vol-Air's Skymaster over the Gambier airport. "We can still turn around and go home."

Click answered by dropping the Skymaster's landing gear. The gear doors popped open, and the aircraft slowed as the wheels came down into the slipsteam. Garrison, in the seat behind the copilot–the copilot this time being Oliver–gazed out the window at Gambier passing beneath the wing.

Click pressed his transmitter button. "Gambier traffic, this is Skymaster Six-Seven-Three Charlie Victor downwind for your north runway."

"Gotcha, Skymaster Three Charlie Victor," came a voice over the Gambier airport frequency. "Wind is out of the north, gusting to twenty miles an hour. That you, Mister Click?"

"It is. That you, Mister Prohaska?"

"Yessir. I got the heater on in the hangar. You'll be

needin' it today."

"Appreciate that. Turning base now." Click ran out ten degrees of landing flaps and pushed the engine fuel mixture controls to full rich. He guided the pusher-puller twin into a turn that lined it up with the runway, wind gusts rocking the airplane. Click fought to hold heading as the Skymaster continued on down. He crossed the fence twenty feet high and held power until the wheels touched the grass, now brown stubble of early winter.

The radio crackled. "Park it in front of the trailer. I'll help ya get tied down so you don't blow away."

"Roger that." Click herded the Skymaster off the runway and did a power turn in front of the humpback trailer, squaring the airplane over a tie-down space. Before he could shut down the engines, a big man bundled in a hooded parka appeared at his left wing, running a rope through the wing's tie-down ring. The man cinched the rope tight. Oliver bailed out the copilot's door to do the same with the right wing.

"Bundled up, Boots?" Click hollered back to Garrison as he snapped off a bank of switches.

"Yes." She came forward and slid across the copilot's seat to the door. Oliver helped her down. Long-distance travel stiffened Garrison, particularly her left leg crippled by polio when she was a child. Her leg had come back enough that she could run track in high school, but never enough that it equaled her other leg. On Garrison's worst days, she had to wear both a back brace and a leg brace. This was one of those days. She moved with a limp around the nose of the airplane to introduce herself to Gene Prohaska.

"Well, Missy," Prohaska said, "let's get you in the hangar where it's not so damn cold."

"I'm certainly for that, Mister Prohaska." Garrison shoved her gloved hands in her coat pockets.

He opened a small door in one of the larger sliding doors. Prohaska ushered Garrison inside, into a warmth that was almost toasty, the hangar lit with large auxiliary lights.

Before them stood the Staggerwing. Prohaska pulled off the canvases and tossed them over his beater. "Some airplane, isn't it?"

"Pop tried to tell me, but I never pictured how sleek it was."

"In its day, which was back in the 'Thirties when I was a kid, sisters of this one with big engines up front–you know, six hundred horses–they won national air races." He stroked the aircraft's propeller. "I'd like to get it flying, but to be honest, I'd probably never get around to it."

"Why not?"

"Oh, just got too many irons in the fire, what with my truck business and real estate dealings."

"That's right," Garrison said. "You sold Teddy Wilson some land up here. I'm handling the estate. You wouldn't happen to be interested in buying it back?"

"Might be if the price is right."

The door swung open. In came Oliver toting two oversized toolboxes and Click with a crate of fabric, dope, and brushes for repairing the holes in the Staggerwing's skin. Click dropped the crate. He slammed the door shut, then stripped his gloves off. "Hey, it's nice in here."

"When's the last time this bird flew, Mister Prohaska?" Oliver asked as he began removing the cowling from the radial engine.

"Probably five years ago."

Oliver sighed. "Will, we could have a problem with dry seals."

"Only way we'll find out is to start her up."

"Yeah, but I want to change out the oil, spark plugs, the battery first, go over all the wiring before we try that. And we gotta look at the fuel lines and oil lines."

"Well, while you do that, I'll patch the holes in the fabric. AJ, want to help?"

She slipped her arm through Gene Prohaska's arm. "Maybe later. Mister Prohaska and I are going to talk a little real estate."

"Shall we retire to the airport office?" Prohaska asked.

"Let's."

"Oh," he said, turning back to Click, "I drained the wing tanks of the stale gas and filled 'em both with new gas for you. My gift."

"Hey, thank you."

After Prohaska and Garrison departed for the trailer next door, Click and Oliver got down to the serious work.

"Would ya kick that bucket over here?" Oliver asked as he fitted a socket wrench over the drain plug in the oil reservoir.

Click glanced up from the crate where he was sorting through brushes. "Whuzzat?"

"The bucket over in the corner."

Click twisted around. When he spotted a dented pail laying on its side among a clutter of junk, he went to it. He inspected the bucket, shook out the leaves, and carried the bucket to Oliver. Click eyed where the oil would stream down and set the metal catcher on the gravel at a spot he estimated to be correct.

The plug came out at that moment. It slipped from Oliver's fingers. Oliver bobbled the plug and it got away, clinked against the side of the pail and down onto the bottom where sludgy oil spread over it.

Click smirked as his partner went fishing. "Butterfingers."

"Yeah, like you've never dropped anything." Oliver came up with the plug. He wiped it clean on a shop rag. "You gonna get on the patching or you gonna supervise?"

"Get on the patching," Click said. He strolled back to his crate of fabric and dope, the fabric nothing more than bed sheeting. There he tore off some patches, then opened a can of dope–a glue-like substance. Click slathered it around a hole the size of a fist in the side of the aircraft and slapped a patch over the hole.

Oliver popped a larger socket onto the end of his socket wrench. He went at ratcheting out the engine's spark plugs.

Click, humming now, patched over a tear in the skin of

the tail.

****

"Coffee?" Prohaska asked after he closed the door on the airport's office trailer.

"Be fine," Garrison said. She slipped out of her heavy coat, all the while gazing around for someplace to put it.

Prohaska saw her. He wiggled his fingers, and Garrison gave him her coat. He laid it across his desk and chucked his own parka in a heap in a corner. Prohaska went over to a metal pot on a hot plate. "It's yesterday's coffee. Powerful stuff, curl your toes."

"Mister Prohaska, I've had to drink my dad's coffee. I think I can handle it."

He waved at a shabby couch swayed from too many fat bottoms having parked on it during the couch's lifetime. "Just throw off some of them newspapers and flying magazines. Make yourself a spot, unless you'd rather have my chair."

Garrison eyed the captain's chair at the desk, the chair missing an arm, and went for the couch. After she pushed enough of the litter aside, she sat down–way down–and came to rest with her chin level with her knees.

"You know, I really oughtta get better furniture in here," Prohaska said when he handed down a mug of steaming brew the color and consistency of dirty crank case oil, "but these old boys that fly out of Gambier International just beat hell out of it. You'd think they'd been raised in the woods by bears."

Garrison wrapped her hands around the china mug, to warm them while she waited for the coffee to cool sufficiently that she could attempt drinking it. She glanced up. "So how did you and Teddy meet?"

"Oh gawd, let's see now." Prohaska shambled over to the opposite wall. He parked his bulk there and leaned back, covering a tool company calendar that featured young women in various degrees of undress. "What was it? I flew down to Knoxville, going after some truck business, yeah. I needed a little gas for the Cessna Three-Ten I was flying at the time, and Teddy was there, gassing up his big Twin Commander. We got to talking."

"But how did trucks and gas lead to a lot on the lake?"

Prohaska stirred his coffee with his finger. He sucked the liquid off, smacking his lips. "Ain't half bad. Oh, it's that male stuff. 'What do you do?' and 'What do you do?' And I mentioned I was developing some property on a lake up here, and he asked what the fishing was like. I was just about to brag on it, and the little lightbub turns on in the old brain of mine, so I says, 'Why don't you fly on up and try your luck?'"

"He catch anything?"

Prohaska's belly shook beneath his Ohio State sweater as he laughed. "I made sure he would. I called up our state department of fish and game and had them sow that lake with the biggest damn bass and lake trout you ever saw. Teddy caught so many, it was nothing to sell him a lot."

****

Click tested one of his patch jobs with the tip of his finger. The patch neither slipped nor gave. He dipped his brush in the dope bucket and went over the patch with one more coat of the liquid that, when dry, would make the patch air and water-tight. One swipe of the brush, and Click went on to the next patch.

"Could use a hand here," Oliver called out.

Click set his brush aside. He pushed around the wing and forward to peer up at his partner standing on box, the mechanic's hands up in a mass of black spaghetti.

Oliver gritted his teeth, straining as he worked. "Jeez, insulation on some of these wires are cracked."

"Want to replace 'em?"

"Got to. Go over to my toolbox. I got a set of plug wires in there I traded Cherokee Aviation for."

Click went to the toolcase–a Sears Craftsman. He pulled open drawer after drawer until he found the one that contained an AC Delco box. Click held it up. "This it?"

Oliver glanced over his shoulder. "Yup."

"What did you trade?"

"Two hours of instruction time for one of their pilots in our Skymaster."

****

Prohaska slurped at his coffee. "Well, you know 'bout me an' Teddy. Tell me 'bout you an' Teddy."

Garrison tried her coffee for the first time. She winced.

"You want I should cut it with some water or maybe some peppermint schnapps?" Prohaska asked.

She swallowed, struggling for breath. "Bit strong."

Prohaska went to the sink next to a fish tank at the back of the trailer. He twisted the hot water faucet on and relieved Garrison of her coffee mug. Prohaska dumped half its contents in the sink, then ran in some hot water. He stirred the thinner concoction with a pencil as he carried the mug back. "This oughta tame it."

Garrison took the mug. Next Prohaska produced a silver flask from his back pocket. "I do have schnapps here."

"Thank you, but no."

"Uh-huh " He screwed the top off, helped himself to a swallow, capped the flask, and slipped it back in his pocket. "You were about to tell me about you and Teddy."

After Garrison forced down a sip of the thinner coffee, she said, "He was ahead of me in high school, so we hardly knew each other, but I knew Anne Bradley, the young woman Teddy eventually married."

"I see. So that's why she came to you when Teddy died."

"That and Judge MacTeer."

Prohaska settled back against the wall calendar again. "Old Ham? What's he got to do with this?"

"The judge is the Wilsons' family lawyer, and he handles all the bank's legal business. Apparently, he thought there might be a conflict if he also handled the estate."

"Oh."

"So now I have to sell Teddy's lake property."

Prohaska took an excessive interest in his coffee mug. After some moments, he glanced up from beneath his bushy eyebrows. Only his left eye looked at Garrison. "And you want me to buy it."

She didn't answer.

"How much you asking?"

"What did Teddy pay for the property?"

"Hey, you know that. You've gone through his records. A thousand bucks. I'll give you five hundred."

Garrison shook her head.

"Well, I'm sure not going to give you a thousand and wipe out my profit."

"A thousand five hundred."

Prohaska squinted at Garrison. "You sure you didn't splash some bourbon of your own in that coffee when I wasn't looking?"

Again, Garrison did not answer.

"All right, a thousand, and that's only because you work with Ham."

"Fifteen hundred."

Prohaska rubbed his thumb against the tip of his nose. Then he brightened. "Miss Garrison, you a gambler?"

"Not really."

"I'll give you two thousand for that property on a bet."

"And what would that be?"

Prohaska came away from the wall. He held his hand out to Garrison and helped her pull herself up out of the depths of the old couch. He walked her back to the fish tank. "See that twenty-dollar gold piece down in the bottom?"

Garrison peered over the edge.

"You pick that gold piece out of there with your hand, and I'll give you two thousand dollars. You don't, you accept my check for five hundred."

Garrison looked up into Prohaska's beefy face, at the one good eye that gazed back and the glass eye that appeared to be studying something beyond her left shoulder. "What's the catch?"

"No catch."

She inhaled and reached her hand over. The moment Garrison's fingers touched the surface of the water, two panfish that had been idling in a corner of the tank broke for the surface, their jaws snapping.

She jerked her hand back as the water whooshed up and out of the tank, onto her pantsuit.

"Oh yeah," Prohaska said, snickering, "they're piranha. I'll write my check for five hundred."

Garrison turned her fingertips up. After she assured herself they were still there, she gazed at the fish tank, at the surface of the water that still roiled, at the two brownish fish that had gone back down to their corner. Garrison leaned to one side for a better view of the gold piece, her eyes measuring the distance between the gold piece and the fish. "If I get the coin out–"

"You want to try again?"

"Maybe. I just have to reach in, right?"

"That's right, Missy. You just have to reach in there. You fish that coin out, I'll give you two thousand dollars."

Garrison, with care, rolled the right sleeve of her jacket above her elbow, then the sleeve of her blouse. But just before she reached into the tank, she picked up a Pilot magazine and pushed that down into the water, shielding the coin from the fish.

The fish charged the magazine. They tore at it as Garrison plunged her bare hand and arm into the water on the coin side. She focused on the coin, grasped it from where it laid on the sand and brought it up, up and out, water streaming down her elbow and onto the trailer's ratty brown carpet. "Two thousand dollars, Mister Prohaska."

"You cheated."

"All you said was I had to put my hand in the water and get the coin."

"Gawddamn lawyer."

Prohaska's scowl morphed into a smile, then he rocked back. Laughter peeled out of him, pulsating the walls of the tiny trailer. "Nobody's ever beat me on that one before."

****

When Prohaska and Garrison returned to the hangar, both again bundled for the cold, they found Click and Oliver sitting in the gravel, changing out the landing gear's old wheels and rotted tires for new wheels and tires they had brought in on the Skymaster.

"You check the brake shoes on your side?" Oliver called out.

Click spun his wheel. "They're fine."

Prohaska leaned his bulk down. "You boys about done?"

"Just got to get the bird off these jacks and the cowling on," Click said. After he tightened the last lug nut on his side, he tossed the socket wrench to Oliver.

Click next went at letting the jack down on his side of the Staggerwing until the new wheel and tire sat firmly on the gravel. He wrenched the jack out and threw it forward. The jack kicked up stones when it hit in front of Prohaska.

The big man stooped down and set the jack aside.

Almost as quickly, a second jack came flying out, Click and Oliver scrambling after it. This jack Prohaska also set to the side while the two mechanics hoisted the cowling over the engine and twisted the locking screws into place.

Prohaska walked around, studying the repair work. "The old bird looks like she's got a bad case of the white measles, don't she?" he said of Click's patching.

Click pulled a shop rag from the back pocket of his coveralls and rubbed his hands clean. "Yup. We'll strip her down to the bones when we get her home, put on all new fabric. Don't know what color to paint her, though. Can't say I think much of the gray-green she is now."

"Damn dowdy. It's an old woman's color." Prohaska guffawed at his joke. "Say, did you know your daughter drives a mean bargain?"

"How's that?" Click asked as Oliver carried his toolboxes back to the Skymaster.

"I offered half what Teddy paid for that land on the lake. She shamed me into full price an' then some, even made me double the original price on a bet to her, but I'll get it back."

"Oh?"

"Yessir, there's a Goodyear executive over in Columbus been badgering me for some land for a weekend retreat. I'll get all my money back and then some or I'm not Big Gene Prohaska."

Oliver came back for the jacks and wheels.

Click took a check from his breast pocket and handed it to Prohaska. "For the Staggerwing."

The seller glanced at the check. After he tucked it in his wallet, he brought out an envelope. "Receipt's in here and all the papers you need. Logbooks are in the bird. You ready to go?"

"Think so." Click opened the envelope. He glanced through the papers. "Seems all in order."

"Well, let me kill the heater and the lights, and we'll get the doors open."

Oliver came back again. Click handed him the crate of patching materials. While Oliver took that to the Skymaster, Click rolled the first door open on the hangar.

Prohaska got the other. He then strolled back and slapped Click's shoulders. "You boys grab the wing tips and I'll pick up the tail."

The truck-and-land hustler worked his way around the end of the right wing and back to just forward of the tail where a handle was fixed to the side of the fuselage. When Prohaska saw Click ready at the right wing tip, he hollered, "Your buddy ready on the other side?"

"Yeah," Oliver called back.

"Let's do it."

Prohaska, a man with the strength of two, grasped the handle. He lifted, and the Staggerwing's tailwheel came up off the ground. With Prohaska pulling forward and Click and Oliver push-pulling on the ends of the wings, they trundled the airplane out of the hangar.

"Heyup!" Prohaska called out and let the tailwheel down. He trotted back into the hangar where, from a corner, he pitched wheel chocks out to either side of the airplane. With these, Click and Oliver blocked the wheels.

While Prohaska rolled the hangar doors closed, Click went around to the left side of the Staggerwing and got inside. He closed the cabin door and worked forward to the pilot's seat. He'd flown hundreds of hours in a Staggerwing like this, so he found all gauges and switches were where they should be. Click opened the window at his elbow. "Clear?" he called out.

Oliver and Garrison stood near the end of the left wing. Prohaska joined them, watching, his glass eye having wandered in its socket so it looked like it was conducting an appraisal of the clouds.

"Clear!" Oliver called back.

Click turned on the electrical switches. He listened to the gyroscopes that drove the artificial horizon and the compass spin up. He cracked the throttle, pushed the fuel-air mixture to full rich, and pumped the primer. Click pursed his lips as he mashed a thumb on the ignition button. The starter burred, turning the heavy engine–four hundred fifty horsepower, more horses than the two engines that powered the Skymaster through the air–but the starter ground away so slowly that the cylinders failed to fire.

Click took his thumb off the button. He called out the window, "Todd, get the booster."

Oliver slapped Prohaska's shoulder and waved for him to follow him to the Skymaster. There the two men lifted out a box that contained three batteries wired in series. They carried this around in front of the Staggerwing's left landing gear and set the battery box on the sod. Oliver pulled a cable from the box. He plugged the cable into a connection beneath the Staggerwing's firewall. Done, he scurried away, rotating his hand above his head as a signal for his partner to try starting the engine again.

Click pressed the starter button. He held it in as the starter, with power from the booster batteries, spun the engine ever faster. A cylinder fired, then a second and a third. Exhaust belched from the stacks beneath the engine. The four hundred fifty horses stuttered and stumbled, then came up into an even, satisfying rumble.

Oliver ducked under the cowling. He yanked the jumper cable from its socket, and he and Prohaska toted the battery box back to the Skymaster.

"Looks good," Click bellowed after he reviewed the needles on the gauges in the instrument panel. The electrical gauge showed the generator charging, and the needles on the temperature and oil pressure gauges rose.

"Ready?" Oliver hollered.

"Yeah!" Click looked out his window. "AJ? Want to ride with me?"

She threw him an okay sign.

"Bring two headsets from the Mixmaster, wouldja?"

Garrison and Oliver trotted to the Skymaster. He climbed on board where he rescued two headsets and handed them out to Garrison. While she hurried away, Oliver latched the door and settled into the pilot's seat.

Prohaska had the Staggerwing's door open when Garrison got back. He helped her up and inside. "Have a good flight."

"What?!" she asked, turning back, straining to hear over the blatting engine.

Prohaska cupped a hand beside his mouth. "Have a good flight!"

"Thank you!"

With that, he slammed the cabin door shut. Prohaska hunkered under the left wing for the wheel chocks. He pulled them away and went to the right wing for those.

Oliver started his engines. He turned his radios on. "Three Charlie Victor on Gambier Unicom. Will, you with me?" Oliver said into his microphone. Static crackled in his headset.

"Staggerwing November Charlie One-Niner-Niner-Six-Seven, roger that."

"You want to take off first? I'll watch from here, make sure your gear goes up."

"That's a plan." Click goosed the big radial of the Staggerwing, and the airplane lumbered forward. When he got it on the runway, he kicked hard on the right rudder. That brought the airplane around so it ambled toward the south end.

"I can't see anything," Garrison said from the copilot's seat. "How do you know where you're going?"

"Easy." Click stepped on the left rudder pedal. The Staggerwing responded, turning slightly across the runway, giving the pilot and copilot a quick look down the runway. Click then stepped on the right pedal. That brought the Staggerwing into a right turn, giving those inside a look ahead out the left windows. Left, then right, left, then right. The biplane wandered down the runway like a drunk, yet each turn gave Click and Garrison a quick look forward.

At the end of the runway, Click brought the Staggerwing into the wind. He stood on the toe brakes, stopping the airplane. There he ran through a check of his switches, gauges, and controls, and did an engine run-up and magneto check. When done, Click pressed his transmitter button. "Gambier traffic, Staggerwing November Charlie One-Niner-Niner-Six-Seven on the active, taking off to the north, departing south."

No response.

"Todd?"

"Go."

Click put the palm of his hand against the throttle and pushed the throttle knob to the firewall. The engine came up into a thunderous roar and hauled the airplane down the runway. Click pressed forward on the control wheel. Up came the tailwheel.

He watched the airspeed indicator rise. At sixty-five miles an hour, he tugged back on the control wheel, and the Staggerwing climbed into the sky. Click pulled the gear lever up, but with the engine blatting so loud, he couldn't hear the hydraulics.

"Gear going up," came Oliver's voice.

One green light flashed on the control column, then a

second and a third. "Three greens. Gear up and locked. Climbing to three thousand feet. Todd, I'll orbit north of town 'til you catch up."

"Roger. Taxiing to the runup area."

Click came back on the radial engine's power. He rolled in some trim, lowering the nose into a shallower climb. "Like it?" he asked Garrison.

"Comfortable."

"This was the deluxe executive aircraft of its time."

"Kind of noisy, isn't it?"

"Yeah. We'll have to pack a lot of soundproofing in the cabin or dispense earplugs to our passengers." Click glanced at his daughter. "Your pants wet?"

"It's a fish story."

"Gambier traffic, Skymaster Six-Seven-Three Charlie Victor on the active, taking off north, departing south."

"Fish story, huh? Keep it for a bit because here comes Todd." Click rolled the Staggerwing into a turn to the left and pressed his transmitter button. "Todd, I'll file flight plans for both of us, then join you on one-twenty-two-point-five."

"Roger."

Click dialed in the Columbus Flight Service frequency. After a briefing on weather between Columbus and Knoxville, he filed his and Oliver's flight plans while Oliver climbed out from the Gambier airport.

Garrison nudged her father. When he turned to her, she pointed at her window, at the Skymaster off the wing.

Click nodded. He dialed in one-twenty-two-point-five. "Todd, you there?"

"Roger."

"We're filed VFR. We should pick up sunshine in mid Kentucky."

"Let's head for home then. I'll stay off your right wing and high so I can keep an eye on you."

Click rolled the Staggerwing out on a south/southwest heading for the Appleton VOR and the aviation route that would take the two airplanes over Portsmouth, Ohio. There

Click intended to pick up the Newcombe VOR and the airway to Hazard, Kentucky, and Knoxville beyond.

"How's the bird running?" Oliver came on.

"Everything's normal."

"Keep her throttled back. Best I can do is a hundred seventy-five."

"Yup. If I were to open her up, I'd be home before you got to Hazard."

"Worse, if you got into trouble, I wouldn't see you crash."

"Cheery."

Click settled into the routine of flying. After some minutes, he leaned toward Garrison until their shoulders touched. "So how did you get Big Gene to go up on Teddy's land?"

A grin came across her face. "I beat him at his own game."

"How's that?"

"I said I wanted fifteen hundred dollars for the land Teddy paid a thousand for."

"And?"

"And Mister Prohaska offered five hundred. But then he said he'd pay me two thousand dollars for the land if I could pick a coin out of his piranha tank."

Click raised his eyebrows. "He's got piranha in that office of his?"

She laughed and took something from her side pocket. Garrison held it up–a twenty-dollar gold piece.

CHAPTER 19

Foul dead fowl

Oliver, in the Skymaster, dropped back and low as the two airplanes came up on the Ohio River.

"Will."

Click pressed his transmitter button. "What is it, partner?"

"Check your oil pressure gauge."

Click studied the face of the gauge, the engine thrumming away. The needle stood pegged solidly on forty pounds per square inch. "It's right where it should be."

"Hmm."

"'Hmm' what?"

"A little oil streaking back under the Staggerwing's belly. You got a leaky seal somewhere, maybe a line."

"Todd, these old radials are famous for slinging oil."

"I know."

"You want us to land and check it?"

"No, let's keep going. Keep an eye on the pressure gauge, though. I'm going to come up on your left, then over top and back down to the right, give you a good inspection."

"Roger."

Click watched the Skymaster slide out of sight beneath his airplane. Moments later, the pusher-puller came out to the left side, climbing.

"Nothing too odd," came Oliver's voice. "Going over the top."

Click tapped the back of Garrison's hand. "Wanna fly

for a while?"

She stared at him, unbelieving of what he had said. "Not on your life. This is a weird airplane."

"Why, because it's got an extra set of wings?"

"No, because it's only got one control wheel."

Click patted the yoke in front of him. "A Beechcraft oddity. Boots, the control wheel is a throw-over. I can swing it over to your side, and you can fly."

"No thanks."

She went silent. Garrison drew within herself, wondering about the man she had met at Gambier, the man whose right eye never looked at her. She wondered, not so much why she had been able to sell Teddy's land back to him, but why he had gambled on the price? What kind of a man was he?

Click broke through the silence. "Coming up on Hazard."

Garrison glanced out her window at the rough hills of Kentucky coal country below. She saw the scars, scars she knew were open-pit mines.

Todd Oliver's voice came over her headset. "I'm going to do another fly-around inspection."

She glanced up to see the Skymaster again sliding down. It went out of sight beneath the Staggerwing.

"Will."

Click pressed his transmitter button. "Go ahead."

"Oil still streaming under the belly."

"Bad?"

"Still appears to be a slow leak."

"Roger."

The Skymaster slid out to the left and climbed back up to the Staggerwing's altitude. Click gazed out at his partner scanning the biplane as the Skymaster went on higher.

"Uh-oh."

Click pressed his transmitter button. "What's 'uh-oh' mean?"

"Fabric loose on top of your left elevator. It's rippling."

"Tears? Holes?"

"No."

"Seems we got a choice, Todd-a-o, land around here and let someone else do the heavy repairs or cross our fingers and hope nothing more serious happens between here and home."

"Your airplane. You're the pilot," Oliver came back. "You decide."

"Forecast is for strong winds out of the north above ten thousand feet. It'll get us to Knoxville faster. I'm for going up."

"Oooo-kay. Go up easy. Don't overpower the engine and bust something."

Click eased the throttle forward, increasing the turning rate of Staggerwing's radial by two hundred rpms. He tugged back on the control wheel and up came the nose into a leisurely climb.

A quarter-hour later, as the two aircraft crossed high above the Cumberland Gap, Click swore.

"What is it?" Garrison asked.

"Look ahead."

She hoisted herself up in her seat and peered over the engine pulling the Staggerwing toward Knoxville.

"See it?" Click asked.

"That's not good."

"We got a solid deck of clouds below, from Norris Lake south to the horizon."

"Pop, what are you going to do, find someplace to land that's clear or go down through it on instruments?"

Click drummed his fingers on the control wheel. He glanced out his side window. Oliver's voice came through his headset. "Will?"

"Yeah?"

"See the cloud deck?"

As Click swivelled toward the Skymaster, oil sheeted up over his windshield. "Shit."

"What is it?"

"Oil everywhere. I'm blind."

"Oil pressure?"

Click glanced down at the gauge, its needle on zero. "Zip, zero, nothing."

"Shut your engine down now."

"Right, dead stick it." Click yanked the throttle back. He feathered the propeller and turned the ignition switch to 'Off.' The big engine shook and shuddered on its mounts, then went silent, the only sound in the cabin that of the outside air slipping by.

Click's fingers danced on the trim wheel as he rolled the wheel back, bringing his airplane into the angle that would get him the most forward distance for each foot of altitude he was going to lose, and, with a dead engine, he knew he was going to lose them all. Click forced his eyes to scan his flight instruments, to feed his brain information on heading, rate of descent, and wing attitude.

Garrison gripped the arm rests hard, so hard her knuckles went white. She edged forward in her seat, studying her father, but Garrison could detect no panic. Could this have happened to him before? "What do you want me to do, Pop?"

"Turn the radio to Knoxville VOR. When we cross it, change our heading to two-three-zero degrees outbound."

Garrison did as she was instructed, and Oliver's voice came over the new frequency. "Nashville Center, Skymaster Six-Seven-Three Charlie Victor declaring an emergency."

A new voice came on, that of someone who could sing tenor in the church choir. "This is Nashville Center. Skymaster Three Charlie Victor, what is your emergency?"

"Three Charlie Victor flying with Staggerwing November Charlie One-Niner-Niner-Six-Seven. The Staggerwing blew its engine. We're over Norris Lake on Victor One-Fifteen for TYS, out of ten thousand and descending."

"Roger, Three Charlie Victor. All aircraft, all aircraft, stay off this frequency. We have an emergency. Say again, we have an emergency. Charlie Victor, what do you want to do?"

"Go on instruments through the clouds below to

Knoxville VOR, then straight in to McGhee Tyson."

"Would you rather divert to Morristown? That airport's in the clear."

"Negative, negative. The Staggerwing's got one chance to land. We want the big airport."

"Can the Staggerwing communicate?"

Click pressed his transmitter button. "This is the Staggerwing."

"Roger, Staggerwing, got your emergency. Maintain this frequency. We're clearing all traffic ahead of you."

"How thick are the clouds?"

"Latest pilot report says you'll penetrate at three thousand feet, break out at two. Visibility below is ten miles, winds light out of the west, altimeter at TYS is two-niner-niner-six. What's your altitude?"

"Out of seven thousand."

"Roger. All traffic for Knoxville has been diverted. You're cleared for a straight-in to Runway Two-Three after crossing the VOR. Knoxville is rolling the fire trucks and an ambulance. Remain this frequency until you're out of the clouds and have the airport in sight."

"Thank you, Center."

"Will," Oliver's voice came over the headset.

"Yeah."

"Your prop's vertical. Rock the starter, get it horizontal. Vertical, you belly in, the prop will bust and flip you."

"Ooo, that's no fun."

"No fun a-tall."

Click popped the starter button, then popped it again until the starter jogged the propeller to horizontal. He leaned all the way to the left wall, checking it.

"Good job. Will, you don't have hydraulics, so you'll have to pump the gear down."

"Oh yeah."

"How long's it take?"

"About a minute."

"Wait as long as you can. Gear down is going to cost you a lot of altitude."

"Right. Todd, I'm blind ahead. In the clouds, I'm gonna be blind all around."

"I'm coming over top now. I'll settle off your left wing with my nav lights on. You follow me down. Woops."

"'Woops' what?" Click glanced out his side window at the Skymaster sliding down into position, the clouds rushing up.

"You've got a rip in the fabric from the cabin to the tail."

"How's my elevator?"

"Still rippling."

Garrison touched her father's arm. "Pop, go into Island Airport. It's closer."

"Can't. One mistake and I either crash into the houses or dump it in the river."

"Oh."

Click pressed his transmitter button. "I'm in the clouds, Todd. I can see your nav light."

He bumped Garrison's elbow and shook his hand at the crank on the floor between them. "That winds the gear down. When I tell you, you turn that crank for everything your worth."

Garrison twisted in her seat, glad she didn't have a control wheel in front of her. She grasped the crank handle with both hands.

"Nashville Center." It was Oliver's voice. "We're over the VOR, coming out of the clouds."

"Roger, Skymaster and Staggerwing. Contact Knoxville tower now. Good luck."

Click's Staggerwing shuddered like a truck bouncing across railroad tracks. "What the hell?"

"What is it, Pop?"

"Trouble?" came Oliver's voice.

"Gawd-awful shaking. It's stopped now."

"Going to tower frequency."

"Same here." Click glanced out at the city's skyline to his right as he twisted one-twenty-one-point-two into his communications radio. "AJ, now!"

She set her jaw and spun the gear-lowering crank.

"Knoxville Tower, Skymaster and Staggerwing here."

A familiar voice entered Click's and Garrison's headsets, that of one of Knoxville's best tower controllers. "Ah, roger. Got the glasses on you. You're three miles out and on the glide path."

"Staggerwing's gear down?"

"Yup."

"Locked?"

"Can't tell."

Garrison, tiring, strained at the crank. "Pop?"

"I've got a green light on the mains," Click said into his microphone. "Yes, a green light on the tail wheel. Gear down and locked."

"Staggerwing, you're low."

"Will! Trees! Pull up!"

Click yanked back on the control wheel.

Garrison braced for a crash.

The Staggerwing hopped up fifty feet, but lost airspeed, the stall-warning horn squalling.

Click slammed the airplane's nose down, and the Staggerwing dove toward the runway, regaining its flying speed. He glanced out the side window at the fast approaching ground. Sweating now, Click again hauled back on the control wheel.

Something exploded beneath the biplane as it crossed the end of the runway. Eyes wide, Garrison stared at her father, and she saw fear.

The Staggerwing's wheels slammed down on the pavement, and the airplane veered right.

Click tromped on the left rudder pedal. He whipped the control wheel to the left–held both controls there–pumped the toe brakes, slowing the Staggerwing, a flopping and bumping shaking the airplane, shaking that slowed as the Staggerwing slowed, that stopped when the Staggerwing stopped.

"What the hell?" Click said. His hand trembled as he groped for his seatbelt's latch.

"You all right, Pop?"

"I gotta pee."

He wrestled himself free of his seatbelt and his seat, and stumbled back into the cabin to the door. Click wrenched it open. He ran for the grass, tearing at the fly of his pants, stopping to relieve himself as a fire trunk rolled up, its wailing siren gyrating down. "You all right?" the driver called out.

Click zipped up his pants. "I am now."

"Hell of a landing. You know you busted a tire on one of the approach lights back there at the end of the runway?"

Click swung around. He stared back where he and his aircraft had come from and saw that a reflector had been knocked off one of the four lights beyond the runway, that the pipe that had held the light up had been snapped forward. Click trotted off to the far side of the Staggerwing.

"Oh, shit."

Garrison climbed down from the cabin. She forced her legs to carry her back around the biplane's tail to the right side. "What is it, Pop?" she asked.

"Blew the hell out of the right main, and that's not the half of it."

When Garrison came up beside her father, she found him staring up at the upper wing. She followed his gaze. A sheet of fabric the size of a table cloth had peeled back and hung like old linen from the wing's trailing edge. "How'd that happen?"

"I don't know."

Oliver, in the Skymaster, had jogged away as the Staggerwing crossed the approach end of the runway. He pulled his airplane back up to pattern altitude, popped its landing gear, and banked around into a steep descending turn to land to the northeast. He now taxied up to the Staggerwing. Oliver killed his engines and stopped in front of the wounded bird. He bailed out, shouting for one of the firemen to bring him a ladder. The two leaned it against the Staggerwing's right wings, and Oliver scrambled up to a bashed-in area in the leading edge of the top wing. There he grubbed inside, among the exposed ribs, and brought out a fistful of feathers. He waved them at Click and Garrison. "Airplanes aren't meant for killin' fowl."

"Bird strike?" Click asked, disbelief in his voice.

"The shudder coming out of the clouds? You hit a goose. Darn lucky you hit him with your wing and not your windshield. If he'd come through the windshield, partner, you and AJ would be dead."

CHAPTER 20

Windstar

Click's friends split on whether to call him 'Goose Killer' for bringing down a twelve-pounder somewhere over Knoxville or 'Rag Man' for the sad shape of his new airplane.

Click thought 'Report Writer' fit him better after he and a Federal Aviation accident investigator waded through thirty pages of paperwork, recording and documenting the flying troubles that caused him to declare an inflight emergency, troubles that screwed up all of aviation within thirty miles of Knoxville's McGhee Tyson Airport for the better part of an hour and a half.

Everything had to be done right to keep the Rag Man away from a stack of fines and license suspensions. Had he and Oliver not documented their repair work to the Staggerwing before takeoff from Gambier, the FAA surely would have grounded Click, all an inauspicious beginning for December.

****

"Can you be there tomorrow?" Garrison asked, a telephone receiver pressed to her ear. She consulted a note in a file on her desk while she listened to the answer. "Good, ten o'clock then . . . Yes, your time. . . . My time in Morgantown? We're in the Eastern Time Zone, too."

Moore came in with a cup of hot water in one hand,

coffee in the other, and a box of Red Zinger tea tucked under an arm. He put the hot water and the tea box on the desk as Garrison returned the receiver to its cradle.

"Got it all worked out?" he asked.

"You sure your sergeant will give you the day off?"

Moore dug in his shirt pocket for the tea ball. He found it and handed it on. "Already done."

Garrison flashed a quirky smile as she unscrewed the two halves of the tea ball. She opened the box, filled half the ball, and screwed the other half back on. This she dropped into the hot water. "Sure you wouldn't rather have tea? This Red Zinger is the best thing to come into the Winn-Dixie."

"I'll stay with coffee."

"You'll be sorry."

"Why?"

"The judge made that. It'll corrode your stomach."

Moore took in a mouthful. His eyes popped as he swallowed. "Whooo. I may never sleep again."

"You want to switch?"

"Hoo-yah. Let me dump this." Moore shot out of Garrison's office and back to the kitchen. He returned moments later with the same cup, only this time filled with hot water. Garrison lifted the tea ball from her cup into Moore's.

"Did you know," she asked as she scratched a dozen words on the note she had been reading, "that there are only three really good appraisers of horse farms in the Lexington area? Three. One of Teddy's partners put me onto this one."

Moore slipped into the leather side chair. "You're trusting Teddy's partners?"

"Oh, no. I located the banker who finances the biggest of the horse farms up there. He confirmed Mister Greeley is the best."

"So what's the plan?" He worked the tea ball up and down in his cup before he set the ball aside.

"Pop's got a charter to Chicago in the morning. You and I can ride along if we can be at the airport by nine o'clock."

"Not a problem. And my job is?" Moore sipped at the tea, a smile lighting his face. "Not bad."

"That's a left-handed compliment."

"No, I mean it. For someone who doesn't like tea, this is not bad."

"Well, would you go over the farm's books and make sure the finances are everything the farm manager has represented?"

"Sure. And you?"

"I mentioned one of Teddy's partners."

Moore nodded and sipped again at his tea.

"He's going to be there tomorrow, too. He wants to buy Teddy's shares if he and I can find the right price."

"He make an offer?"

"A million dollars."

****

"A million dollars!" Click squalled into the microphone of his headset. He had fiddled with the switches on his radio panel, cutting three of his passengers out of the circuit so only he, Garrison in the co-pilot's seat, and Moore sitting behind were in on the conversation.

"Pop, from what I've been told," Garrison said, her elbow on the armrest, "Teddy put together a syndicate of eleven investors to buy what was then the Five Oaks Horse Farm. Each of the eleven put up a half-million dollars, and they gave Teddy a full share for assembling the thing and agreeing to be the managing partner."

Click shook his head as he gazed out the windshield of the Twin Commander, the airplane eating up the sky on its way north into the bluegrass country of Kentucky. "Why can't I fall into something like that?"

"I don't know. But look, the more I learn about all the things Teddy was into, the more I realize I never really knew him, and Anne knows nothing of this venture."

"Amazing." Click twiddled with the autopilot. That changed the heading two degrees to the west.

"Anyway, Mister Ellsted," Garrison went on, "he's the

partner who wants to buy Teddy's shares. Mister Ellsted told me one of the other partner's business got into trouble last year, that he needed money, so Teddy bought him out for cash. That's why Teddy has two shares instead of one and why Mister Ellsted is offering a million dollars instead of a half-million."

Click glanced at his daughter. "Good golly, Miss Molly, the estate taxes are going to be something horrendous."

"Probably. Even if the IRS gets half the proceeds from the horse farm, Anne will still have five hundred thousand she can put in the bank."

Click whistled. "That ought to make her the richest widow in Morgantown. Maybe she and I can get together."

Garrison swatted her father.

Click clutched at his shoulder. "Parent abuse. Parent abuse."

Garrison swatted him again.

"Hey," he said, "enough of that. You think this thing is legal?"

Moore broke in. "Will, a real estate agent would get six percent of the deal. If Teddy cut out the agent and did all that work himself, then took another three percent for a fee for managing the new business for his partners, that's not unreasonable."

"I still find it god-awful amazing."

"Hey, I've done some checking. Monied people go nuts when they get a chance to get in on the thoroughbred business. They'll throw money at it with no thought of tomorrow."

"And it's legal, you say?"

"It appears so," Moore said.

"Hot damn–" An indicator beeped on the Twin Commander's instrument panel. Click touched a button that cut out the warning. "We're twenty miles from Lexington, Boots. It's time I went to work."

He turned the autopilot off and rolled the trim tab forward. That put the airplane into a gentle descent to take it from fifty-five hundred feet to three thousand before the

Twin Commander crossed the Lexington navigation station. Click flipped a switch that cut in the overhead speaker in the passengers' cabin.

He hacked hard, clearing his throat, then spoke into his microphone much as an airline captain would. "For our Chicago passengers, we're coming up on Lexington, the capital of Kentucky horse country. You'll be able to see the city off our left wing as we get closer. We'll be landing at Bourbon County Airport northeast of Lexington in about fifteen minutes."

Click glanced out his window at the city skyline on the near horizon. "As quickly as we get our Kentucky passengers off, we're back in the air. I'll have you in Chicago in time for an early lunch."

He flipped two switches. The first cut out the overhead speaker. The second cut in a communications radio. "Lexington Flight Service, Twin Commander November Fourty-Four-Two-One Echo."

Static, then a new voice came over the headsets of Click, Garrison, and Moore. "Two-One Echo, Lexington Flight Service, go ahead."

"Two-One Echo is ten DME south of the Lexington VOR, canceling flight plan."

"Roger, I'll take care of that. Where are you landing?"

"Bourbon County."

"All right. You can expect the wind to be about the same as here at LEX–light and variable out of the south. Temperature fifty-two degrees, and the altimeter is three-zero-zero-one. Call me when you're off and I'll open the remainder of your flight plan to Chicago."

"Roger."

"And welcome to the Bluegrass State."

"Thank you." Click twisted the new setting into his altimeter as did Garrison on the altimeter on her side of the instrument panel. He flipped a switch that cut in his second communications radio. "Bourbon County, Bourbon County, this is Twin Commander November Four-Four-Two-One Echo over the Lexington VOR, inbound for your airstrip."

A woman's voice answered over the headsets. "This is Bourbon County, Four-Four-Two-One Echo. Do you have a Miss Garrison on board?"

"And a Mister Moore," Click answered. He banked the Aero Commander to the right, to a new heading of thirty-five degrees. Click kept the airplane in its descent, pushing on down to an altitude of eighteen hundred feet.

"There's transport waiting for your passengers. Four-Four-Two-One Echo, we have almost no wind this morning at Bourbon County. May I suggest you land to the west?"

"Roger, will do."

"The mint juleps are waiting."

"Darn, and I can't stay."

"We wish you could."

Garrison arched an eyebrow at her father.

"Just a little harmless flirting," Click said. He pointed over the nose of the aircraft. "Does that look like it to you?"

Garrison sat higher in her seat. She scanned the near horizon. "I don't see it."

"There. A couple miles up the road from that town. Doesn't that look like an east-west airstrip to you?"

"Oh. Isn't that a windsock on the top of that building? It sure is slack."

"That's the way I like it, no wind." Click throttled the engines back. He rolled in trim, bringing the nose up into level flight. He popped the landing gear. As the Twin Commander slowed, Click fed out ten degrees of flaps to slow the airplane even further. He banked to a new heading of ninety degrees.

Click held that course until he passed the landing strip, then throttled back further and turned the Twin Commander onto a base leg. He added more flaps and banked on around to two hundred seventy degrees–heading due west–for a final approach. Click held that heading and power setting, allowing the aircraft to slide down out of the sky. The Twin Commander crossed the end of the airstrip, and the wheels touched down so easily the passengers in back didn't know the airplane was on the ground.

Click brought off all the power as the Twin Commander rolled westward toward the far end of the runway and a short turnoff that led to a small terminal building. Several people clustered near two white Suburbans–a welcoming committee, Garrison presumed.

One man stepped out. He waved both hands at the aircraft, beckoning the pilot to bring the airplane his way. He moved away from the others, directing Click into a turn, then wig-wagged his arms over his head.

Click pulled the throttles and mixture controls all the way back to the stops. That starved the engines into silence. When the propellers stopped turning, he snapped the ignition switches off but left everything else on. "Get the door, Scotty," he called over his shoulder.

Moore and Garrison took off their headsets. They unsnapped their lap belts and left their seats, Moore to open the cabin door, Garrison to go back into the cabin. They collected their coats and hats, and Garrison her briefcase, from the back, before they went on outside.

A hand came out as Moore held Garrison's calf-length coat open for her. "Buck Laramour," the man said. "We talked on the phone."

"Yes, Mister Laramour." Garrison shook his hand. "This is my accountant, Scotty Moore."

"Mister Moore, welcome. I'm the farm manager." Laramour glanced at the airplane. "Your pilot going to wait for you?"

Garrison settled her fake fur hat over her hair. "No, he's got three passengers he's taking on to Chicago."

"I see. Well, come this way." He led Garrison toward the Suburbans while Moore went back to the Commander, to close the cabin door.

Laramour, a lean man about Garrison's height–dark, with an oversized mustache one expected to see on the face of an Old West cowboy–wore jeans, highly-polished boots, a cattlemen's hat, and a waist-length jeans jacket with Windstar Farm stitched in gold across the back.

Of the two men waiting at the cars, one was short and

as lean as Laramour. He stood in Hush Puppies, green twill trousers with a sharp crease ironed into each leg, a golfer's cap, and a bright orange and white nylon jacket–insulated. Stitched over the right breast the name Beans Greeley.

The second dressed similarly to Laramour, only his jeans were faded and his boots appeared never to have seen polish. This man wore a battered Fedora, and the puffy bags under his eyes suggested he knew too well the taste of Wild Turkey.

"This is your appraiser, Beans Greeley," Laramour said, waving toward the smaller man. Garrison and Greeley shook hands. "And our trainer at Windstar, Hank Martin. He's been with the farm almost as long as I have, what, fifteen years?"

Martin mumbled an agreement. He rubbed his hand on the leg of his jeans before he offered his hand to Garrison.

Moore trotted up. Behind him, the Twin Commander's engines burst to life. All turned to watch as the airplane swivelled around on the taxiway and rolled back to the runway. It did not stop, but turned left, the engines coming up into a full-throated bellow, pulling the aircraft away and into the air. They watched it climb and bank off to the north.

"Mighty fine airplane," Laramour said. "Teddy's, isn't it?"

"The estate's now," Garrison said.

"I suppose. Beans, Hank, this gentleman is Mister Moore, Miss Garrison's accountant." The farm manager pushed Moore into the circle for another round of hand-shaking. Laramour turned to Garrison, indicating the Suburbans. "What do ya say we get up the road and give you the nickel tour?"

Before she could answer, Greeley interrupted. "If you don't mind, Miss Garrison, I'd just as soon get to work. The longer I'm here, the more I cost you."

"Certainly."

"Hank," Laramour said, "why don't you drive Beans wherever he needs to go?"

The trainer touched a finger to the brim of his hat, then he and Greeley went to the second car, the appraiser moving with a pronounced limp, his left knee not bending.

"What's the matter with Mister Greeley?" Garrison asked after she settled into the right seat of Laramour's Suburban. Moore in the second seat, leaned forward, elbows on knees, listening.

"Beans?" Laramour asked as he slipped into the driver's seat. "You didn't know? Well, unless he told you, of course you wouldn't. Beans was a helluva jockey in his time, until a horse fell on him in a race. Crushed his leg and hip, and that ended his career."

"That's unfortunate," Garrison said.

"Depends how you look at it, Miss Garrison. That old rascal, after he mended, he went to the business college at UK. Then he got into real estate and found he had a gift for understanding the value of things in the horse business."

"And that led to–"

"That's right. The last five years, he's been an appraiser and a damn good one. Demands and gets a top fee. Of course, you know that by what you're paying him."

Laramour stepped down on the accelerator. He guided his Suburban after Martin's that had already turned onto the highway and disappeared to the northeast. "Windstar Farm's a couple miles on," he said, bringing his car up onto the pavement.

Rock fences laid to either side. When Laramour noticed Garrison gazing at them, he asked, "You got anything like them in Tennessee?"

"Not in Ballard County."

"They're dry-laid. The flat stones are stacked in such a way that you don't need any mortor to hold 'em in place. We've got a lot of limestone under the soil here, and that's what the fence builders used."

The Suburban rolled past the pillared and iron-gated entrance to a horse farm–Swickter Thoroughbreds, a sign read.

"Anybody ever tell you why we have all these horse

farms around here?"

"I've wondered," Garrison said, her gaze moving to a series of paddocks empty of horses.

"It's that limestone shelf this whole area sits on. That limestone so close to the surface, it makes the soil sweet, so Mama Nature grows the best horse grass in all the world here."

"The bluegrass," Moore said.

Laramour glanced up at the mirror, at his passenger's image. "That's right. That's our place, just ahead on the left."

The farm manager took his foot off the accelerator. He pulled the clicker down and slowed the car more, braking for a graveled drive that came out to the highway through a gap in a stone fence.

Laramour made the turn, then rolled the Suburban on at a lazy speed toward a set of buildings several hundred yards on. He waved toward the trees that stood sentinel at the sides of drive. "Magnolias," he said.

"My, tall, aren't they?" Garrison said.

"Sixty feet."

"The magnolias down in our area are much smaller, but I think they have larger leaves. Pop and I measured one once–twenty inches long and ten inches wide. We call our magnolias umbrella trees." She changed the subject. "I'm curious about the history of this place."

"Well, let's see," Laramour said, "I came here in Nineteen and Fifty-Two, just a farmhand, Buck the next year as a groom. We both kinda worked ourselves up. Old Man Bennett–that's Daniel Bennett–he owned the place. Lost more money than he ever made."

"Why is that, Mister Laramour?"

"He just could never come up with that one horse that would be the big winner. Well, anyway, the last ten years, Mister Bennett didn't have any money to keep the place up, so it got pretty shabby. Then three years ago, with his health bad and no kids who wanted the farm, Mister Bennett decided to sell out."

"So that's where Teddy came in?" Garrison asked.

"Yup."

The farm manager guided the big car into a graveled yard bordered by barns and a machinery shed. A Dalmatian dashed out from one of the barns toward the travelers. "That's Beauregard. Everybody's pet," Laramour said.

The dog swung around the Suburban and trotted along on the farm manager's side as the car rolled toward the front of the central barn–a Gothic structure, white with green trim.

Laramour noticed, when he brought the Suburban to a stop, Garrison studying the exterior of the barn. "White and green, that's the colors of our silks."

"I didn't know that."

He leaned back in the seat. "You asked about Teddy. I had seen him at a couple horse sales, and we got to talkin', and I mentioned this farm was coming up for sale. The rest, as they say, is history."

Laramour got out, as did Garrison and Moore. She left her briefcase on the seat, and they moved toward the barn's open doors. "Mister Bennett, bless his soul, found out his horse business was only a jot better than worthless, but his land was pure gold. I never saw him happier than the day he sold out. Follow me and meet the farm's namesake."

The three went on inside, Beauregard beside Laramour, the dog's tail wagging with a slow, steady rhythm. "Teddy and his partners said they wanted a showplace, so we bulldozed the old barn and built this palace. Inhale, my friends. Any way you cut it, it still smells like a horse barn, but Teddy always said that to his partners that was the smell of money."

Garrison covered a laugh.

"Well, behind the palace," Laramour went on, "we built a closed-in arena, so we can exercise and train our horses no matter the weather. Our equipment shed was a wreck, so we bulldozed that and built a new machinery barn. We replaced our tractors and our field equipment and our trucks. We put up all new fencing, had a dozen guys working one summer to rebuild the stone wall you saw along our highway frontage. I kept telling Teddy this was costing us big money, but he just said, 'Don't you worry about it. These boys are in the business to lose big money. They want a tax writeoff.'"

Beauregard bounded away toward a stall halfway down the aisle of the barn. He turned back and barked.

"Old Beau wants us to hurry."

The trio picked up the pace, Garrison and Moore looking to either side at the faces of the horses curiously watching them.

"They know you're company," Laramour said. "Hank's always wanted to train a winner. He's had some come awful close. Three years ago, he sees this one where Beau is–Patch's Beauty, entered in a stakes race. Hank said he saw something in this two-year-old stallion, and he wanted him. Well, I tell ya, I couldn't see it, but he talked me into putting one of our horses up against him–one time around the track–and we won the damn thing."

They stopped at the stall where the dog waited. Above the open top-half of the door hung an upturned horseshoe and a plaque on which was painted the name Windstar. The horse leaned his head out and down, wiffling as he and the dog touched noses.

"Stable mates. Wherever Windstar goes, Beauregard goes."

Garrison reached a hand out to stroke the star on the horse's forehead. "But I thought you said his name was Patch's Beauty."

"It was for the first couple months we had him. Hank worked with him, and the damn thing began to win ten-cent races, you know, at county fairs. His times were good, particularly when the track was wet. No horse could keep up with him in the slop.

"Well, Hank worked with him over the winter. In the spring, he showed me his practice times and said 'let's give the new owners a thrill and enter him in the Derby. He's qualified.'" Laramour reached in his jacket pocket. He took out an apple and gave it to Garrison. She offered the apple–

a Golden Delicious–to the horse. "To my way of thinking, Patch's Beauty is kind of a sissy name for a stallion, so we put down Windstar on the entry form, and, damn, if he didn't win the race running away."

Garrison chuckled at the story. She continued stroking the horse's broad face as he crunched on the apple.

"Well," Laramour said, "these old money boys were walking mighty tall, telling Hank and me we got to enter Windstar in the Preakness and the Belmont, you know, go for the Triple Crown. Damn if Windstar didn't win the one and come in second in the other. Well, that put everybody who was anybody in the horse business to calling us, begging us to breed Windstar to their mares. We had a money machine on our hands."

Garrison patted the horse's neck before she stepped back. "That had to be good."

"Nooo. Remember we're in business to lose money, not make money. But Teddy, he figured out a way."

Both Garrison and Moore looked at Laramour. "How'd he do it?" she asked.

The farm manager stroked his chin, a half-smile on his face. "He raised everybody's pay."

"Well, surely that wasn't enough?"

"It wasn't, so Teddy gave out bonuses. Then he ordered me to spend more money on farm improvements. When we had to have still more expenses to eat up that income, he set up a consulting company."

Laramour nodded. "With that company, Teddy charged Windstar Farm whatever was needed to assure the loses he'd promised the partners. If he hadn't died, he and I'd be going over the books in a couple weeks, figuring out what the charge would have to be for this year."

The farm manager motioned for Garrison and Moore to follow him. "I'll take you to the arena. One of our grooms is exercising a nine-month-old colt sired by Windstar. Hank thinks this one is our next winner."

"Not changing the subject," Garrison said as the three walked along, the dog again at Laramour's side, "but when we drove in, I noticed the house was rather dowdy."

"That's our next project. The bid for the restoration came in at three hundred thousand dollars and some change. I tell ya, when we're done, the Big House is going to be the mansion it must have been when Mister Bennett's father built it in the Nineteen Twenties."

"Are you going to live in it, Mister Laramour?"

He glanced up, surprised. "Me? Oh, no. No, no, Teddy worked out a time-share where each partner and his family gets to live in the Big House for one month each year. I got a nice little place in town."

They moved through the double doors at the rear of the barn and on into an arena bathed in sunlight that streamed in through a series of skylights. Large fans hung from the polished-beam ceiling, idle in the cool of winter, waiting for summer's heat to go to work. Laramour led Garrison and Moore to the side, to one of two areas of grandstand seating. There they leaned on a railing and watched three colts prancing along at the sides of their grooms.

"That second one, see," Laramour said, "he's got the same star on his forehead as his daddy. Big colt for his age, and strong. If he develops next year like he should, no horse in his age class will beat him."

Garrison gazed around the arena. "This is quite something."

"Well, we wanted to be able to have sales here and shows. We're appealing to the same money crowd our owners are a part of, so, as you see, no bench seating. Everything is theater-style."

Garrison touched the farm manager's arm. "Maybe we should see the books."

"Of course."

Laramour waved to the grooms, then led Garrison and Moore back into the barn and out through the front doors to the Suburban. Beauregard slipped away when they passed Windstar's stall. He hopped the half-door to bed down with the horse.

The farm manager drove his company across the graveled lot toward a low building tucked away in a grove of pin oaks, the building painted Windstar white with green trim. He wheeled the Suburban into the half-circle drive in front and stopped under a canopy at the front door.

"We have everything ready for you," Laramour said as he ushered Garrison and Moore inside. Ahead of them, on the wall facing the entrance door, was a lighted trophy case and, in the center, the cup from the Kentucky Derby.

"Really, for us, this is where everything started," Laramour said, extending his hand toward the case. "The farm may have been here for half a century, but it was just a horse farm until Windstar won that trophy. If Windstar's Dancer adds one to it and the stallion he might sire–sorry, I kinda get carried away."

He guided his guests into the reception area. "Alice," the farm manager said to the young woman at a mahogany desk, "this is Miss Garrison and Mister Moore."

Alice Witherspoon stood. Tall, gracious, wearing a red dress suit with a Christmas bells pin on the lapel, the former Miss Kentucky held out her hand. "We've talked on the telephone," she said to Garrison. "It's so good to meet you at last. May I take your coats?"

Moore helped Garrison out of her long coat. He held it while she stuffed her hat in the sleeve, then handed the coat to the receptionist and shucked his own.

"Mister Laramour, everything you asked for is in the conference room," Witherspoon said and carried the coats to a closet.

The farm manager took off his cattleman's hat. He carried it at his side as he went on to a set of glass doors. Laramour opened one and held it for Garrison and Moore. Ahead was a table long enough to seat ten people on either side. The wall beyond, a window-wall that looked out on gardens covered in leaf litter. Garrison assumed, come spring, the gardens would be raked clean and planted. Beyond the gardens and a lawn, she saw the Big House, its paint peeling, a shutter hanging askew.

Garrison swivelled around to a massive portrait of Windstar on the interior wall and, to the side, in a frame, a list of his races–his wins and losses, his losses only three. On an end wall hung another portrait.

"Who's that?" she asked.

"Mister Bennett," Laramour said. "I insisted we have it painted and displayed there. Teddy agreed. With Teddy gone, I don't know if the other partners will let me keep it up."

Moore motioned toward the account books and filing boxes arrayed on the table.

"Yup, that should be everything you need," Laramour said, "from the day the partnership bought the farm to today–bills, receipts, copies of checks, state and federal tax reports, employee records, the works."

The farm manager gestured to a copy machine in the corner of the room. "Feel free to make copies of anything you need. I'll be glad to stay if you need me, but if you don't, a horse farmer's work is never done."

He moved toward the door.

"Ah, Mister Ellsted?" Garrison asked.

Laramour's hand went to his forehead. "Oh, I'm sorry. He called shortly before you got here. Said business at the bank was holding him up, but he'd join us for lunch. And if it's all right with you, lunch will be right here. We have a caterer coming in."

"You needn't have gone to the trouble."

"Mister Ellsted insisted." Laramour put his hat on and went on out.

Garrison turned to the boxes of files as she put her briefcase on the table. "Where do we start?"

"Well, I'll tell you what I want to see, the P-and-L statements for the last three years," Moore said. He went to the first box and thumbed into it. "Why don't you look for the property tax statements, see what's happened to the valuation of this place?"

Garrison pulled over a box labeled 'Taxes.' She removed the cover and read the tabs on the folders. At last, she pulled one out.

Moore found the a series spreadsheets and laid them side by side. He leaned down to study the numbers.

"According to the county assessor," Garrison said, reading from one paper, "this farm wasn't worth much the year Teddy's group bought it."

"That's because Bourbon County's assessed valuation for taxes is twenty-percent of its real value."

"You sure?"

"Oh yes," Moore said without looking up from the profit-and-loss statements. "I called and checked."

"Well, even multiplying this number by five, it doesn't come up to a million dollars."

"What about the next year, the year they built that barn and all that stuff?"

Garrison took out another statement. "Oh, this is better. The valuation tripled."

"And this year?"

Garrison looked at that statement. "Almost doubled."

"See? With the improvements, and that horse, the valuation's getting up in the neighborhood of where it ought to be." Moore took a pad and pen from his suitcoat pocket. He scratched a heading and began recording numbers. "And these guys, hey, they don't care what the farm's tax bill is. They're writing it off on their personal taxes. Well, look at this."

Garrison glanced up from the property tax statements to see Moore's eyes glistening. She came to his side. Her gaze followed his pen down to the previous year's profit-and-loss statement. He put a checkmark next to an item labeled 'Consulting fees,' then circled a number–three hundred sixty-seven thousand, two hundred twenty dollars.

"Did Teddy pay taxes on that, do you suppose?" Moore asked.

Garrison pressed her palms on the table top. "The only income taxes he paid in the last six years were on what he made at the bank."

"Then where's this money?"

CHAPTER 21

Beans and the deal maker

Account books, files, and tax statements all laid open the length of the table.

Moore leaned back, the sleeves of his white shirt rolled above his elbows, his tie loosened. He locked his fingers behind his head. "I'll tell you, short of running an audit, there's nothing wrong with these books that I can see."

Garrison sat half the table away, hunched over the partnership agreement. "Do we have anything?"

"Yup. Two."

She glanced up.

Moore held up an index finger. "One, Teddy set up everything he could on a fast depreciation. The more he can show, the greater the potential loss for the year."

"A paper loss, I know," Garrison said.

"Right, because you still have all these fine buildings and the new equipment boosting the real value of the farm."

"The second?"

Moore made a pistol with his hand. He fired that pistol at Garrison. "The consulting company."

"Ahh yes, and the money mystically disappears."

"You know," Moore said, his fingers going to his earlobe, massaging it, "Teddy may have spent the money, remember? Laramour said he bought out one of the partners for cash."

"We still have to trace it."

"I can call the Secretary of State's Office, see if Teddy incorporated up here."

"Would he really do that?"

"I wouldn't, not here or anywhere else if I wanted to stay below the tax man's radar. The moment you incorporate, there's reports to file and that includes copies of your corporate income tax statements, even if you don't make any money."

Something outside the window caught Garrison's attention–a flick of red. A cardinal? "You don't think the farm would pay Teddy in cash?"

Moore came forward in his chair. He pulled over an account book and paged into it. "December, December, December–yup."

Garrison pushed her chair back and came around to look over Moore's shoulder. "Yup what?"

"A cash withdrawal in the amount of–" He went scrambling in a bills box. From the box, Moore pulled a December file. He then dug into it and produced a slip of paper. "Our boy didn't even bother printing up letterhead. He just hand-wrote the bill for the consulting company on blank paper."

He placed the paper next to the journal entry. "Cash, all right. Can't be traced."

"Another safety deposit box somewhere?"

"Not necessarily."

"What makes you say that?"

"Teddy could have put the money in a coffee can and buried it in the garden. Who'd think anything of him out spading in his garden?"

Garrison tousled Moore's hair. "You have one devious mind."

"Hey, I'm a cop." He looked up into her eyes. "The way this place goes through money–and that includes the money Teddy floated off–every partner last year could claim, give or take a few nickels, a two-hundred-thousand-dollar loss."

Moore touched some numbers on his notepad. "See here? A new problem this year."

"What's that?"

"That horse of theirs. He's bringing in bags of money in stud fees, money they gotta get rid of."

He circled a number. "By my arithmetic, Teddy, if he were alive, would have to bill the farm for more than four hundred thousand dollars in consulting fees to assure his partners of the losses they want."

Garrison leaned on Moore's shoulder. "But Teddy's dead."

"Yes, and some of the partners may have to pay income taxes."

"Oh, that's sad."

"Makes my heart bleed."

A rapping came at the glass door. Garrison saw the farm appraiser waving, so she motioned him in.

Beans Greeley took off his cap as he limped through the doorway. "Some place, isn't it?" he said, brushing his hair back over a balding spot.

"I'm certainly impressed." Garrison pushed several file boxes out of the way to give the appraiser some table space. She gestured to a chair, and Greeley sat down.

He peered at the chair, studied it, then tested it, springing up and down on the seat.

"They didn't go cheap, did they? Three, four hundred dollars a piece, I'd say." Greeley laughed. "My car isn't worth as much as the furniture in this room, and I drive a pretty nice car."

Garrison slipped into the chair next to the appraiser. "So, tell us, what do you think the farm is worth?"

He waved a hand over the clutter on the table. "Anything here tell you what they paid for the place?"

"Four-point-five mill," Moore said.

"Then they established a four-million-dollar line of credit at the Fifth National Bank of Lexington," Garrison added.

"That's easy enough to do, when one of your partners owns Fifth National." Greeley took a notepad from his jacket pocket. He opened it to near the middle. "Four-point-five for the place, yup, the rumors going around Lexington three years ago pegged it around there. I remember the farm back then. I have to tell you, Miss Garrison, I believe the partners paid high for what they got."

"And now?"

"Lotta changes. With all the new buildings and the improvements, and with Windstar, as long as that horse is in the deal, I can bring you three people who'd pay you eight-and-a-half to nine million and not quibble." Greeley looked up. "Ten if the mansion were already restored."

Garrison pulled her legal pad over. She wrote nine on it and divided by twelve. "So each share is worth seven hundred fifty thousand dollars."

"I'd say so."

"Don't forget, Teddy's got two shares," Moore said, "so double that for him."

Garrison doodled. A sparkly star revealed itself on her pad. "Mister Greeley, do you think Mister Ellsted would pay a million and a half?"

"Well, he can." The appraiser rubbed at the side of his nose, one eye squinting shut. "He's got the money, no question. But whether he's willing to go that much–"

"Mister Greeley, my job is to get every dollar I can for the estate and for my ultimate client, Teddy's widow."

"Then, Miss Garrison, what you need is some leverage. You ever work one of these deals before?"

"Nothing of this size."

"Well, you surely know that, as executor, you're now the managing partner for Windstar Farm." A Cheshire grin bowed up the corners of Greeley's mouth. "If Sam hesitates–"

"You know Mister Ellsted?"

"Miss Garrison, the thoroughbred business is a verrry small club. We all know each other. As I was saying, if Sam hesitates, you tell him you're dissolving the partnership, that you're doing it right now today. Tell him the farm goes on the market."

Another rapping came on the glass door. This time, a

large man in a tailored, gray herringbone suit and vest, a man whose hair was more salt than pepper, and cut short, stood on the other side.

Greeley gave a small wave. "That's Sam."

Garrison went to the door and pushed it open.

The big man put his hand out. "I'm Sam Ellsted."

Garrison shook his hand. "I'm AJ Garrison, and you know–"

"Yes. Beans, how's the world treating you?"

"Fine, Sam," Greeley said.

"And the other person here is my accountant, Scotty Moore."

Ellsted reached for Moore's hand and shook it before he swung back to Garrison. "Sorry I'm late. Damn-fool crisis at one of the coal mines over by Hazard. They needed a whopping big loan and needed it fast, and, well, lending money is how I make my money. But I did bring lunch."

The banker motioned for three people in chef whites to come in. With them came Alice Witherspoon. She went around the room collecting file folders and putting them in boxes. Moore hopped up to help her.

Two of the caterers rolled in a serving table with deep pans, covered and warming over sterno flames. The third rolled in a cabinet. From it came white table clothes. With the help of her colleagues, the caterer's assistant snapped them open and let them flutter down until they covered the length of the mahogany table. They then set out place settings for six–bone china, glasses of lead crystal, and gold tableware.

"Come, sit," Ellsted said. He pulled a chair out for Garrison and held it while she sat down. He then sat to her left.

Beans Greeley took the chair to Garrison's right.

Moore and Witherspoon sat across from the others. While they opened their napkins, Buck Laramour dashed in. He sailed his cattlemen's hat at a corner of the room and slid into the only vacant chair at a place setting.

Ellsted grinned. "Cutting it pretty close, huh, Buck?"

"That happens. Rod Moleson just came in with the lime spreader. I had to point him to the right pasture."

Ellsted motioned to the caterers. Two took the covers off the pans, and the third speared what appeared to be half a beef. The man lifted it, dripping steaming hot juice, from one of the pans and set the beef on a cutting block. He whisked a carving knife across a sharpener several times and tested the edge with his thumb before he proceeded to slice the meat.

"Hope you like prime rib," Ellsted said. "Nobody does prime rib like Roscoe and his crew."

The man doing the carving waved his knife.

A caterer came to Garrison. As he took her plate, he asked, "How would you like yours?"

"Medium, please."

The plate came back, as did the others, with a slab of beef sufficient for two, and on came the Caesar salads, bowls of vegetables, and a platter piled high with bubble bread.

Ellsted bumped shoulders with Garrison as he sawed off a hunk of steer on his plate. "You're going to want to keep a little room open for dessert," he said.

Garrison sampled a pickled baby ear of corn. "Why's that?"

"We're going to have mud pie. It's chocolate the likes of which you've never tasted before. Tell me, how do you like our little place here in bluegrass country?"

"I'm very impressed."

"Teddy did us all a favor getting us in on it."

Garrison buttered a piece of the bubble bread. "Couldn't you have bought it on your own?"

"A couple of us could, but hell, then we'd have had to run the damn thing. With our businesses, we don't have time for that. This is a plaything for us, you see."

"And a tax writeoff."

"That, too." The banker helped himself to some of the bubble bread.

"So, you don't mind the fees Teddy was taking?"

"Oh hell, no. You need a little juice for your beef." Ellsted waved at a caterer and pointed at the crystal cup next to Garrison's plate. "You ever been up this way before?"

"This is the first time."

"Beautiful country. But lest you go home believing thoroughbred horses and racing account for all the money around here, let me dissuade you. It's coal. Those old boys make their pile in the mountains, then retire here to Lexington. And, of course, we finance most of the mines in the eastern part of the state."

"Is that how you and Teddy met?" Garrison dipped a bit of beef in the juice cup. She put the beef in her mouth.

"Uh-huh. Teddy went after some of my customers and, goddamn him, he got 'em."

"Yet you could set that aside and go into business with him?"

"Hell, Miss Garrison, I figured anybody who could beat me, that's someone I wanted as a partner, not a competitor. Then one day Teddy says we ought to buy this farm, and, damn, if he hasn't got the whole deal worked out in his head. This boy was good."

"So I'm learning."

"Shame he had to go crash into that tree."

Garrison motioned to one of the caterer's assistants. "May I have a glass of milk, please?"

The woman reached below her serving table for a pitcher. She filled a crystal glass and brought it to Garrison.

Ellsted glanced at her plate. "You on a diet?"

"Oh, this is so much more lunch than I can handle."

He waved the head caterer over. "Roscoe, would you pack this young lady's plate to travel? In fact, you pack all the extra food, and we'll send it home with her."

Garrison raised a hand, to fend off the offer.

"No, I insist," Ellsted said. "And, Roscoe, you can bring out the mud pie now and, of course, Miss Garrison, you'll want a dab of mint ice cream with that." To the caterer, he held out his hands, suggesting a large bowl.

Garrison nudged the banker. She held her hands out, close together indicating a small cup.

Dessert went as amiably as the main course, only to change when the caterers began clearing the place settings. "I suppose you'd like to do a little business," Ellsted said.

"I'm ready if you are." Garrison went to the side of the room for her briefcase. From it, she took a legal pad.

"I offered a million for Teddy's shares. I stand by that."

Greeley turned away, chortling, covering it by bringing a hand to his face.

Ellsted snorted. "Come on, Beans, what is it?"

Greeley shook his head. "Sam, you're low. I appraised the farm and the business at nine million."

"You're goddamn high."

Garrison interrupted. "Mister Ellsted, based on Mister Greeley's appraisal, Teddy's two shares are worth one and a half million at a minimum."

"Not to me."

"That's all right. You don't have to buy them. There are others who are interested."

"Who?"

"Mister Ellsted, you don't expect me to tell you everything. This is a negotiation."

"Only I'm not negotiating. One million, you have your money today, that's it."

"It won't do."

"All right, a million one."

Garrison shook her head.

"A million one-five, that's my best offer."

She sighed, as if she were greatly disappointed in this person. "Mister Ellsted, you leave me no choice."

"Pardon?"

"You know Teddy's powers and authority as managing partner devolve to his estate. Now I don't like to do this, but as the executor, I'm exercising the estate's right to dissolve the partnership."

Ellsted pushed back. "You wouldn't."

"Watch me, Mister Ellsted. Mister Greeley has assured

me we have three people, each ready to buy the land and the business at his appraisal."

"We'll sue."

"That's your right, but before you get the papers filed at the courthouse, the farm will be gone and the settlement checks disbursed to the partners. Your issue will be moot." Garrison, with Ellsted glaring at her, motioned to Greeley. "Make the calls."

The appraiser stood. "I can get them on a conference call. We can hold an auction, get you more."

"Wait a minute, wait a minute." The banker drew a hand down his face. He exhaled mightily, then reached into his inside pocket. Out came a checkbook. "Beans, come a day I'll get you for this."

"No, you won't, Sam. You know my appraisal's fair."

"A million five?" Ellsted asked as he wrote 'The Estate of Teddy Wilson' on the pay-to-the-order line.

"For the shares," Garrison said, "but I also want four hundred thousand dollars for Teddy's consulting fees for the year."

Ellsted slammed his pen down. Ink blotched out onto the white tablecloth. "Oh, come on now. He's been dead for almost half a year, for God's sake."

Garrison walked to one of the windows. From there, she studied a pin oak clutching onto the last of its leaves as if they were things of great value. "Mister Ellsted, I leave here with two checks, one for one million five hundred thousand dollars–your check, Mister Ellsted–and one from the farm for four hundred thousand dollars."

"Goddammit, woman!"

Garrison did not turn around. She continued speaking, with her back to Ellsted, her voice flat, all emotion gone. "Sir, do not raise your voice to me. I leave here with your check and the farm check, or a check for one-point-nine million dollars from the proceeds of a sale. You choose."

Ellsted cast a smoldering look at Greeley, Greeley who had limped to the far side of the room. The appraiser stood there, near Garrison, his back against a window, his arms folded across his chest. From Greeley, Ellsted cast his gaze at the receptionist dithering with her napkin. "Alice, write the goddamn check. Buck will sign it."

****

Click examined the checks while the Twin Commander cruised on autopilot toward Knoxville, the sun long below the western horizon. "Hon," he said to Garrison, "may I never sit across the table from you on a business deal."

Moore leaned forward between the pilot's and co-pilot's seats. "You should have seen her work him. She had a handful of aces, and that banker knew it."

"I hoped I had aces," Garrison said.

"Oh, you did, you did. With that appraiser who knew the market, ready to back his appraisal by producing buyers with the money–"

Click passed the checks back to Garrison. "How much of this is yours?"

"Maybe two thousand dollars for today's work, although it was more fun than work. Pop, that farm's a beautiful place. And the horses–"

The moon laid some twenty degrees up from the eastern horizon, almost full, a warm yellow, the color of ripe sweet corn. The ruler of the night sky appeared to be wearing a hairpiece.

"Must have a cloud deck out there," Click said as he gazed ahead.

The hairpiece receded from right to left as the Twin Commander's engines milled away, Garrison, Click, and Moore lost in watching the moon. Then the hairpiece disappeared, and the moon came into possession of its high forehead. The night's reflector of the sun inched higher in the sky, the moon's buttery color beginning to pale.

"Oh, look at that," Garrison whispered.

Three lights alternately flashed like fireflies, on and off, on and off, one light above the other and the third above that, separated by how much distance one could not be sure, the lights on a vertical line to the left of the moon.

Click nudged Garrison. “WBIR’s television tower. We’re almost home.”

CHAPTER 22

Old business

Garrison sat hunched over a file folder open on her desk, rereading the newspaper clipping of Doctor Taylor's death. She stopped, scratched a note on a legal pad, and drew a large question mark after it.

Snow-booted Millie Purkiss scuffled in, a half-dozen envelopes and a copy of the Morgantown Chief in her hand. "The morning mail," she said.

Garrison glanced up. As she did, she saw the woman's boots and jabbed her pencil in their direction. "It's not snowing in here, is it?"

"Miss Garrison, do you know how cold it is in that room you and the judge call my office?" Purkiss placed the mail on the corner of her co-employer's desk. "It's the only room in the house that doesn't have a heat vent, and the cold air washing down off that big window–every morning this week I've had to wear my coat until enough heat came in out of the hallway to make my office feel like March instead of December."

"Why don't you have a space heater?"

"The judge won't get one."

"Why not?"

"He says it's a frivolous expense. He says the cold is good for us. He says it's invigorating. Miss Garrison, my feet aren't invigorated. They're frozen."

Garrison sat back. "Are you going out this morning?"

"To the courthouse to get warm. I have some papers I

have to deliver to the clerk of courts."

"Would you do a favor for me?"

Purkiss rubbed her arms.

"Would you go by Hub's when you come back?"

"Sure."

"Would you buy the best space heater Hubbie's got and ask him to charge it to me?"

"I can't spend your money."

"I can." Garrison flashed an assuring smile. "We'll keep this between you and me. The judge doesn't have to know."

"That's very kind of you."

"If I may ask, what was that room before it became your office?"

"A storeroom for steamer trunks and other things the Freybergs didn't want to carry up to the attic. The last Missus Freyberg made it into a sewing room. In winter, she just closed the door and never used it, according to history."

Garrison beckoned Purkiss around to her side of the desk. "Speaking of history, I've been reading the newspaper story again, and there are two things that puzzle me."

The secretary put on her glasses.

"This paragraph," Garrison said, "this one next to the last, about Doctor Taylor tracing his family's history. Why is that in the story?"

Purkiss read the paragraph, and her hand went to her cheek, her eyes sorrowful. "You didn't know, did you? You were in college."

"Didn't know what?"

"In Doctor Taylor's last years, he got real interested in the Taylors of earlier generations. I guess all of us, when we get old enough, we get to wondering where our families came from and how they came to be here rather than somewhere else. Haven't you ever wondered how different your life would be if your grandparents or your parents had settled somewhere else?"

"I've never thought about it."

"Of course not, you're too young. I can tell you this, in the doctor's last years he'd spend hours and hours and hours at the library. All of the genealogy collection and our county history, it's there largely because of the work of Doctor Taylor."

Garrison pushed the eraser of her pencil against her notepad.

"What was the other thing?" Purkiss asked.

Garrison tapped an earlier paragraph. "Doctor Taylor had forty thousand dollars in his pocket. Why?"

"Oh, the doctor always had a pocket full of money. Said he knew what it was to be poor and that he didn't have to be that way anymore."

"Fifty dollars, a hundred dollars, that I can understand, but forty thousand dollars?"

"I'm afraid I can't help you there," Purkiss said.

"Do I have any clients this morning?"

"Not until one."

Garrison took her billfold from her briefcase at the side of her desk. She opened the billfold's card pocket and fingered her way through until she found her library card. With Purkiss watching, she tore the card in half and dropped the pieces in the wastebasket. "Oh," she said, "I'm afraid my library card's been damaged. I better get a new one."

****

A flood of small children and their mothers–the children clutching picture books in their mittened hands–washed out of Morgantown's city library as Garrison came up the walk. She stepped aside, into the snow that had fallen the night before, to get out of their way. She waved at several children she knew.

One stopped. A boy. He held up his book. "See what I got? Pirates."

"Wonderful. Do you read?"

He grinned from beneath his stocking cap. "Yeah."

From the corner of her eye, Garrison caught the mother shaking her head and mouthing the words, "but he's learning."

Garrison crouched down to the boy's level. "Thomas, would you come by my office and read to me?"

"Yeah."

"When are you coming to the library next?"

He looked up to his mother for help with the answer.

"Thursday morning next week for storytime," the young woman said.

Garrison touched the front of the boy's coat to get his attention. "Thomas, after storytime next week, you have your mom bring you by my office, all right?"

"All right."

"Then you can read your book to me."

The boy hugged his book, grinning, as Garrison stood up. "Marissa," she said to the woman, "you'll bring Thomas by?"

"We wouldn't want to impose."

"It's not an imposition. It'll give me a chance to find out what I missed while I was at UT and you were starting a family."

The woman touched Garrison's arm. "It's the best thing, AJ."

"You don't have to sell me."

"Well, I've got to be getting Thomas home," the woman said.

She moved away down the sidewalk, and Garrison stepped from the snow back onto the concrete. She stamped her feet, glad she had bought calf-length leather boots rather than the flats she had considered. Her pant legs masked the upper portions of her boots, so she could wear them anywhere—even in court.

Garrison went on inside the stone-and-timbered building, into a bright, expansive, carpeted book room. The building had originally housed Morgantown's city offices, with the library no more than a closet on the second floor, as Garrison remembered it when she was a child. In Nineteen Sixty, the city offices moved out into a new building that also housed the police department and a council room large enough that it could double for police court.

It was Taylor who stepped up to provide the money to modernize this building and put an addition on the back that tripled the ground-floor space. The architect hired for the job converted half of the second floor to a community room with a kitchen and the other half to a climate-controlled room where the library maintained its rare books and its map collection. Taylor, so the story went, even provided enough money that the library could install an elevator, making the second floor accessible to those in wheelchairs and on walkers.

Garrison went up to the checkout counter where a woman, with a wild pile of hair on her head, handed three books to an urchin unrecognizable under a snowsuit and muffler, the muffler wrapped over his–or her–nose and mouth.

"You hurry back," the woman said.

"Mmmfphm mphfmmf," is all Garrison heard.

The woman waved her fingers at the child and his–or her–mother as the two left.

"Missus Cunningham," Garrison asked, "do you remember me?"

The woman turned from her work. She gazed at Garrison, puzzling. "Amanda Click, how you've grown up." Martha Cunningham cupped her hand under her chin. She smiled at the slim woman before her. "Now that you're living here, are you going to start using our library again?"

"If I can get a new card. I'm afraid something happened to my old one."

"What, your dad's dog get a hold of it?"

"Something like that."

Cunningham took a blank card from a box beneath the counter. Garrison stopped her before she could remove the cap from her fountain pen. "Could you put AJ Garrison on the card rather than Amanda Click?"

"Ah-ha, you've become your own woman and taken up your mother's last name," the librarian said. Her eyes flashed pride as the letters flowed in script from her pen's nib.

Cunningham blew on the ink to dry it. "Here. Now you can check out anything we have in the library. You've not been in our building since we've expanded, have you?"

"I'm afraid not."

"Come. Let me show you around." She swept out from behind the counter, the hem of her flowing dress swaying about the calves of her legs. This refugee from the theater was as tall as Garrison, but big boned. She dressed for show–bold colors, a long skirt, a scarf worn off the shoulder, a great clustery pin, and reading glasses that hung from a jeweled chain around her neck. Garrison thought the woman's pile of hair might be auburn, but there were streaks of white, suggestive of Frankenstein's bride.

"Oh, our library has changed so much."

"I remember it as the little room upstairs," Garrison said as she pulled off her hat. She shook her head, fluffing out her hair.

"Yes, and we have Doctor Taylor to thank for it all, God rest his soul. Over here we have the periodicals." Cunningham waved toward the windowed area at the front of the library. "References over there–big with the school children. With all this space, we've more than quadrupled our collection."

She led on back toward the new addition, pointing out the tables and overstuffed chairs among the stacks where people could read and work. Garrison loosened her muffler as they walked.

"Back here is our children's library and our storytime area. Today, I was reading a Babar story to the little ones." Cunningham stopped at a glassed-in room. "This is our pride, The Morgantown Room. We wanted to call it The Taylor Room when Doctor Taylor wouldn't let us rename the library in his honor, but he refused that as well. He said this was the community's library, not his."

Garrison turned back as she opened her coat. She admired all she had been shown, and the 'all' included a chandelier suspended in the two-story high lobby, the chandelier and a portion of the curving staircase that swept up to the second floor visible from where she and the librarian stood. "This must have cost a lot of money."

"Oh, it did," Cunningham said. "I worried about that, but Doctor Taylor never questioned anything we wanted."

"It's truly amazing."

"It is that. You know he sold his hospital to the county and made a pile of money. He told me, 'Martha, I want to spend it all before I die, and I want to spend it all where I grew up. Morgantown,' he said, 'has been good to me.'"

"I understand Doctor Taylor got into genealogy."

"Oh, yes. Just about everything we have in The Morgantown Room we have because of him–city histories, county histories, family diaries, wonderful collections of private letters, picture albums, census data going back to the first census conducted in the county in Seventeen Ninety, can you believe that? That was five years before the county was formed." Cunningham opened the door. She escorted Garrison inside.

Garrison set her briefcase on a table and went over to the county history books. She took one down. "You know, I wonder if the Click family and the Taylor family could be related anywhere along the line."

Cunningham paused. She tapped the side of her nose. "I really don't think so. Your family's from up in the mountains, right?"

"Yes."

"There are four generations of Clicks buried in Paradise Cove that I know of."

"Maybe five," Garrison said.

"And the Taylors were lowlanders. The first Doctor Taylor came to Morgantown in Eighteen Fifty-Three. None of the Taylors ever strayed far from here." She went to a filing cabinet. There, as she settled her glasses on the bridge of her nose, she pulled a drawer open and removed a file folder fat with official-looking documents and papers. "Here's everything related to the Taylors that the doctor assembled. You're certainly welcome to look through it."

"I'd like that, thank you." Garrison took the folder. She

opened it next to her briefcase.

"Well, I'll leave you, then," Cunningham said.

There on the top Garrison found copies of Taylor's birth certificate and that of his wife, Eldora Richardson Taylor. Beneath the certificates, copies of their baptismal records, their school graduations, college diplomas, and Taylor's medical licenses and Army records.

Next came a hand-drawn, hand-inscribed family tree. Garrison perused it. Nowhere could she see that the Clicks and the Taylors crossed, but the Taylors and the MacTeers did. A Hattie MacTeer married a John Taylor in Eighteen Eighty-One. Could that be someone related to the judge?

She opened her briefcase. She took out a legal pad and jotted down a few words about her discovery.

Further in the file Garrison unearthed a note about a watch belonging to one Hattie MacTeer Taylor that went to her husband, John Taylor, upon her death, a watch that her husband willed to their son, Raymond, upon Taylor's death. The note described an inscription on the inside of the watch's cover, *Presented to Robert MacTeer for exceptional service, Seventeen Seventy-Eight, General George Washington.*

The General's Watch.

Garrison scratched out more notes.

Hammond MacTeer opened the door and leaned in. "I see you found our storehouse of great treasures."

She laid her pencil aside. "I didn't know about this place."

"Well, you were away at college. Millie said you were here. Find anything interesting?"

"I think so." She turned her pad to MacTeer.

He came into the room, unbuttoning his overcoat and shucking his hat. MacTeer pulled out a chair and read Garrison's notes. "Oh, yes."

"So you were related?"

"Aren't many old Ballard County families that didn't intermarry or make babies together in the hayloft at some time. Yes, the doc and I were third or fourth cousins five times removed–something like that. I didn't know it until

Doc came across this and told me."

"Hattie MacTeer?"

"Well, as I came to learn, my family pretty well wrote her out of our history because Hattie married John Taylor who was, how shall I put this–" MacTeer gazed up at the ceiling as if the words might be there. "He was rather, uhm, disreputable. Hell, old John was a thief. Made his money going South, stealing it from those damn poor unfortunates who lost The War."

"And the watch?"

MacTeer paused. He looked again at Garrison's notes. "Well, I'll be damned. It got into the Taylor family."

"You didn't know?"

"Hah, never would have believed it. I figured it just got lost." MacTeer took his lady-slipper watchcase from his vest pocket. He removed the watch and opened its cover. "That's why I had my copy made up. But if the notes you have are right, I got the inscription wrong. I got the date after the General's name. Shoot."

"I'm sorry, Judge."

"Can't be helped." He put the watch back in its case and the case in his vest pocket. "Feel like going for a drive?"

"Where to?"

"Been a helluva long time since I been out by Sam Houston's school. Sam Houston, the first president of the great nation of Texas and its first governor when we made Texas a state. When he was a young man–before he went west–he taught just down the road at a little country school in the next county. Some of the neighbors put together an association and restored it. You ever been there?"

"No," Garrison said as she put her notepad in her briefcase.

"It's a nice little place. Maybe we can bum the key and get inside."

CHAPTER 23

Follow the money

O.C Peamantle noticed the lights on in the Freyberg mansion as he walked by.

"Oh, what the hell," he said and turned back. He tracked through the quarter-inch of powder on the sidewalk to the porch. Peamantle pounded on the oak and beveled-glass door, and stamped the snow from his shoes while he waited for someone to answer.

The door opened. There stood Garrison without her blazer, the cuffs of her blouse sleeves turned up, her feet in pantyhose. "Out late, aren't you, Mister Editor?"

"Workin' late, aren't you, Miss Defender of the poor souls abused by old John Law?"

"You caught me. Come in." She stepped aside. Peamantle entered, his hands jammed in his pockets, a certain smell of bourbon about him. He wore neither an overcoat nor gloves to ward off winter, just a duffer's cap to protect his bald spot from frost.

"Have you been drinking?" Garrison asked after she closed the door.

"Some. I'm off duty."

"Millie left some coffee in the kitchen. Let me get you a cup."

"That'd be welcome if it's strong."

"Strong for my taste." Garrison led her visitor down the hallway.

"Booze, the newsman's curse. Killed half the good editors I know," Peamantle said, following along, never taking his hands from his pockets.

In the kitchen, Garrison took down a mug that had a picture of the Scales of Justice on it, a lawyer sitting on one pan and stacks of money and coins on the other. She handed the mug to Peamantle and went after the coffeepot.

"Some mug," he said, eyeing the picture.

"The judge got it at a bar convention." Garrison poured in the steaming brew. The newspaperman waved for her to stop at half, so she poured the remainder of the coffee down the sink and slurried out the pot under the faucet. "I know you, O.C. You didn't stop by just for scintillating conversation. Bring your coffee to my office."

Garrison turned the pot bottom-side up in the drainer before she led the way back up the hallway and into the back parlor. She motioned at a chair and, for her part, settled on the leather couch Judge MacTeer had added to her suite of furniture.

Peamantle eased down into the side chair. "What's it been since the last time we visited some?"

"A month?"

"Something like that." The editor sipped at the coffee and grimaced. He took a flask from his side pocket. Peamantle unscrewed the cap and poured a splash in his mug, then a second splash. He caught Garrison's look of reproach. "Keeps the tigers at bay."

"We don't have any tigers around here. Black bears, but no tigers."

"See? It works. You haven't told me what you learned in Gambier. You've been up there, haven't you, or your boyfriend?"

"He's not my boyfriend."

"You may say that, young lassie, but I've seen the way he looks at you." Peamantle dragged a finger across the top of his flask. He popped the drops of bourbon into his mouth and smacked his lips. "This is great stuff. What have you learned?"

Garrison tucked her feet beneath her. "Well, as my father would say, the damnedest thing."

"Oh?" The editor stirred his high-octane coffee with a pencil from his breast pocket.

"You know Teddy made a flight up to Gambier in mid-May, every year for six years."

"Yes." Peamantle sucked his pencil dry before he stuck it back in his pocket.

"Well, it appears Teddy carried a check up each time from the county, each check for somewhat less than a quarter-million dollars, ostensibly to buy road equipment."

The newspaperman looked up. "The hell he did."

Garrison frowned.

"Look, my innocent, the county bids and buys in the fall. They've never bought a truck in the spring in all the years I've been here. You sure they were county checks?"

"I've asked for copies."

"And?"

"All I can tell you is the banker who cashed them said they were federal checks made out to the county."

Peamantle set his coffee to the side, on Garrison's desk. "Sonuvabitch."

"What is it?"

"Gawddamn. You can't trust a politician as far as you can throw him."

"You know something?"

He came forward on the arm of his chair, wagging a finger. "Those damn checks are federal revenue-sharing checks."

"You sure?"

"Ninety-three point four percent. Look, Morgantown got its first revenue-sharing check seven years ago come May. I asked old Ham when the county was getting its, and he told me the county didn't qualify, and no federal revenue-sharing checks ever came through. Gawddammit, I know because I publish the county's budget and its audited statement every year."

Garrison pushed a finger into the hollow of her cheek.

"You think Teddy was using truck buying as a ruse to cash the county's checks out-of-state? Why would he do that?"

"You've never heard the expression among government officials, 'It's my turn to steal for a while?'"

"No."

"Well, welcome to the real world." Peamantle gulped from his mug, baring his teeth as the fire washed down his gullet. "You know Teddy was spendin' more money than he was making. You ever figure out where the extra money was coming from?"

"Only a part."

Peamantle set his mug aside for a long draught from his flask. Again he bared his teeth. "The little bastard was probably getting a cut of the county's check. He was the middle man, had to be."

"O.C.–"

"He was a banker, for gawd sake. He could put it together. Now we got to prove it." The editor screwed the cap back on the flask. "I stand corrected. You gotta prove it."

"Why me?"

"Because, my dear, you are an officer of the court. Me? I'm just a lowly ink-stained scribe, a scribe who's had too much to drink." Peamantle raised his flask in salute to Garrison. "Here's mud in your eye."

He thought better of it, pocketed the slim bottle, and hoisted himself up from his chair. "I'm goin' home."

****

Garrison watched Peamantle, after he poured himself out the front door, go down the walk, watched him pause at the end as if he were trying to decide whether home was to the left or to the right. At last he turned right, stumbling as his toe caught against his heel. "I'm all right!" he called out, waving to Garrison.

Only when he was well out of sight did she close the door, unsure what she should do with what she had learned.

Garrison pulled on her leather boots and her black

wool overcoat. She recovered her fake fur hat and walked out of her office, down the hall, snapping off light switches as she went. At the front door, she brought out her keys. Garrison locked up, then went on to her Volkswagen, her cold, heaterless Beetle. Well, she thought, it isn't far to home.

She started the engine and, while it warmed, took a file folder from her briefcase. Garrison swept the snow from her windows with the folder. When done, she settled back inside and buckled her lapbelt. Headlights came up in her mirror, blinding her.

A moment later, a tap came on her window glass.

Garrison rolled the window down, and a new light flashed in her eyes.

"Don't look at me, honey," a voice said. "Look straight ahead."

Garrison twisted away. She stared out through the windshield, her hands tight on the steering wheel. "Uncle Bunch?"

"Honey, I been sent to warn ya. You gotta stop what yer doin. Yer into something way too big, and yer gonna get yerself hurt if you don't quit this pokin' around, askin' questions. You gotta promise me, honey. You gotta promise."

"Uncle Bunch?" she asked again.

"You drive away now, you hear?"

The light waved for Garrison to go. She let out the clutch and watched the mirror as she picked up speed, watched the headlights recede as the Beetle moved away, the headlights at the side of the street, another light–a lone light, a flashlight–in the middle.

****

Garrison sat huddled on the old family couch, hugging Bart to her–Bart, her father's retriever–the dog looking up at her face, confused by the attention. She heard the back door creak open and clutched the dog more tightly as footsteps came her way.

Something dropped in the hall.

Her body jerked at the sound. Only when Garrison heard a whistling and new sound, the sound of shoes being kicked off did she relax.

A stocking-footed Will Click came around the corner and into the room. "Boots?"

"Dad?"

"What are you doing up this late, and why do you have my smelly dog in the house?"

"I'm scared."

"Just because I didn't call? Hey, I'm sorry, kid. I just got in from Chicago. I thought my guys' business meeting was never going to end." Click stripped off his flight jacket and tossed it in a chair. He threw his cap after his jacket. "Turns out they stopped at a strip bar on the way to Meigs Field and drank for two hours. Thank God they slept all the way home."

He went down on one knee and whistled.

Bart leaped from the couch. He bounded across the room to be slap-patted by his master.

"Come on, Stinky, you're no house pooch," Click said. He got to his feet and led the dog down the hallway and into the kitchen.

Garrison heard the back door open and close, then the refrigerator door open. She also heard the phsss of a beer that had its pop top pulled away.

"This isn't for me," Click said when he came back in the room, a Budweiser in his hand. "It looks like you need it and maybe something stronger."

Garrison rose from the couch. She threw herself into her father's arms, her body trembling as the dam on her emotions broke.

****

Bunch Jeffords, in his fur-collared winter deputy's jacket, pushed open the door to Will Click's trailer office. He stood there, chewing on a stick of Juicy Fruit. "You wanted to see me?"

"Hey, Bunch!" Click hollered, waving from his work at his desk. "Get in here before you let all the warm air out."

Jeffords stepped inside. He closed the door behind him.

"Bunch, you ever been flying?"

Jeffords held up a timid finger. "One time. Ko-rea to Japan."

Click tossed his papers into a drawer. He grabbed up his flight jacket and cap as he came away from his desk. "Well, come fly with me. I gotta take my Skymaster up on a test hop, and I'd enjoy the company."

"I'm on duty."

"Oh, come on. Bunch, our mountains from the air, they're spectacular in their winter garb. You're gonna love it."

"I don't know."

"You worried about the sheriff?"

"A little maybe."

Click took Jeffords by the elbow and herding him outside. "I think he can spare you for thirty minutes."

"He's gonna yell."

Click winked at Jeffords. "Who's going to tell him?"

The two went on to the Cessna pusher-puller twin parked in front of the office trailer. Click opened the copilot's door and clambered in. He slid across to the pilot's seat, then leaned back. Click slapped the copilot's seat as the signal for Jeffords to climb in.

The deputy glanced to the side, unease showing on his face. He took a deep breath, saw a handhold on the door frame, and hauled himself up.

"Bunch, just reach out there and pull that door shut, wouldja? It'll latch," Click said as he secured his lapbelt. When he heard the door close, he added, "You buckle up, now. Wouldn't want you falling out and hurting yourself."

Jeffords glanced at Click, as Click turned on switches and pressed in knobs. He found the two ends of his lapbelt and drew them together, secured them in the belt's locking mechanism. An engine started, then a second engine. Jeffords glanced over his shoulder at the rumbling coming from behind.

Click spoke into his microphone. "Knoxville Ground, Skymaster Six-Seven-Three Charlie Victor at Vol-Air. Two on board. Ready to taxi."

A voice came back over the speaker above Jeffords' head. "Gotcha, Three Charlie Victor. Cleared to Runway Five. Wind light and variable out of the north. Altimeter Three-Zero-Zero-Two. Clear forever and ceiling unlimited, a great day to fly."

"Roger, Ground, we're rolling." Click goosed the engines. He swung the twin out and onto the taxiway heading to the departure end of the runway. As the Skymaster rolled along, he ran through his checklist of controls, instruments, and radio settings. When done, Click dialed in the tower's frequency and spoke into his microphone. "Tower, Three Charlie Victor ready to go. Send me over the mountains. I'm going on a brief test flight."

"Roger. Hold short for a Southern Airways Fairchild."

****

Garrison, with Moore a step behind, rapped on the glass of Judge Rayfield's door.

"Come," a voice from inside said.

She opened the door.

Rayfield, in his shirt sleeves at his desk, gesturing Garrison toward his side chair. "Just reading the paperwork on this damn lawsuit between the Knott brothers you suckered me into deciding. AJ, you should be ashamed of yourself."

"I'm just doing what my client wants."

He set his reading glasses aside and pinched the bridge of his nose. "What brings you and the super trooper by? Incidently, Scott, why are you in civvies?"

Moore pushed his hands in his back pockets. "I'm off duty, sir."

Rayfield grunted.

"Judge," Garrison said, "I need your advice."

"A lawyer asking my advice? That's a first. Go ahead."

"You know I'm handling Teddy Wilson's estate."

"I do. Tell me, when are you going to close that thing out?"

"I don't know."

"Why not?"

"Mister Moore has been doing some investigating for me. We've turned up information that suggests Teddy may have been stealing from the county, or he was being bribed, or something. There's a million and a half dollars involved."

Rayfield stared at Garrison. He motioned for her to close the door. "Why am I not going to like this?" he asked.

****

A high-wing turbine twin whistled across in front of Click's Skymaster. Bunch Jeffords jerked up, startled. The twin touched down on the runway and rolled on.

"Lordy, we gonna get hit?" Jeffords asked, his hand grasping at the lone arm rest on the side of the door.

Click slapped the deputy's knee. "Not a chance."

A voice crackled over the speaker. "Three Charlie Victor, you're number one to depart after the Fairchild clears the runway. Into position and hold."

Click let off the brakes. The Skymaster rolled out onto the runway. He kicked the right rudder, bringing the airplane into the wind. "Tower, Three Charlie Victor. Want an eastbound departure."

"Roger. There's no traffic out there. Three Charlie Victor, the Fairchild is clear of the runway. You're cleared for takeoff. Have a nice flight."

"Be back in thirty minutes."

"We'll be here."

Click pushed the throttles forward to the top of the power quadrant. The engines responded, spinning up to full power, bellowing as the forward engine pulled and the rear engine pushed the Skymaster down the runway and into the sky.

Jeffords grabbed for the bottom of his seat, his stomach

sinking.

Click glanced at his passenger, Jeffords with his eyes squeezed shut and his lips moving as if he were mouthing a prayer. Click swept up the landing gear. He bent the Skymaster into a climbing right turn and eased the throttles back to a less demanding power setting. "Look outside, Bunch. It's beautiful."

Jeffords forced an eye to open. He squinted out his window and down.

****

Rayfield wadded his sixth sheet of paper and launched it across his office. The wad bounced off a filing cabinet and fell into a wastebasket. "You want me to believe that Ham and the fiscal court and Teddy and this guy up in Gambier are chopping up federal revenue-sharing checks and putting the pieces in their pockets? Checks that aren't recorded anywhere except in a bank in Ohio that's not in our jurisdiction?"

Garrison glanced at Moore leaning against the wall, paring his fingernails. He nodded to Rayfield.

"Shit. Do you know how long I've served with these guys, all of us here at the courthouse? If this is true, there's going to be so much stink it's going to get on all of us." The judge launched another wadded paper at his wastebasket. "Can you prove any of this?"

Moore shook his head. "The canceled checks would be in a federal warehouse somewhere."

"Of course, and you have to have them to know who endorsed them."

"To get the checks, we'd have to have a federal attorney and the FBI."

Rayfield pulled open a drawer in his desk. He took out a small binder and paged into its contents. "I can make some calls, but if they find anything, they'll run with it. We won't have any say-so."

"That's right."

"If Ham and the boys are stinking up my courthouse,

gawdammit, I want them up in front of me."

Moore pocketed his knife. "AJ doesn't like this one, but what if Judge MacTeer was selling the county's equipment and pocketing the money?"

"You can prove that?"

"Maybe. Look, on a hunch, I had a buddy in State Police headquarters go over to the Secretary of State's office. He checked some corporation records for me." Moore took out his notepad and laid it open on Rayfield's desk. "See here? Hammond MacTeer has a little business up in Spangler–ABC Sales Inc. There's no telephone, but there is a P.O. box."

"What's this got to do with anything?"

"I did a little poking around. I found the office up over a garage. Last night, I went up there and read the files by flashlight."

"Oh, this I'm not going to like," Rayfield said.

Moore turned a page. "I found bills of lading for trucks and road graders and backhoes going back six years, bills of lading for ships outbound from New Orleans for Venezuela."

Rayfield closed Moore's notepad. "Illegal search. There's not a damn thing there I can use. Trooper, if someone saw you, you could serve time for this."

"Judge," Garrison said, "what if we could go at this another way?"

Rayfield threw up his hands.

"What if you were to give us a search warrant for the county road department's books? If we can go through the department's documentation on its equipment and we find any discrepancies, you can order an inventory. If we can physically count the trucks and backhoes and road graders and check their motor numbers against the records, if they're off by so much as one, you can order the arrest of the department head."

"Ah, squeeze the little guy. Squeeze poor old Henry Tingle and he gives us the big guy. I hate this." Rayfield opened a desk drawer. He took out two badges and slapped them down. He also took out a fistful of court orders.

"AJ, I'm making you a special prosecutor so we can bypass the county attorney," Rayfield said as he scribbled away. "I doubt Mark's in on this, but I'm not taking any chances. Here's your badge."

The judge pushed a badge toward Garrison and tossed the other to Moore. "You, my good man, are now my court deputy. I'm writing out an order that attaches you to the special prosecutor. Call your supervisor and take a leave of absence. I don't want you wearing a State Police badge when you're working for me."

"But I need my paycheck."

Rayfield glared at Moore. "The hell with your paycheck. I can pay you, pay you both, not much, but it'll keep wienies and mustard on the table." He went back to writing. "Scott, you work for me, you don't wear jeans. You wear a suit. Got that?"

"Yessir."

"So get your suit out of the closet."

Garrison stood. She moved to Moore's side while Rayfield finished his final order. He signed it with a flourish and held it out. "Your search warrant. Got an accountant you can take with you, somebody with a good pair of eyes?"

"O.C. Peamantle," Garrison said.

"That blister on the butt of city and county government? I can't stand him, but the bastard's honest."

The new badge holders, search warrant in hand, moved toward the door, but Rayfield stopped them. "You realize, if this goes bust, I'm looking at unemployment after the next election."

****

Click leveled the Skymaster at three thousand feet. He trimmed it to hold that altitude and snapped on the autopilot. "Bunch, you can relax now. Everything's all right."

Jeffords, his face scrunched up, slumped in his seat. He gazed around the cockpit and out the windshield to the horizon, the muscles in his face and neck relaxing. He loosened his death grip on the seat. "Kinda nice," he said, his voice like that of a frog.

"Isn't it, though?"

"What we doin' up here?"

"Last night, coming home from Chicago, that door popped open. I had a passenger sitting where you are. He thought sure he was going to fall out."

Jeffords retightened his fingers on the seat bottom. "You fix it?"

"I tinkered with the latch this morning. I think I got it, but the only way to be sure is to test it in flight."

Click reached across Jeffords. He slapped his hand against the door.

Jeffords pulled back.

Click slapped at the center, at the top, at the latch. He hit the latch, and the door swung out into the slipstream.

Jeffords swallowed his gum. He shrank from the open door, shrank away from the wind howling in.

Click raked open the latch on the deputy's seatbelt. He slammed against Jeffords' shoulder, shoved him into the door. "Gawddammit, Bunch, you threatened my girl! What the hell's wrong with you?"

The plane dipped with the shifting weight, and Jeffords' hat whipped away into the wind.

The autopilot responded to the shifting and brought the wing back up.

Jeffords let go of the seat and grabbed Click's arm.

"Talk, Bunch, or you're going out the door, gawddammit. They'll never find your busted-up body here in the mountains." He jacked the deputy further into the slipstream. The wind grabbed Click's cap and tore it away.

"Don't do this, Will! I didn't have no choice! I didn't."

Click, with his free hand, came up with a Crescent wrench from the floor. He menaced Jeffords. "I bust ya an' you're gone."

Jeffords stared at the wrench, fear writ large. "The sheriff made me do it. Honest, the sheriff made me do it."

"Bogle? Why the hell for?"

"I don't know."

"And I should believe you?"

"I'm jus' tryin' to git by, Will. I'm jus' tryin' to git by."

Click dropped the wrench. He pulled Jeffords back into his seat. When the deputy let go of the Click's arm, to cover his face, his fear, his tears, Click reached across for the door. He got hold of the latch and yanked the door out of the slipstream, slammed the door closed. The latch locked.

Click glanced at the gauges on his control panel. "Bunch, you ought to get down on your knees and thank the Almighty you never could lie for beans."

Chapter 24

Follow the trucks

"You in a suit? I haven't seen this in a while," Garrison said as she and Moore clattered up the steps to his apartment.

"Just be glad I haven't porked out. It's my college graduation suit."

"And your momma bought it?"

"No, my dad." Moore pushed the door open, and Garrison trailed in after him. He strode off. "Don't make yourself too comfortable. I'll only be a minute."

She loosened her muffler. While she waited, she drifted around the front room, running a gloved finger along the bookcase and across the top of the television. She looked at her finger.

Dusty.

"I haven't washed dishes for a couple days, either," Moore called out.

How did he know? "You only have three plates. You better wash them unless you intend to eat out of your beer mugs."

"Is that a problem?"

Garrison picked up a brochure. "What's this from UT?"

"Oh, they're offering night classes in criminal justice. I'm thinking of signing up." Moore came into the room, fussing with his necktie. "This all right?"

"As long as it doesn't have a hula dancer painted on it." Garrison glanced at the tie as she brushed a collar point down for him. "Your shirttail's out."

"Oops." Moore tucked it in as he went back to his bedroom. When he returned, he wore a suit coat. "Acceptable?"

"Other than the lapels are too narrow."

"So?"

"It's out of date."

"It's all I've got." From the coat tree, he took down a tan London Fog and slipped his arms into it.

"Turn the collar up, you'll look like Humphrey Bogart in 'Casablanca,'" Garrison said.

Moore slapped a ball cap on his head.

"But not with that."

"Hey, it's this or my trooper hat." He held his arm out to Garrison. "Shall we?"

But she motioned toward the kitchen. "May I use your phone before we go?"

"Sure."

"I want to leave a message for Pop, that I might be home late."

****

Garrison pointed to a cross street. "Would you turn up here?"

Moore spun the steering wheel of his pickup. "Any particular reason?"

"Missus Taylor lives up here. Let's go see her."

He jerked his truck around a pothole. "But the warrant–"

"The road department's not going to run away. There, the second house on the right."

"Big old place, isn't it?" Moore said as he guided his truck to the curb.

"The Taylors were always taking in student nurses and, when the hospital shut down that training program, they took in students from the college. Missus Taylor still does."

The two got out and went up the front walk to the porch. There they wove their way around something bulky, wrapped in canvas, on their way to the door. Garrison guessed the pile was porch furniture waiting for spring.

She pressed the bell button.

A hand pulled back the sheer curtain that covered the door glass and as quickly let the curtain fall back into place. The door opened.

"Amanda, how nice," a slight, round-shouldered woman said, a cardigan over her print dress. "Come in, come in. And Scotty."

Eldora Taylor held out her hand to Moore. They shook as he and Garrison came on into the front room, a room large enough that one could hold a church meeting there. Some years back, Garrison remembered, the Taylors remodeled their house. They had the workmen remove the wall between the front and back parlors and the wall between the parlors and the hallway. That opened up half the main floor. The easier to entertain, they told their friends.

Missus Taylor held out her hands. "Let me take your coats."

"We can only stay a few minutes."

"But at least those minutes can be comfortable."

Garrison and Moore surrendered their coats and hats to their hostess. She laid them over the arm of a couch. "It's been so long," Missus Taylor said.

Garrison glanced around. The room smelled of furniture polish and brown sugar. "All the tables?" she asked.

"Oh, my bridge club's coming over tonight. Four foursomes. When the doctor died, everybody thought I'd drop out, but I talked my sister into becoming my partner. She's gotten to be quite the player. Come, sit down." She guided Garrison and Moore to chairs at the side of the room, in front of a fireplace burning low. "I do like a fire in the winter, don't you?"

"It's pretty."

"And warm. Lets me keep the thermostat turned down a little." Missus Taylor settled on a Queen Anne's chair. She folded her hands in her lap and gazed at Garrison. "How are you doing now that you're a lawyer?"

"Keeping busier than I expected."

"Well, I follow your exploits in the newspaper. What you did for Irene McCoskey, that was really wonderful." She turned to Moore. "And I suppose you're writing as many speeding tickets as ever?"

"Trying to keep the highways safe for when you drive to Knoxville."

She smiled and patted his knee. "We old ladies appreciate that."

"You're not old, Missus Taylor," Garrison said.

"Sixty-three come next month. I swear, some mornings I feel like I'm seventy. I have arthritis in my back. Could I get you two a little something? I'm baking coffee cakes for my bridge club, and I already have one out of the oven."

"It smells wonderful, but no thank you," Garrison said.

Missus Taylor looked to Moore, but he waved a hand. So she settled back, glancing again to Garrison. "Now, Amanda, if I were a betting person, I would be betting you didn't come by just to check on my health."

"I didn't. A friend has asked me to look into Doctor Taylor's death."

"You mean murder. That's what it was. I've been mad at everybody down at the courthouse for three and a half years because nobody'd do anything. How can I help you?"

Garrison picked at a cat hair on the leg of her pants. "I don't know, but I was down at the library the other day, reading your family's file."

"Oh, that file is interesting, isn't it? The doctor discovered so much when he started digging."

"There was a mention of a watch that came down in the doctor's family."

Missus Taylor pulled forward in her chair. "Yes, the General's Watch. The doctor was so proud of that, always showing it off."

"He had it?"

"Of course."

"But Judge MacTeer said the watch was lost."

"Oh, Hammond knows better than that. He tried to buy it from the doctor, but the watch is lost now."

"What do you mean?"

"I assumed the doctor had it with him the night he died, so I asked Deputy Jeffords, and he told me he didn't find a watch when he went through the doctor's pockets. I've looked through the doctor's office for it, I've looked through the house. It wasn't anywhere."

"Well, I'm curious. I know the watch came into your family through Hattie MacTeer, but how did it get to Doctor Taylor?"

"Oh my, that's a long story." Missus Taylor's hand went to her cheek. "The way the doctor explained it, the watch came down to Zachariah MacTeer, Hattie's father. Well, Hattie was an only child, so she inherited the watch and brought it with her when she married John Taylor, the doctor's great-great uncle. The watch then goes to their son Raymond who, in Nineteen Twelve, married Henrietta Watson."

Missus Taylor's gaze turned to the flames dancing in the fireplace.

After some moments, Garrison asked, "And?"

"Oh, yes, poor Raymond. He died after The Great War, of influenza. Poor Aunt Nettie, that left her alone, and she became, umm, what is the polite way I can put it? Odd? "

"She's not the cat woman, is she?"

"The very one." Missus Taylor shook her head as if she couldn't quite believe it. "She had a hundred and twenty-three cats running around her house when she died, and she had named every one of them. But the watch. When the doctor finally figured out Aunt Nettie had it, he went to her and persuaded her to give him the watch, to keep it in the family since she had no children."

"When was that?"

"Oh, maybe four years ago. Aunt Nettie died the next year."

"And the watch is gone."

"Yes. It makes me so angry."

"I'm sorry."

"Amanda, you needn't be."

"And the forty thousand dollars Doctor Taylor had in his pocket that night?"

"I've wondered about that, too."

"Do you know why he had so much money with him?"

"I have no idea." Missus Taylor leaned forward on the chair's arm. "He always kept two hundred dollars in a money clip in his pocket, his security money, the doctor called it. I've never seen him with more."

"Did the sheriff return it to you when he closed his investigation?"

"Amanda, he never did. He said Hammond–Judge MacTeer–had told him he should keep it as evidence until he could explain it."

"I've been trying to find some explanation for it, too. Well–" Garrison stood. "Missus Taylor, you've been so very kind, but Scott and I have to be going along. There's another matter we're working on this afternoon."

Missus Taylor rose and went after her guests' coats. "Am I going to read about it in the newspaper?"

****

After Moore and Garrison were back in his pickup and on the way to the newspaper office, he asked the question that had been eating at him since they had left the Taylor house. "Why are you so interested in a watch?"

She gazed ahead at the first streetlight flickering. "Scott, try as I might, I can't explain it, not just yet. But I have a feeling, like all that money Doctor Taylor had, it's terribly important."

"First things first. Let's get O.C. and get out to the road department before everybody leaves."

****

Moore pulled up to the curb in front of the newspaper

office.

Garrison bailed out. She went inside and shagged Peamantle back to the truck.

The trio then drove south out of town, to the gravel road that led to the county garage. Moore turned off the highway. Ahead, two vehicles stood in front of the Quonset building that was the garage, a small Datsun and a black Ford pickup.

"The pickup, that's Mister Tingle's," Garrison said.

Peamantle, riding shotgun, peered through the windshield at the other vehicle. "So who do you suppose has the slanty-eyed car?"

"O.C.–"

"Hey, I just believe people ought to buy American. It wasn't that long ago we fought the Japs."

"O.C., I'm not going to argue with you. Anyway, we'll find out soon enough who owns the car."

Moore guided his truck in next to the Datsun.

"Lights on," Peamantle said. "Somebody's still home."

Moore checked his watch. "Just the heads. The drivers and mechanics leave at four-thirty."

Peamantle nudged Garrison. "Tell me, are you really sure you want me on this?"

"I am. Can we go on in?"

He opened the passenger door. Peamantle stepped down, then reached back to help Garrison.

"Ahh, you are gentleman," she said, giving him a warm smile.

"Only when I'm sober."

Moore came around the truck to the shop door. He opened it and followed Garrison and Peamantle inside. The trio stopped at the counter.

"Anybody home?" Garrison called out.

A head popped around the corner of an office door halfway down the garage. "Yeah!"

"Mister Tingle?"

"Right! Come on back."

Moore lifted a hinged section of the counter, and the

three went on through. To their left, a jungle of vehicles. Ahead and beyond the office, hoists and winches and workbenches littered with tools and engine parts, all wrapped in the sweet aroma of grease tinged by the acrid smell of diesel fuel. Moore moved between a nude wall calendar from a truck supply company and Garrison. "Maybe you shouldn't look at this," he said.

"Ahh, but I can." Peamantle took out his spectacles. He peered at the model on the December page. "Hmm, better than most."

Garrison and Moore went on into the office, a table at one side. Coffee cups and crumpled lunch bags told their own story. File cabinets jammed the back wall with a map of the county above them. Beyond a metal secretary's desk, Tingle–the manager of the county road department–and another man hunched over a second desk, working on what appeared to be a schedule of jobs.

Tingle looked up. "What kin I help you with?"

"Mister Tingle, do you remember me?" Garrison asked.

"Yer that young lawyer from out at the cemetery, back in the fall. You were with the judge." He pushed the bill of his cap up, revealing a high, shark-belly white forehead. "What kin I do you for?"

"Mister Tingle, could we look at your files?"

"Oh, that I don't know. They're not my files, you see. They're the county's, and you don't work for the county," he said, waggling a finger, "any of you."

Garrison set her briefcase on the secretary's desk. She opened it and took out the warrant. "I have a paper that says I can look at your files."

Tingle patted the other man's shoulder as he left him. The roads manager took the paper from Garrison and opened it. "A search warrant? What've we got that would interest anybody?"

"Your equipment inventory."

Tingle swept a hand back toward the cabinets. "Well, have at it. Is it all right if I get Sam out of here? He's got a wife waitin' dinner on him."

"Yes, that's fine."

The three went to the filing cabinets. There they read labels on drawers in an effort to decide where to start.

Tingle went back to his partner. "How about you close up an' take off," he said.

The squat man pushed his chair back. He shoved the job schedule in a drawer and went toward the shop.

"Stop back before you leave, wouldja, Sam?" Tingle asked. He scratched something on the back of an envelope. "I got one more thing for you."

"Right." The man went on out. The door of a locker rattled open, then closed. When the man returned, he was zipping himself into his parka. "Whatcha got, Henry?"

Tingle folded the envelope. He handed it to his partner.

The man lifted the fold open. He glanced at the note. "Right," he said and stuffed the envelope in his pocket.

"See ya in the mornin'," Tingle said.

"You bet." The man backed away out of the office, staring as he went at Garrison, Moore, and Peamantle, Garrison and Moore at a table reading files, Peamantle still at a cabinet.

Tingle came over to his company, to Garrison and Moore. Both had shed their coats and Moore his suit jacket, a harness apparent that supported a shoulder holster. Peamantle remained off at a distance, his elbow on a cabinet, a drawer open and a sheaf of papers in his hand. He whistled the march from 'Aida' while he read.

"Ma'am," Tingle asked, interrupting, "mind if I call my wife since I'm gonna be here a while?"

"Go ahead."

Moore twisted his file to Garrison. "I think I found something."

****

Peamantle stuffed the folders he'd been reading under his arm. He strolled out into the shop. There two bare hundred-watt bulbs cast eerie shadows in the cavernous interior. Peamantle went up to one of the dump trucks and peered at the number on the door.

"Hey! Get away from there!"

He whipped around. "Sorry," he said to Tingle standing in the office doorway. "Big trucks always fascinate me. You wouldn't mind me asking a question, wouldja?"

"Question? Guess not." The roads manager pushed his hands in his back pockets as he came over.

"They let you drive these?" Peamantle gestured at the trucks in the shop.

"Uh-huh."

"Must be something."

"Yeah, particularly the big ones we got up in the mountains. We got the big blades on those suckers, for pushin' snow that drifts six-feet deep."

Peamantle patted a fender. "How many of these rigs you got?"

"Well, let's see." Tingle glanced to the side, appearing to be running a mental inventory. "We got four in here, six out back, two in Spangler, and three up at Genesis."

Peamantle put his arm around Tingle's shoulders and strolled with him back to the office. "That sure is a lot to look after."

"Keeps us busy."

"I'll bet it does."

He left Tingle and went on to the table. There he bent down to Garrison and Moore. He laid his files open. "Bingo."

"What do you have?" Garrison asked, her voice hushed.

Peamantle pushed out a paper. "A Nineteen-Sixty inventory. The county owned twelve trucks at the end of that year."

Next he fanned out a handful of papers. "Purchase orders. In the intervening years, the county bought forty trucks, right at five a year."

Peamantle fanned out a second handful of papers. "Liquidation orders. The county sold thirty run-out trucks during the same years."

Gravel crunched in the driveway beyond the shop door.

"You do the arithmetic," Peamantle said, his voice low.

"Yeah," Moore said, "the county should have twenty-two trucks."

A door opened, then closed.

"But it doesn't. If Tingle over there told me the truth, the county owns fifteen."

A new voice joined the conversation. "Am I comin' in on a party?"

Garrison, Moore, and Peamantle glanced up toward the office door. "Sheriff," Moore said, greeting the new arrival.

"You people lookin' for something in particular?" Sheriff Bogle asked as he pushed his bulk through the door and on into the office.

"Did the judge send you?" Garrison asked.

"Uh-huh."

"He didn't say anything to us."

Bogle turned the papers on the table and bent down. He studied them. "Well," he said after a moment of reading, "he's not one to tell you everything. Find some discrepancies, have you?"

"It appears so."

Bogle sucked on his teeth. "Figured you might."

He straightened up, and as he did, he brought a revolver out from beneath his mackinaw. Bogle jabbed the weapon into Moore's ribs. "I'll just relieve you of that damn cannon you got in yer armpit, sonny boy."

Moore glanced at Garrison, shock on her face.

The sheriff shot his hand across and lifted Moore's weapon from its holster. "Henry, you still got that pit out back?"

"Yeah," Tingle said.

"We're gonna fill it up. Git you an endloader goin'."

As Tingle hurried out the door, Bogle waved his gun for the others to also head for the door.

"You don't think he's going to," Garrison whispered to Moore as she and Peamantle came away from the table.

"He's going to."

"What are we going to do?"

Bogle came up beside Moore. "What you two hissin' about?"

"Just this miserable weather," Peamantle said, before Moore or Garrison could answer.

"Hurry it up. Weather ain't gonna bother none of you much longer."

Gravel crunched in the lot outside.

"I don't suppose it would matter to tell you I'm not one of them," Peamantle said.

"Nope. It's kill the lawyers, then kill the editors. Keep the world safe for democracy."

"Aw, come on, Clarence."

Bogle rammed his revolver into Peamantle's back. He shoved him out into the shop. A motor ground away, pulling a garage door up and back into the ceiling of the shop. Ahead, Tingle climbed into the cab of an endloader. He started the engine.

The door from the parking lot swung open and in stepped Click and Oliver. "Just picked up your message," Click said to Garrison and Moore coming his way. She ran to him and threw herself into his arms. "What it is, Boots?"

Bogle stepped out from behind Peamantle. "Damn shame you two had to come by."

Click peered through the dim light toward the new voice. "Clarence? So that's your cruiser out there. Where the hell do you get off threatening my girl?"

"Where the hell do you get off raisin' your voice to me? Gawddammit, Click, I got the gun, so turn your ass around there and hike out that big door." Bogle again shoved Peamantle forward.

The newspaperman tripped. He fell against Moore and from him against a truck. There as Peamantle pulled himself up, he raked a hand along the edge of the truck's bed.

Bogle, a snarl curling his lip, waved his pistol at the editor. "Gawdammit, git with the others or I kill ya here."

"Okay, okay," Peamantle said as he shuffled back into the line of march, back next to Moore. He opened his hand, showing a fistful of sand. Some dribbled away before he curled his fingers closed.

Moore opened his mouth, but Peamantle shook his head.

****

Outside, the endloader's diesel engine roared as Tingle rammed the machine's bucket into a gravel pile. When he had the bucket full, he jiggled it back and up, lifting the bucket to beneath the level of the rig's headlights. Tingle backed the machine around until its lights bathed the garage's trash pit.

****

The five edged on, harangued by Bogle, Peamantle stumbling from one person to the next, whispering to them.

Headlights came around the far side of the garage. They turned at the end of the property, their glare flooding the group. Click raised an arm.

The headlights stopped moving, then a car door opened.

"Sheriff?" a voice called out.

"Bunch!" Bogle hollered. "Get yerself over here. We got some disposal work to do."

Bunch Jeffords came forward, stopping when the headlights of his cruiser silhouetted him. "Sheriff, I can't let you do this."

"You ain't got a helluva lot of choice, Bunch. With what they found out, we're going to prison, and I'll be damned if I'll have that. Now get over here."

"Why'd you kill the doc?"

"What?"

"Doc Taylor. Why'd you kill him?"

"What the hell you talkin' about?"

"Clarence, while you worked in the jail this afternoon, I took your Forty-Five. I test fired it. The bullet matches the one that killed Doc."

Peamantle wheeled. He whipped his handful of sand

into Bogle's face, and the five captives dodged away, out of the headlights as the sheriff clawed at himself, spitting and swearing. After Bogle cleared his eyes, only Bunch Jeffords remained, still outlined by the headlights of his car.

Bogle, squinting, brought up his gun. He jerked the trigger, and two blasts answered his.

Bogle and Jeffords both fell away, Jeffords twisting back onto the hood of his cruiser. The sheriff stumbled, then toppled to the ground in front of the endloader.

Moore ran out of the night toward Bogle, and Click, Oliver, and Garrison to Jeffords.

She got to him first. "Uncle Bunch, are you all right?"

Jeffords winced. He gripped his left shoulder, blood seeping between his fingers. "Hon, I've had better days."

"The sheriff's dead," Moore called out. He came up and raced to the endloader. Moore yanked Tingle from the cab and threw him to the ground. "Goddamn you, stay there," he bellowed and ran back to Bogle, to recover his pistol.

Jeffords whispered, "Hon, you better git me some help. I ain't feeling too good."

"Dad, call the ambulance."

"Hell, get him in his car." Click jerked a door open. "With the siren, we'll get him to the hospital in ten minutes." He and Oliver muscled the deputy into the back seat, Oliver going in with Jeffords. Click jumped in the front seat. He jammed the transmission into drive and sprayed gravel as he raced away, the siren wailing into the night.

Peamantle strolled up to Garrison alone in the light from the endloader's headlamps, dust roiling in the breeze. He scribbled on galley paper he carried. "Helluva story, this one. Wish I'd brought a camera."

"O.C.," she said, "it's not over."

"Hmm?"

"Far from it."

****

A light still burned in Hammond MacTeer's office as

Garrison drove up in her father's pickup. She abandoned the truck on the street and hurried to the mansion, the front door always unlocked when someone was there. She went in, into the hallway, to MacTeer's office.

The old lawyer glanced up, a tumbler of amber liquid and a Jack Daniel's bottle in front of him. "I see you escaped the clutches of our dear sheriff," he said. "Damn shame, all of it. But where are my manners? Come. Sit." He motioned with his tumbler toward his side chair. "Where's your trooper?"

"Out at the county garage, doing what a policeman does when somebody's been shot," Garrison said, her voice flat, lacking emotion. She slipped into the chair.

The bags beneath MacTeer's eyes drooped more than usual. "You'll forgive me for not standing. I'm kinda tired." He stirred his whiskey with his finger. "Can I pour you a drink? No, that's right. You young ones are beer lawyers, not whiskey lawyers."

"It was the watch, wasn't it?" Garrison said.

A hollow laugh welled up from MacTeer.

"You ordered the sheriff to get the watch for you," Garrison said, "whatever it took."

"So you figured it out. I knew you were smart, but I bet myself I was smarter."

She stared up at the shrine behind MacTeer, the niche in his bookcase occupied by the bell jar, the watch stand inside it still empty. "Where's the General's Watch?"

MacTeer set his drink aside. He pulled open a bottom drawer and brought from its bowels a velvet case that he laid on his desk. He lifted the top, revealing a silver watch, its exterior highly tooled with flourishes and fancy scroll work. MacTeer brought it out. "Mine I had made in gold, but the real one was silver. It's said that Paul Revere did the tooling and the inscription."

He pressed a button on the side, and the cover opened. MacTeer held the watch up to the light. "The inscription is right. The date is before the General's name."

With love for things of unmeasurable value, he placed

the timepiece on a paper so the watch stood upright, its cover still open.

"Doc never should have had it," MacTeer said, the weight of the world in his voice. "He wasn't one of us. His family didn't found this county like mine did. The Taylors, they were damn carpetbaggers. Old Doc felt the watch gave him standing."

"So you knew he had it, and that ate at your soul."

"Damn him, he wouldn't give me the watch. He wouldn't sell it to me, either." MacTeer stared level into Garrison's eyes. "So, I sicced Clarence on him. The sheriff owed me his job."

"But murder?"

"Sometimes you have to do things."

"Judge, something I don't understand. The forty thousand dollars in Doctor Taylor's pocket–"

"Yesss. You thought he walked on water, didn't you? Hon, that was Doc's share of the federal revenue money we fiscal court judges divvied up that night."

"You told the sheriff to keep it for evidence."

"Missus Taylor didn't need it, and there were people who were going to have to be paid."

"Who?"

MacTeer gave a sideward jerk of his head, as if to say I'm not going to tell you. He picked up his tumbler. MacTeer held it up and studied its contents. "Amanda, you're not gonna win this one. I'm gonna cheat the jailer."

He tossed the drink back. The fist with the tumbler came down to the desk, MacTeer sucking in wind through bared teeth. He slumped back into the deep comfort of his leather chair. His eyes closed, and the muscles of his face went slack.

"Judge?"

He didn't answer.

Garrison came closer. She put her fingertips against the artery in his neck and saw, to the side–on the desk–an open pill box next to the whiskey bottle. With the back of her hand, she slid the box to the edge of the desk, nudged the box and watched it tumble over, down into a jumble of papers in the wastebasket.

She picked up the General's Watch and closed the cover, all the time gazing at MacTeer, wondering what justice he might find when he rapped on heaven's gate. She went to the niche. There she lifted the bell jar and put the watch on the stand her mentor had reserved for it. After she replaced the bell jar, she turned on the light that illuminated the niche.

Again Garrison gazed at MacTeer. She touched his shoulder, gave it a soft squeeze, then turned out the light on his desk.

CHAPTER 25

One more flight

A fuel truck rumbled away from her father's One-Fifty as Garrison came down the airport access road toward Vol-Air. She turned in and parked in front of the trailer office.

She watched him from her car before she got out, her father in insulated coveralls, the hood pulled over his head, polishing the windshield of his two-seater Cessna.

Garrison turned the collar of her own coat up against the late December chill as she stepped out. "Hey, Pop!"

Click waved his spray bottle. "Hey, Boots!"

"What do you think?" She held her hands out to her car the way a model would who was showing off a new vehicle on television.

"Hot-damn," Click said. "Yours?" He stuffed his cleaning gear in his coveralls' pockets and hustled over.

"Yes. I finished today."

Click slipped his arm around Garrison's waist and hugged her. "Finished what?"

"Teddy's estate. I filed the papers with the judge, and Anne paid me."

He looked at the car. "So you went out and bought this?"

"No, Anne gave me this in payment. It was one of Teddy's. A sportster isn't any good when you've got children."

"But you do know what you got there? That's a

Corvette, my dear daughter."

"That's what the title says."

"A Nineteen Fifty-Three Corvette, first model they ever made–wire-mesh headlights, fins like a Flash Gordon spaceship. Chevy built only three hundred of 'em, did you know that?"

"I'll trade you stories," Garrison said. "Chevrolet gave this one to Governor Clement, did you know that?"

"Hon, you got me there."

"Somehow–and I don't know how–Teddy managed to get hold of it."

"And now it's yours. For real?"

"For real." Garrison's grin reinforced her words.

Click walked around the car. He ran a hand along its soft, sleek lines. He caressed the convertible top, wiggling his eyebrows in Groucho Marx-fashion as he did. "Sweet, sweet, sweet. Tell you what, before you take me for a ride, let's go flying."

"Are you crazy?"

Click swept his arms out. "It's a beautiful day. The One-Fifty's gassed up. It's ready to go."

Garrison shook her head as she came around to her father. She took his arm and together they strolled on to the waiting airplane.

"That car beats a paycheck, doesn't it?" Click said.

"Do you know it's older than my Volkswagen?"

"Oh, but it's got class. It suits you, a successful young lawyer. Incidentally, you're flying."

"Why?"

"Don't ask, just do it. You take the left seat." Click opened the cabin door. He helped Garrison step up and in. "Talk to Ground and get the altimeter setting while I do a quick walk-around."

She pulled the door closed and turned her attention to the control panel. Garrison snapped the master switch on. That powered up the flight instruments and the radios. She swept her hat away and dropped it behind the seat so she could settle a headset over her ears.

"Knoxville Ground," she said into her microphone, her thumb on the transmitter button, "this is Cessna Six-Seven-Two Charlie Victor on the ramp at Vol-Air. Your current altimeter, please."

"Roger, Two Charlie, altimeter is three zero point zero six. What's your pleasure?"

She glanced over her shoulder, out the rear window at Click wiggling the rudder and inspecting its hinges. "I guess Pop and I are going out flying."

"Roger that. Runway Five is the active. Wind light and variable out of the northeast. Visibility thirty miles and scattered clouds at ten thousand feet. Call when you're ready to taxi."

"Two Charlie Victor."

Click opened the door on the copilot's side. He pulled himself in and flipped his hood back. "Nothing fell off, so start 'er up."

She glanced to either side of the propeller, then opened her window. "Clear!" she called out.

"All clear," Click answered.

Garrison turned the ignition key, engaging the starter. The engine, still warm from the last flight, burred to life. She gave the engine enough power to start the airplane rolling. "Knoxville Ground, Two Charlie Victor ready to taxi."

"Two Charlie Victor cleared to taxi. Move it along. You have a Piper Aztec behind you, coming out of Cherokee Aviation."

Garrison added more power. She turned the One-Fifty out onto the taxiway and headed to the run-up area. Click handed her his spare set of sunglasses.

"Oh, thanks," she said. "What do you want to do?"

"Just some touch-and-go's." He pulled his knees up to keep his feet off the rudder pedals and crossed his arms. "How about opening up the heater?"

Garrison glanced down. She found the heater control knob and pulled it all the way out, swirling warm air into the cabin and around their feet and ankles.

Click passed the checklist to Garrison as she swung the airplane onto the pad where all departing aircraft stopped so their pilots could do their final engine run-ups before they rolled out onto the runway.

She went down the list, taking each action called for.

Click, for his part, gazed out his window at the Piper twin pulling in beside. The pilot nodded, and Click waved in return. He'd never flown an Aztec. The thought rambled through his mind that maybe he ought to thumb a ride sometime.

"Everything's ready, Pop."

That startled him out of his reverie. Click moved his attention to the second radio, its frequency set to the tower. "Let's go then," he said.

Garrison turned a toggle switch that cut out the ground frequency and cut in the tower. She pressed her transmitter button. "Knoxville Tower, Cessna Six-Seven-Two Charlie Victor, ready for takeoff."

"Roger, Two Charlie Victor." A tower controller. "Hold short of the active. Twin Beech on final."

Garrison glanced out Click's window as she increased the One-Fifty's power. She turned the airplane away from the Piper twin and guided it to the hold-short line. There she stopped. At almost the same moment, a Beechcraft flashed by her windshield, wheels down and flaps out.

"Two Charlie Victor, take the active. Cleared for takeoff after the Beech clears the runway."

"Roger." Garrison let the One-Fifty roll forward, out to the center of the runway and into the wind.

"Tower, Aztec Five-Five-Seven-Zero Echo, ready for takeoff."

"Roger, Seven-Zero Echo, you're number two. Pull in behind the putt-putt and hold."

"All right."

Click pressed his transmitter button, calling the Aztec. "Daniel, where you going?"

"Saint Louis, and you?"

"Local. AJ's going to shoot some touch-and-go's."

"'Bout time you let her go up on her own, isn't it?"

"Yeah. Have a good flight."

The tower controller broke in. "Two Charlie Victor, cleared for takeoff. Make a right turnout. The Piper's going left."

Click pointed ahead. Garrison pressed the throttle to the firewall, and the One-Fifty raced up to liftoff speed. As the aircraft hopped into the air, she saw a lawn chair in the snow to the side of the runway. "What's that out there for?"

"I don't know," he said.

"Aztec Seven-Zero Echo, the Cessna's turning. You're cleared for takeoff."

"Seven-Zero Echo, thank you."

Click twisted around to look out his window. He watched the twin Piper, already four hundred feet below, speed down the runway and into the air. When he could no longer see the airplane, he turned his gaze toward the Smoky Mountains. With no summer haze to shroud them, their outlines cut like the edges of knives across the horizon.

"Have you seen today's Chief?" Garrison asked.

"Not yet."

She handed him a folded newspaper she had taken from her pocket.

Click opened it. He whistled at the headline: COUNTY FISCAL COURT REMOVED; STATE TROOPER NAMED SHERIFF.

"Scotty?" he asked.

"That's right." Garrison leveled the One-Fifty at pattern altitude. She banked the aircraft to the right and brought it around into a right downwind.

"Boots, did you know this was going to happen?"

"That I did not."

"So is this going to change things between the two of you?"

"Pop, I'm trying to fly." Garrison pulled back on the power and rolled the trim wheel forward. The plane's speed came up. Too much, too much, she told herself, keep it under ninety.

Click scanned down the story while Garrison tugged back on the throttle, her eyes focused on the airspeed indicator. The One-Fifty crossed the southwest end of the runway, and she pulled the carburetor heat on, the engine power dropping two hundred rpms. Garrison nursed the power back some more. She rolled the trim back, slowing the airplane for the correct descent.

The tower controller broke in. "Two Charlie Victor, you're cleared for the touch-and-go. Turn left on climb-out to fly standard patterns."

Garrison–busy–motioned for Click to return the call. He pressed his transmitter button. "Two Charlie Victor," Click said, acknowledging the change in instructions.

When the altimeter read sixteen hundred feet, Garrison banked the One-Fifty to the right, onto the base leg, her attention on her speed and her descent–*Keep it steady, keep it steady.* She moved her gaze to the runway off her right wing.

"So about you and Scotty–"

"Pop, not now." At fourteen hundred feet, Garrison again banked the One-Fifty to the right. She brought the airplane in line with the runway. "I don't like this. I'm high."

Click folded his newspaper to a quarter of its size and stuffed it between the seats. "So what do you do?"

Garrison put her fingertips on the flap handle. She pushed down and held it, watching the extension needle go from zero to ten degrees to twenty, feeling the nose pitch down into a steeper descent. "Is that enough?"

"See how it goes," Click said.

"You're not much help."

"You're the pilot."

"Dad!"

"You're doing fine."

Todd Oliver's voice came into the headsets. "Knoxville Tower, Skymaster Six-Seven-Three Charlie Victor, fifteen northeast with the numbers."

"Roger, Three Charlie Victor, continue on. Two

Charlie Victor is in the pattern shooting touch-and-go's."

"Who's flying?"

"Will and AJ."

Garrison brought the One-Fifty across the approach end of the runway a hundred feet high. "More flaps?" she asked, sweat beading out on her forehead.

"You're okay."

She tugged back on the control wheel as the airplane came closer to the runway. She brought the nose up, flaring the One-Fifty for landing as if the airplane were a robin. The tires on the main gear screeched as they touched the concrete and spun up to speed.

Garrison pulled the throttle all the way back. She pushed the carburetor heat off. "Ready to go again?"

"No, stop and let me out."

"What?"

"Stop and let me out," Click said. "You can fly this thing on your own."

"The heck I can."

"Boots, you can." Click pushed on the brakes. He brought the little airplane to a stop at the side of the runway and bailed out.

When he turned back to close the door, she yelled at him, "Dammit, Dad, I can't do this!"

His face flushed, yet he pointed down the runway. "Go. Solo. Now!"

"But, Dad–"

Click slammed the door and hustled away.

"On your own, huh?" the tower controller asked.

"Oh, shut up." Garrison rolled the trim wheel forward. She shoved the throttle to the firewall, and the One-Fifty raced away much faster than usual. Then she remembered, only one on board. The aircraft is lighter. Everything is different. She pulled back on the control wheel, and the little airplane leaped into the sky.

****

Behind, on the ground, Click strolled across the runway

to the lawn chair. From there he watched the One-Fifty fly the circuit. He had done this so many times, cut more novice pilots loose than he could remember, but never his daughter. Now she had grown up in all ways.

He took a small thermos of coffee from the cargo pocket on the leg of his coveralls. Click screwed off the cap and poured himself a generous quantity. As the One-Fifty turned downwind, he help up the thermos cap. "Here's to you, Boots."

****

From a thousand feet above, Garrison saw that someone was sitting in the lawn chair, but who?

The tower controller broke in. "Two Charlie Victor, cleared for touch-and-go. Three Charlie Victor, you're number two behind the One-Fifty."

"Roger. Grease it on, AJ."

"Stuff it, I'm busy." She pulled the carburetor heat on, reduced power, rolled the trim wheel back, watched the airspeed slow, set up her descent, watched the runway–*Come on, come on, don't drift on me*–banked onto the base leg. Garrison swiped at the sweat on her forehead, then inched the flaps out and rolled in more trim.

She established her power at fifteen hundred rpms. Garrison took a breath. She glanced at her airspeed–*Seventy miles an hour, right where I want it. Now inch in more flaps, gotta turn final, line up with the center of the runway. Yes, that's it. A bit more flaps, a bit more trim.*

Garrison stared at the earth rushing up toward her–*Have I done everything? What have I done?*

She brought the One-Fifty over the approach end of the runway fifty feet high. She pulled off all power, and the airplane dropped. It hit hard on its tires, so hard that the One-Fifty sprang back into the air.

"Oh God." Garrison punched in a burst of power that carried the plane further down the runway. The One-Fifty settled again, more slowly, the tires touching, rolling.

That's better. Come on, let's get out of here.

Garrison set her jaw in a sharp line. She closed the carburetor heat and, just as she was about to put the throttle to the firewall, she glanced out her side window toward the person in the lawn chair, the person–a man–holding something in the air, saluting her. "Dad? I'm in here sweating and you're drinking coffee?"

She slammed the throttle in, and the One-Fifty raced away.

"Three Charlie Victor, the One-Fifty's climbing out. You're cleared to land."

"Roger, Knoxville Tower. I want to turn off by that old man in the lawn chair."

"I can okay that."

****

The Skymaster whistled down the chute, its rear tires greasing onto the runway. Oliver, with full flaps out for maximum drag, worked the brakes. He slowed the pusher-puller twin and swung it off the runway, into the snow just beyond Click. He taxied back and stopped beside him.

"How ya doin', father of the pilot?" Oliver asked after he rolled off the command seat of the Skymaster and down to the ground.

Click kept his gaze fixed on the One-Fifty speeding along its downwind leg. "Got your camp stool?"

Oliver kicked his way back to the rear of his aircraft. He opened the baggage door, and, from deep inside, brought out a canvas chair folded flat and his own thermos. Oliver snapped the chair open and set it down next to his partner. "How's she doing?"

"Better than she thinks."

"Isn't that always the case?"

Click chuckled. "No. I've cut a few new flyers loose who could have gotten my instructor's ticket pulled if a flight examiner had been around."

The One-Fifty turned onto the base leg, then bent around to final approach, Click and Oliver watching, each sipping coffee.

"Good flight?" Click asked.

"Yup. No problems getting into Wheeling. My passengers decided to stay for two days, so I gave 'em a choice. They could hire the plane and me to wait for them and pay my expenses, or buy two round trips and send me home. They sent me home."

The One-Fifty touched down as whisper quiet as had the Skymaster.

"Wave," Click said. He brought his hand up in a gentle greeting, but Oliver wig-wagged his arm over his head as the airplane flashed by, its engine again at full power.

****

Garrison gave a quick nod to the waving, then tugged back on the control wheel. That brought the trainer off the runway into an easy climb.

The tower controller came on. "Good job."

"Thanks."

"Full stop this time?"

"Three landings is all I have to do, isn't it?" she asked as she banked the One-Fifty into a climbing turn toward pattern altitude.

"Right."

"Full stop then. God, I'm tired."

"Relax. Enjoy it."

"Easy for you to say." Garrison brought the One-Fifty into a second banked turn, this time for the race downwind, doing all she had been taught to level the One-Fifty and slow its airspeed. 'Keep it down. Cruise in the pattern at twenty-two hundred rpms.' She could hear the voice of her father in her head as clearly as if he were sitting beside her. 'Crossing the end of the runway now. Carb heat on, power back to seventeen hundred, roll in the trim, eighty miles an hour.'

She banked to the base leg. 'Ten degrees flaps now, roll in more trim, seventy miles an hour.'

Garrison guided the One-Fifty around to final approach. 'Line up on the center line, twenty degrees flaps, power back to fifteen hundred, more trim, sixty-five.'

The fence at the end of the airport slid beneath the One-Fifty. 'Power back, let her touch down on the numbers.'

The One-Fifty did, right at the top edge of the big Five painted on the runway. The Cessna rolled on, slowing. Garrison turned the airplane off into the snow and applied power to taxi up next to the Skymaster.

There she cut the engine. Garrison let all the tension of the last fifteen minutes flow from her body while she snapped off one switch, then another until there was nothing left to do but get out of the airplane.

She opened the door.

There were Click and Oliver, Oliver his gloved hand held high. She stepped down and slapped his hand in a high five, then threw herself into her father's arms.

"I did it!"

About The Author

Jerry Peterson once flew light aircraft for a living. He also was a teacher and a newspaperman. For the better part of a decade, he lived and worked in eastern Tennessee where he sets his newest crime novel series. While there, he attended graduate school at the University of Tennessee where he claims he was the oldest student on campus. He now lives and writes in his home state of way-south Wisconsin, the land of brats, beer, and books. Visit Jerry's website online at http://JerryPetersonBooks.com.

Upcoming Titles

Coming soon, *A James Early Christmas,* a collection of stories of the season; and *Rage,* the second book in the AJ Garrison Crime Novel series. In that book, Garrison finds herself appointed to defend a high school student accused of murdering his English teacher.

Read it now right here, chapter 1 of *Rage*. . .

RAGE

Seven o'clock

Remember the Alamo, remember the Maine, remember me . . .

Those words–a kind of memory stone–rolled through Thad Cardwell's mind as he turned the blade of his art knife against a whetstone. It wasn't his art knife, exactly. He had put it in his pocket during class and just managed not to remember to leave it at the end of the hour–borrowed it one might say. Besides, it was sharper than anything he had and sharper still now, as sharp as a scalpel. He drew the knife through a sheet of paper, cleaving the page in two.

Neat.

The boy–tall, gawky, his hair a thatch that broke teeth out of pocket combs–opened his history book. He sliced away at a pattern he'd drawn in the center of the pages, deepening an excavation, humming aimlessly, tunelessly as he worked. He'd wanted to be in the choir, but when he couldn't tell whether a C was above or below a G, the choir director thanked him and suggested he pick up another shop class.

Another shop class.

Right.

He'd 'borrowed' a small bottle of Elmer's glue at the Ben Franklin store and pasted the edges of the book's pages together so nothing moved as he deepened his incisions. He stopped and threw the new mess of scraps he'd cut from the heart of the book into a plastic bag. This he would have to dispose of.

Cardwell gazed at his work. He set the art knife aside and ran his hand around the inside of the cutout, pleased at how smooth the form was. The point and the blade on the art knife made all the difference.

And now the test.

Cardwell picked up the Luger from the blanket beside him, not his Luger. He didn't own a pistol. He had 'borrowed' it, too, from the drawer where his uncle kept it and, last night, carefully pressed eight bullets into the magazine. Now he placed the gun in the cutout. Admired it.

A perfect fit.

"Thad?"

His mother's voice, calling to him from downstairs. For as long as Cardwell could remember, it was his mother and he, and his older brother, but Rob was gone now, in the Army, somewhere in Vietnam.

"Thad?"

"I hear ya, Ma."

"You gonna have breakfast before you go to school?"

"Don't think so. Not hungry, really. Besides, John'll be by in a couple a minutes."

"You sure?"

"Yeah."

He closed the cover of his history book and put it in with the others he intended to carry to school. Cardwell took his plaid jacket from the bedpost and pushed his arms into the sleeves. The jacket, shabby from age and wear, had come down to him from Rob. He took his blue-and-white striped cap from his jacket pocket and slapped the cap over his hair. Kids called it his feed cap and it was. His uncle had gotten it free from the co-op mill.

A white cat rubbed up against Cardwell's pant leg.

The boy bent down. He tickled the cat under his chin, and the cat purred with gusto.

Cardwell swept him up, cradled him in his arm, and stroked his belly, the cat smiling its perpetual smile.

"Kit, I gotta go," the boy said. He opened the window and set the cat outside, on the roof over the porch. "See ya when I get home from school, huh?"

He closed the window and grabbed up his books and binder, and tucked them under one arm as he clattered down the stairs.

"Thad, you all right?" his mother asked from back in the kitchen.

He stopped at the front door. "Yeah . . . yeah, I'm all right."

"You hurry home after school. It's church night, tonight, you know."

"Yeah, I know." He pushed on outside and down the stone path to the gravel road.

Thaddeus Pease Cardwell. Thaddeus had been his grandfather's name, an honored name, his mother had said. Pease, that was her maiden name, and she didn't want it forgotten. She had been an only child, and there was no one else to carry the name on.

Thaddeus Pease Cardwell, TP to some. Cardwell knew what that stood for. Pees-alot to others. He and John Gilland were called the Hick Club, not by their choice, but because both lived so far out from Morgantown, in Teller Cove, he up under the lee side of Cullowhee Mountain, Gilland further on, on Reed's Creek below Long Ridge.

The two had ridden the bus to the county high school, always exiled to a front seat–behind the driver–until Gilland turned sixteen and his brother went off to the Marines and left him his 'Fifty-Two Chevy half-ton, not a bad vehicle on most days, but when it rained, water splashed up through the rusted-out floorboard on the passenger side. Cardwell had gotten into the habit of putting his foot over the hole, but still there were stormy days when he walked into school with one pant leg wet up to the knee.

Cardwell heard the half-ton rattling his way. Rattling, yes. Much of the joint between a rear fender and the truck box had rusted away. Gilland had patched it with Metal Weld, advertised as a body-shop super-glue, but that had broken. Next he'd taped the joint with duct tape, but that hadn't held either. Cardwell had talked to Mister Romines, the ag teacher, about bringing the truck into the shop, to weld new sheet metal under the box and the fender.

Cardwell waved as Gilland pulled to the side of the road. Gilland shoved the passenger door open. "Gitcher math done last night?" he asked as Cardwell slid onto the seat and slammed the door shut.

"Huh-uh."

Gilland, a chunky youth topped by a Cincinnati Reds baseball cap that kept his unkempt mane in some sort of order, pushed the floor shifter into first. "Well, why not?"

"I was workin' on my history." Cardwell pushed the book up on the dash.

"Well, what the hell for? We ain't got a test in there for another week."

Cardwell said nothing. He just leaned his elbow on the door's armrest and gazed off toward the side of Cullowhee, his eyes not taking anything in.

Gilland shifted the transmission into second. "You kin copy my homework if you want."

When Cardwell didn't answer, Gilland came back with, "You in some kinda funk?"

"Maybe . . . yeah, I guess I better copy your homework."

****

Get Geronimo, get Pancho Villa, remember me . . .

A new set of words rolled through Cardwell's mind as Gilland busied himself with herding the truck off the pavement of the high school's entrance road and into the gravel lot.

The building before them lifted the spirits of no one. Plain brick and flat roofs, it had the look of a prison–industrial cheap, cheaper than anyone knew at the time the school was built a decade previous. The contractor had scammed a fifth of the funds, covering with low-grade materials and shoddy workmanship. The building showed the proof–cracks in the foundation and walls, roofs that leaked. When it rained, the janitor and the principal raced through the building, distributing buckets to teachers to catch the drips and downpours. In one upstairs hallway, students had to squeeze to one side to get past a tub the janitor put out as a water catcher. On one of those soaker days, students dropped rubber ducks in the tub, and one a block of wood with a paper sail on which he had printed 'SS Morgantown High.'

Gilland pulled the handbrake up and turned off the

key. "Five minutes. We better git on inside."

Cardwell didn't answer.

Gilland got out and turned back. He gathered up his books and his sack lunch. "You comin'?"

"In a bit. Thinking of a poem. I may write it before I go in for English class."

"Old Lady Blevins don't care shit for yer poems. Hell, she don't care shit for you." Gilland closed the door. He called back through the open window, "See ya in math. And how 'bout you catch me for lunch, huh?" He held up his brown bag. "I brought extra."

Cardwell waved him on.

Gilland galumphed away. He disappeared inside with the last of the late rush.

Cardwell opened his binder. He took out a pen and touched the point to his tongue, not because he liked the taste of ink, but out of habit. Then he wrote a title, 'Escape,' and dashed off five lines. He read them back, smiling as he did, pleased with the meter and the a-b, a-b-c rhyme scheme.

The bell rang, and he closed his binder.

Made in the USA
Charleston, SC
05 May 2016